CW01512110

First Edition: September 2022

ISBN-13: 978-1-953145-21-6

THE ASSASSIN'S BRIDE

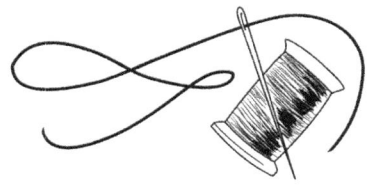

BETH ALVAREZ

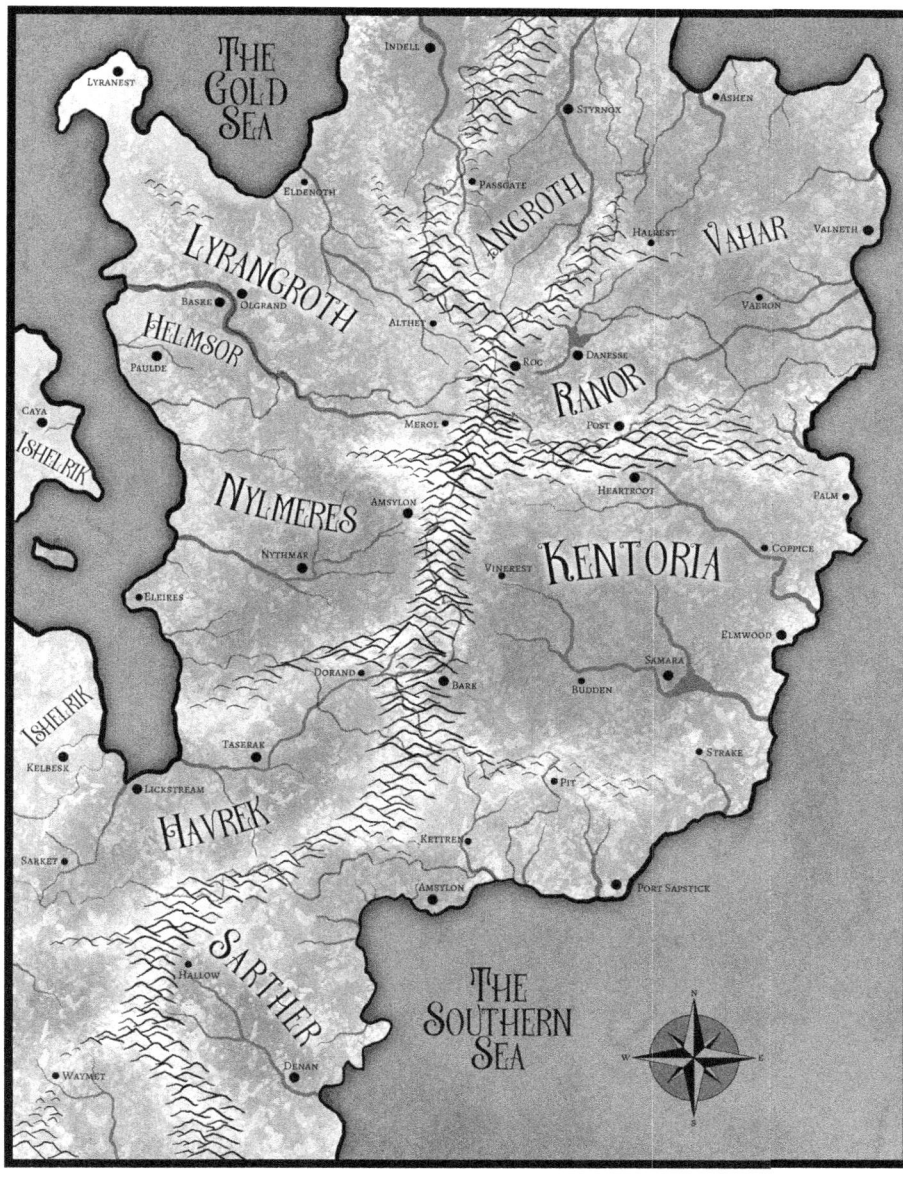

CHAPTER ONE

OF THE FIVE kings who had ruled in the past three years, Gaius Rothalan was said to be the worst. Not because he was a bad ruler, but because he was merciless.

When Thea had petitioned for an audience with the crown, the third king of those five had still been the man wearing it. Now she stood outside the palace with her letter of audience crumpled in her hands, unsure if it was worth setting foot inside the throne room.

"In or out," the guard at the gate said, as if her tiny moment of hesitation were a burden. "You're the last one today. The gate shuts after you."

Flustered, Thea gripped her paper and hurried into the courtyard. Afternoon sun dappled the cobblestones, casting everything in shades of gold. The manicured maples that lined the walkway fluttered their orange and yellow leaves in the wind, promising more color in the coming days. Autumn had arrived a bit early this year. Everyone swore it meant winter would be hard. All the more reason to ensure her business was settled now, she reminded herself. The harder the winter, the riskier the travel. Should the winter prove as cold as the sugarmakers claimed, being turned out of her home due to a clerical error no one had been able to resolve could end with an icy death.

"You're late," called another guard as she approached the palace doors.

Thea was never late. She was also in no position to argue with any of the king's guards, so she kept her jaw clamped tight as she turned the letter of audience for his inspection. He waved her on like it didn't matter. She supposed it didn't. The first guard wouldn't have allowed her through the gate without that letter.

"Won't be anyone left in the sitting hall this time of day," the guard said. "Go on down the hall and straight to the throne room. Don't knock, he's waiting. Best pray he's not annoyed."

"Thank you." She glanced to the door, half expecting the man might open it for her, but he remained at the foot of the shallow stairs. She continued on her own, letting herself into the palace.

Though the rich red granite of the palace exterior led her to expect it would be dark inside, high, narrow windows let in enough warm light that it didn't take long for her vision to adjust. The notion of a sitting hall left her anticipating a waiting room, but instead, a long corridor ran straight to the next set of doors. Benches lined the walls.

"Sitting hall indeed," Thea murmured to herself as she made for the doors at the far end. All she had to do was go in. The letter granting her audience was all she held, but notes filled the pockets of her skirt. With fortune, the king would be willing to let her read them. Knowing his reputation, she might be allowed two sentences.

She paused outside the doors, drew a deep breath, and willed her hands not to shake. A stray thread on her sleeve caught her attention, a small reminder of the dozen or so garments she still had to stitch magic into, and she plucked it off with a wince. She'd done her best to be presentable and professional. Now all she could do was hope.

Thea squeezed her eyes shut and pushed into the throne room.

A gurgle greeted her and her eyes flew open.

Before the throne, a man in black jerked a blade from the king's chest. Two guards lay beside Thea's feet, slow-spreading pools of crimson beneath their bodies. The crown fell from the king's head and rolled lazily across the room. She watched, frozen, as it tipped over right in front of her and wobbled circles against the floor.

Her chest grew tighter, until she couldn't breathe. A low throb echoed in her ears, the sound of her own pulse drowning out the rattle of the crown and the sick saw-smack of the knife.

The crown stopped and the air rushed back into her lungs.

Thea screamed.

The killer spun toward her with the king's severed head in hand. Instead of the murderer's face, she was greeted by a silver executioner's mask.

She screamed again and an instant later, he was on her. His free hand closed on her arm with the strength of a vise.

Guards burst through the door at her back. They shouted in alarm as they all but tripped over the bodies of their comrades. The assassin spat a curse and released her arm. The guards drew weapons, but he was fast, and a flurry of punches and kicks drove the men to their knees.

Thea turned to flee, but the man in black caught her arm again before she could. He drew a breath as if to speak. Instead of his words, a shrill whistle split the air, and he swore again. "Run!" he snarled, dragging her through the door.

The whistle piped again and a clatter of boots rose in the hall. Thea dug in her heels and strained against the assassin's grasp. He was stronger than she expected and when he pulled again, he almost dragged her off her feet.

Guards spilled into the far end of the sitting hall. More footsteps rose in the throne room behind them, accompanied by cries of dismay as they found what remained of the king. Thea's eyes swung down to the head in her captor's hand before she caught herself. Her stomach lurched and she lost her will to fight.

The assassin bore enough battle lust for both of them. He released her long enough to launch himself at the guards, his strikes precise and devastating. They tried to swarm him, but the hall was too narrow for more than a few to face him at once.

Thea spun back toward the throne room. She made it two steps before he had her again.

"I mean to kill only once more," he snapped. "Your blood will not be on my hands."

They burst from the palace and descended the stairs before the gate guard intercepted them. A fist to the face sent him crashing to the ground. Then they were beyond the gate, running for some narrow alley while a chorus of screams rose from the city's people. What was she doing? By the Light, she was running from the law!

Shadow swallowed them and at last, they slowed. Thea jerked her arm free and clapped her hands to her middle. She felt for her pockets, then looked at her palms. Empty. Her paper was gone. "My audience!" she cried.

"Audience?" The assassin turned toward her. His arm shifted and she screwed her eyes shut, lest he make her look at the king's severed head.

This was not how the day was supposed to go.

When she pried her eyes open to see if she could run—from him, this time, instead of the guards—she saw him fold shut the flap of a leather satchel, sealing the head away from view. He wiped his hand against his hip and looked back the way they'd come. "We must go."

"We?" she repeated, incredulous.

The sounds of the city beyond their cranny grew louder. The baying of hounds rose above the thunder of boots and armor. Before she could protest again, he snagged her wrist and led her farther down the winding alleyways. She thought of fighting back, but the cries of the dogs put a lump of fear in her throat and the sight of the leather satchel that bumped at his hip made her knees feel like water. She wobbled on her feet, but his grip never faltered.

What little strength she had collected in her voice and escaped as a single protest. "Let me go."

Her captor said nothing. Nor did his hold on her abate. Step by step, he led her deeper into parts of the city she had never seen. In the dark, narrow alleys of Samara, the cool autumn air turned sour with the stench of rotting garbage and damp, decaying leaves. The hounds' keening grew distant and faded.

They emerged between shacks near the lake. The streets here were little more than mud, but they were empty. Soft breezes whispered through the leaves and stirred the water to lap against the shore, both sounds something that should have been peaceful. Instead, they put Thea on edge. Whoever lived on the city's outskirts, they were gone for the day, earning their keep elsewhere.

There was no one nearby to hear if she cried for help.

A small lean-to against the back of a rough house was where they stopped, though only for a moment. The assassin's hand closed on the lock and she didn't see what he did, but a snap split the peace and the lock fell to the ground. He jerked open the door and thrust her inside.

Panic surged in her chest as she stumbled into a pile of firewood and he slammed the door shut behind them.

"Don't kill me!" she gasped, her hands up, palms out, as if she held any power to stop him. She hadn't even been able to prevent him from dragging her through the city while fear held her tongue.

He snorted. "I've told you already, your blood will not be on my hands." The lean-to was poorly constructed, with wide gaps between the vertical boards that comprised the walls, providing enough light to see him clearly. He swept the uncomfortably familiar executioner's mask from his face and cast it to the floor.

Thea had expected many things from the assassin, but that he might be handsome wasn't one of them. The notion that killers ought to be as frightful on the outside as they were on the inside sprang to mind, but she quickly stuffed it down. Her brother's killers had been handsome, too. It hadn't changed his wrongful death.

He left the mask on a stack of firewood and raked his fingers through his dirty blond hair. When he looked at her again, he exhaled hard. "You weren't supposed to be there. No one was supposed to be there."

"I had an audience," Thea protested.

His brows rose. "Then you were late, because audience hours were over."

"I was not late!" She clenched her hands to fists and stomped one foot, only realizing after she'd done it that showing belligerence to a man with a severed head tied to his belt might be unwise. Her throat thickened and she gulped. "My letter said the king would see me at five."

"It did not say five."

Her jaw tightened until it ached. "Well I can't prove you wrong now, my letter is gone." And so were her chances of having her problem solved. The gravity of everything that had just transpired bore down on her shoulders until she thought she might collapse.

Her letter was gone, and so was the king. The last of the Rothalan line had been murdered right in front of her. The kingdom would be in turmoil before the sun set. And here she was, standing in a wood shed with the man who had done it, arguing over whether or not she'd read her letter wrong.

Thea made herself wet her lips with her tongue. When she spoke again, her voice shook. "I won't tell anyone I've seen you. Please, spare me. I'll make no trouble."

"No." The single word was spoken without hesitation, firm as the ground beneath her feet.

Her heart beat faster. "But you said—"

"That I won't kill you, yes. That's fun, isn't it." The sarcastic edge in his voice took her off-guard. Again, he slid his fingers through his hair. Why was he so troubled? He had no right.

"Then why did you bring me here?"

The look he gave her made her feel the answer should have been obvious. "You were the last person to enter the throne room. The only person the guards knew was present. You stood in the throne room with murdered guards at your feet. What do you suppose would be done to you, had I left you behind?"

Her hand rose to her throat before she could stop it.

"Precisely." He turned as if to pace, but there was nowhere for him to go. The twitch of a muscle in his cheek betrayed his frustration. "Had I left you there, you would be executed by morning. Had I left you there, knowing I bore the power to spare you, I would be as guilty of your death as I am of his." His hand hovered above the satchel, then went for the mask. He contemplated it for a moment, then gritted his teeth and left it where it was.

Thea gripped her skirt in both hands. "Then you've spared me and done your part. Leave me here. I'll escape on my own, go back to my shop—"

"To where the guards will be looking for you?" He arched a brow. "You showed a letter with your name on it to every guard between me and the front gate. Whoever you are, you're a wanted woman now, and there's no going back."

"Thea."

"What?"

"My name," she replied hotly. "Who I am."

"I don't care who you are. All I care about is getting both of us out of this mess, so I can keep my conscience clear."

Her eyes widened. "Your conscience? You have a man's head in your bag!"

He glanced down at it with a frown, as if he'd not yet considered its moral implications. By the Light, what sort of assassin had she gotten herself tangled up with?

7

Either he reached a conclusion or he decided it didn't matter, for he glowered at her a second later. "The hounds are still after us and the scent of blood will lead them this way with ease. At this moment, you have two choices. You may stay here, or you may come with me. If they catch you, you will be executed. If you stay with me, I'll take you somewhere safe before I continue on my quest."

"Your quest," she repeated.

The flat stare he gave her indicated he would discuss it no further.

A distant howl caught her attention. They both turned toward it, though there was nothing to be seen beyond the lean-to's slats. In the moment of silence that followed, she grew aware of her heartbeat drumming in her ears.

Against her better judgment, she found herself turning her gaze to the silver executioner's mask that lay on the wood. It was the same, she was sure of it. How strange that the mask that had haunted her nightmares since her brother's wrongful death might now lead to hers, too. How might things be different, if Ashvin had been presented the same opportunity? A chance to face the crime he was accused of—a crime he'd not committed, but for which he'd surely be punished—or a chance to flee?

As if to hasten her decision, the assassin slid his hand over the mask's features. He removed it from the wood pile and thrust it into his bag. Had he stolen it from the palace, or were such masks all the same? Did it matter if they were? She stared at the bag until she realized he'd placed the mask in with the king's head, then tore her eyes away.

The choices were cooperation or death. In truth, that was no choice at all. When she finally spoke, her voice was quiet, defeated, and the simple words made the assassin's shoulders sag with relief.

"I'll go."

CHAPTER TWO

DESPITE THE URGENCY that clawed at her heart every time she heard a dog wail, the assassin moved slowly between the shabby buildings at the city's edge.

"We have few choices," he said after a time. "We have to leave Kentoria."

Thea could have sputtered. In another time, her family had been well off enough to travel. Her father had been a noble, part of the merchant class, a man who traveled widely and forged connections along most of the eastern sea. But those connections had been lost with him. Beyond Kentoria's borders, she had nothing.

"I don't hear you making any suggestions otherwise," he continued when she did not reply. Had they not been in such a dire situation, she might have sworn he sounded playful.

"I have nowhere to go." She didn't know what else to say.

"Family beyond the kingdom's borders?"

Thea shook her head.

He stared at her, his storm-gray eyes unreadable. Eventually, he glanced away. "Kentorian, born and bred. Few like you outside the upper castes."

The comment dug under her skin. She followed him to the

shadowy side of the next building before she spoke again, her voice a harsh whisper. "What makes you think I'm not upper caste?"

"You're a working woman in a peasant's dress. There are chalk stains on your skirt and a piece of string in your hair."

Thea fought back a gasp, but she couldn't stop her hand from snapping up to her auburn locks. Searching for it with her fingertips was futile, but she still probed her loose curls, just in case. "What shame is there in working to support myself?"

"None." He peered around the corner, then gave her an earnest look. "It just means you aren't upper caste."

Not anymore, at least. That lifestyle had perished with her brother. She bit the insides of her cheeks and made herself exhale. How many times would Ashvin's execution plague her today? For as long as she was in peril, she supposed.

Instead of moving on, the assassin lingered at the corner of the building, his brows knit with frustration. Thea tried to follow his line of sight, but she saw nothing to warrant such concern. Whatever it was that vexed him, it existed only in his thoughts.

She cleared her throat. "Say we were to leave Kentoria," she ventured. "Where would we go?"

"Why? Have you suddenly thought of some wealthy distant relation you'd like to drop in on?" The question earned her a grim look, but the sarcastic note had returned to his voice. He was proving to have far more personality than she supposed an assassin ought, but she paused to consider that she'd never encountered any before. At least, not outside of fiction. The sudden thought of her bookshelves at home put a new sort of grief in her heart. Books were expensive. How would she ever replace that collection?

"It's more that we can't travel without supplies," Thea said. To her frustration, he moved as she spoke. She picked up her skirt and hurried after him. "We're a good twenty miles from somewhere we might be able to shop."

"Shopping should be the least of your concerns." Instead of

leaving the city, he skirted its edge through the same alleyways they'd only just escaped. Or, perhaps these were different alleys. They all looked the same to her.

"We could return to my shop," she suggested. Maybe then she could save a favorite book or two.

"That is the absolute worst place we could visit, barring a trip back to the palace itself."

"Then where are we going?" They'd already ventured some way through the alleys, with their disorienting twists and turns. "Shouldn't we be headed the other direction?"

He sighed. "We are deliberately leaving a difficult trail. We've gone all the way to the water's edge. It might gain us time. Leaving from that side of the city would mean circling the lake, and that's far too exposed. We'll go by way of the groves."

"With all the workers there?"

"It's a better suggestion than your shop." He snorted softly. "What sort of plan was that? Do you mean to barricade the door while you sew up some disguises?"

She could. Disguises she made with her own two hands would be unparalleled, but that sort of magic was forbidden, and for good reason. The thought was there, but fleeting. The time it would take eliminated the possibility.

She hesitated too long.

He paused and turned to face her, his expression both thoughtful and wary. "You are a dressmaker?"

Thea opened her mouth to confirm or deflect, but no sound came out. He was observant. The chalk, the loose thread stuck in her hair. Had he pieced it together from that alone?

He took a step closer and reached for her. She flinched, expecting to be struck. Instead, he pulled the long blue thread from her hair and twisted it between his fingers. He studied it, then clasped it in the palm of his hand. "No," he said slowly. "A Threadmancer."

Her pulse quickened and she moved backwards out of reflex. How did he know? The power she stitched into clothing was undetectable, save by other Threadmancers or the most skilled of artificers. Surely he felt nothing from a single strand of leftover thread.

"You are," he continued, a new gleam in his eyes. "You could sew disguises like no other."

"I'm just a seamstress," she lied, though with the way her heart hammered its way up to her throat, she knew it was too late.

"Can you sew in illusions?"

Offense twisted her face. "I am a law-abiding person."

"You aren't abiding by the law right now."

"I've done nothing wrong," she protested.

He moved closer. "You're running from the guard."

"Because I have no choice. You've essentially kidnapped me."

"Essentially." A low chuckle rumbled in his chest. "And now, you'll make what we need so we can escape the kingdom."

Now she felt faint. "Sewing illusions is a criminal offense punishable by death." Virtually every kingdom had outlawed it, a choice with which she happened to agree. An assassin with illusory garments could be an unstoppable force.

"But you know how to do it."

Every Threadmancer did. And every Threadmancer knew when to bend the rules. To stitch just enough magic into a bride's gown to ensure her natural beauty was unrivaled at her wedding. To alter a wealthy old nobleman's coat in just such a way that it slimmed him like no other garments did. But those were trade secrets, nothing a Threadmancer who valued their head might admit.

Just when she thought she had no way out of an explanation, a dog's howl erupted at the far end of the alleyway.

The assassin cursed and grabbed her arm. His other hand went for his bag.

Her stomach lurched when she realized what he sought. "Don't!"

He graced her with a glower before he slid the mask over his face, its surface smeared with blood. "If I'm seen well enough that my face makes it onto a poster, it'll be that much harder to escape. Move."

The thought of her own countenance posted on boards for wanted criminals made her sick. "But—"

"Move!" he snarled through clenched teeth. He grasped her elbow and twirled her in a new direction as the sound of the dogs grew louder.

There was hardly room to run, but he still flowed through the alleys, dragging her along behind him. Thea stumbled more than once, but he never let her fall. They darted across busy streets and behind familiar buildings, winding farther from the shopping district she'd called home since her brother's death.

"Keep going," he whispered. "Show me where."

Taking him home was the last thing she wanted to do now, but when she stalled at the side of a busy avenue, something pressed against her back.

She stiffened, envisioning the same knife he'd used to kill the king.

This time, when he spoke, he leaned close beside her ear. The iron scent of death clung to his mask. "Don't make me ask again."

Thea turned. Instead of crossing the road, she led him back a few paces and turned into another alleyway. The angle of the sun overhead told her where they needed to go. "We have to go back into the city. My shop is in the heart of the market district."

He made an unhappy noise, but let her take the lead.

Heading back into the city was the most dangerous thing she could imagine, aside from refusing to aid him further. His proximity to her back made it clear hesitance would be punished. She did not dare try his patience.

By some miracle, they circumvented the dogs, though she had no doubt they would not be far behind. Even she could smell the blood that stained his mask. Her stomach turned over at the thought and she put it firmly out of mind as she opened a tiny gate off an alley. It led into a small garden, a space linked across the backs of a handful of shops. Silently, she prayed the space would be empty.

She swallowed hard and stared straight ahead, holding her breath as if it might make a difference in whether or not they were seen.

The back door to her modest shop was just ahead, and the hounds and their baying were far behind once more.

"They'll pick up our trail fast," the assassin murmured as she retrieved her key from her pocket and unlocked the door. "We've been seen crossing streets. We'll get what you need and then we must move."

She didn't appreciate the sentiment. "Of course." Once again, the idea she could surrender instead of prolonging the inevitable crept through her mind as she pulled open the door and slipped into the tiny kitchen. It was idiotic at best. If she surrendered, she would surely be executed.

And if she wronged the assassin behind her, she'd die by his hand. If she cooperated and fled, she might still die trying to flee the country, but there was a tiny, glimmering possibility she could make it beyond Kentoria's border and start over.

He slid into the kitchen behind her and wasted no time in barricading the door.

Thea watched as he moved the chairs and small table. The way he stacked them made it impossible the door would even budge. "Is that really necessary?" If anything, it would slow down their escape.

"No questions. Get what you need to work your magic." He looked toward the front room, as if contemplating barricading that door, too.

She hurried to the front before he made up his mind.

The room was dim, but she knew the placement of everything she needed by heart. She pulled a basket from underneath the counter and opened a drawer to retrieve her best shears and a packet of good needles. A box of thread went in next, then pins and her best measuring tape, alongside a jar of buttons and toggles she'd surely need.

Last of all, she stood before the racks of fabric that lined one wall. Her collection of fabrics had become a source of pride, each one selected for quality, texture, and color. The notion of leaving them behind struck her even harder than the thought of losing her books. Which she still needed to pack, assuming he gave her enough time.

"I need to go upstairs," she said after she folded her last fabric selection into the basket. She hadn't seen him appear in the doorway, but his looming presence was unmistakable. He was silent, stealthy, as an assassin should be, but she still felt his eyes on her back. That he was being threatening on purpose was the only thing that made sense.

"Be swift. We have little time."

She was tempted to grumble. It was easy for him to say; he didn't need to decide with only a few minutes' notice which parts of his life were important enough to pack and take with him. Thea suspected she could get away with taking a single bag, and that was assuming she could convince the assassin to carry her sewing basket part of the time.

And why shouldn't he? She hurried up the stairs and stifled the urge to snort. He was the one who wanted her to sew disguises. He should bear at least part of the burden.

The absurdity of it all hit her hard the moment she reached the top of the steps. By now, she was wanted for a crime she didn't commit, unable to clear her name and guaranteed to be wrongfully executed by a merciless crown. And here she was, standing at the top of her stairs, worrying about books and which pair of shoes would be best suited to running while she fled her homeland alongside a murderer.

She didn't even know his name.

Thea shook her head as if it might clear her madness, then stuffed her two favorite books into a satchel she'd made herself. It was shabby, one of her first sewing projects, but she was fond of it. Then she changed into a clean dress, just in case her skirt had picked up blood from the guards. Or the king's head, as her companion toted it around. She fought back a shudder as she put on her most comfortable boots, crammed extra undergarments into her bag, and returned to the stairs.

The assassin waited at the bottom, already holding her sewing basket, his mask in one hand. "Is that everything?" The question was low, urgent, yet not as sharp as she expected.

"Chalk." She snapped her fingers. "I forgot my chalk."

Before she could descend the stairs, he turned to retrieve it for her. Her drawers were always tidy, so it wasn't hard to find.

He slipped it into the basket. "Now, we must—"

A knock at the door cut him short. "Thea?" a soft voice called from outside. "Are you in? I've brought either a consolatory cake or something to go with celebratory tea, depending on how your audience went."

Forget the assassin's knives, Thea thought. The look he sent her was enough to kill on its own. "My cousin," she whispered.

He drew breath to either tell her to sneak away or pretend she wasn't home, or perhaps curse at her or threaten her in some way, but a jingle and clatter announced that the door would soon be unlocked.

Thea grimaced. "She has a key." It had never been a problem before. Elia helped her around the shop from time to time and was the only member of Thea's family who still seemed to care for her. Why wouldn't she have her own key?

His murderous glare darkened, but he dipped backwards into the kitchen and out of sight.

Thea hurried to greet Elia at the door.

"Oh!" her cousin exclaimed. "You are in. Oh, is that a good thing? Or bad? That means your audience was rather short."

"The king was unable to see me," Thea blurted. It wasn't a lie, but her cheeks still colored.

To her good fortune, her cousin mistook it for anger. "After all this time? By the Light, he really is the worst of the Rothalan kings, isn't he?"

Thea reddened even more. "I don't want to talk about it."

"Well, you don't have to. I'll make us some sulking tea." Elia tried to step inside, but Thea crowded her back out the door.

"I don't want company, either! I just want to be alone. This day has been terrible for me, Elia. You can't even imagine." Thea's voice cracked and tears threatened her eyes, but she refused to cry over how fast everything had gone wrong.

Her sweet cousin's face crumpled with dismay. "Oh, Thea. I'm sorry. I'm so sorry, I didn't mean to... I forgot. The last time you went to the palace was..." She trailed off and gave a resolute nod. "I understand. I know it's hard, but we'll work through it tomorrow, after you've had some time. Here."

Thea hardly caught the paper-wrapped cake Elia shoved into her hands. She fumbled it close against her stomach while her cousin seized her face and kissed her soundly on both cheeks.

"You eat this and I'll stop by to see you tomorrow, all right?" Elia said.

"Yes," was all Thea got out.

"Bless you, you poor thing. Don't worry about it at all. We'll sort it out. You know, I'm going to go right over and tell my father about this. He'll know what to do, and we'll get you in to see the king in no time. And next time, I won't let you go alone."

"Thank you," Thea managed.

Elia patted her cheeks and picked up her skirts to tromp down the street, toward where her father would be drinking the afternoon away in a private parlor, likely with all the rest of the city's politicians. Had they heard by now? Thea didn't want to stay long enough to find out.

She slammed the door and locked it tight.

"Within minutes, she'll know what's happened in the palace," the assassin's deep voice offered from the shadows.

Thea exhaled hard. "Then we'd better go before she gets back. Out the back door?"

"Better than being seen going out the front." His eyes fell to the wrapped parcel in her hands and one of his brows drew upward.

She shoved it into her satchel and hurried to join him without a word.

"The city will be thick with guards. This is our one chance to escape. Once we're past the maple groves, we'll be able to slow down, but we cannot afford any missteps." He removed the barricade from the back door as swiftly as he'd put it up.

Thea gripped the strap of her bag. "What's your name?"

He fumbled a chair, but caught it before it hit the ground. Of all the questions she might have asked, he hadn't expected that one."What?"

"Your name," she repeated. "What am I to call you?" Or call for help, when the guards inevitably seized her? She grimaced. What a foolish notion. As if he would ever turn around to help her.

His mouth worked a moment before he answered. "Gil."

A name far too ugly for a face as handsome as his. An alias made sense, but she felt a tingle of curiosity over why he'd chosen *that*.

"Very well, Gil," she said, as breezily as she dared. The last of the barricade came away. As she held open the door, she had the fleeting thought that her sewing basket on his arm made it look as if they were departing for a picnic.

Just the three of us, she thought with a wry smile.

Her, her peculiar savior, and the dead king's severed head.

CHAPTER THREE

GIL LED her through the familiar narrow roadways behind her home with remarkable grace, pausing only now and then to evaluate the best course to take. Despite the baying of the royal hounds, he was calm and unbothered, unhurried to make any decisions. Yet he did not waste any time, either. Each calculating pause was no more than a moment, just long enough to evaluate the road ahead, the turns they could take, and the sounds that filtered through the noise of everyday life. The rattle of armor or footsteps too regular and distinct made him turn. A dog's whine made him retreat. But every step led them unerringly farther, and Thea followed close at his heels.

She dared not wonder at how abruptly her life had been upended. To pay it any mind at all might have brought her to tears. Instead she watched her footing and held tight to her bag. Gil still carried her sewing basket, an act of chivalry she was sure her back would appreciate before the day was out. With fortune, she would convince him to bear that burden for the rest of their trip.

How far was it to the border? She hardly knew. She knew how big Kentoria was on paper, but the distance between dots on the map was too hard to reckon without tools. Or the map in front of her, she supposed. She had only a vague notion of where things were in relation to one another. All she was sure of was the capital's location beside the lake and the river that fed it, and the heavily-traveled road that led east, toward the coast.

"Where are we going?" Thea barely dared speak. The question escaped so softly that at first, she wasn't certain Gil had heard. After a moment, though, he glanced back at her with a speculative glint in his eyes. At first, she'd thought them the gray of storm clouds. Now she took it back. They were cold and sharp, the scuffed steel of a razor-edged blade.

When he finally answered, his voice was as calm as the rest of him. "Away. For now, that's all you need to know."

Thea wasn't sure she agreed. Refuge would be easier to find where dogs couldn't track them, where politics wouldn't require them to be handed over to whatever noble took Kentoria's throne now that Gaius Rothalan was dead. Most of the bordering countries were on amiable terms with her homeland; if not allies, at least they weren't antagonistic. Only the small country of Ranor to the north held Kentoria in poor regard, though their forces were so minuscule that they dared not prod the hornet's nest at their feet.

Would somewhere like Ranor let them in? Hide their passage and force the scattered remnants of the Rothalan bloodline to dig for answers? The dense parts of Samara shrank away, replaced with the warehouses, lumber yards, and sugar shacks that had come to represent the kingdom in a way nothing else could.

As she stared past the structures and their workers and into the hills of maples dressed in red and gold, Thea realized she wouldn't see them again. The heart of Samara, the only home she'd known, now lay behind them. Everything ahead was unfamiliar, and panic frayed the edges of her heart.

"Keep walking." Gil's mask lent his voice an odd resonance, but the rich depths of his smooth baritone remained solid beneath it. Steady. Reassuring in ways it shouldn't have been.

She chased away the thought by changing the subject.

"Shouldn't you take that off? The dogs will smell you from a mile away."

"I see no reason to continue to discuss my choices after I have explained them once."

"What if someone doesn't understand?"

"Then that's a failing on their part, not mine. I am many things, in addition to being a killer, and one of them is well-spoken." He put out an arm to keep her from passing him when he stopped. Her basket swayed on his forearm.

Thea started to ask why they'd halted, then decided to look around instead. They'd stopped at the back side of a pavilion where lumber from culled maples sat in tall stacks to dry. She poked a finger at a bead of sap on the end of a board. It had already hardened. From there, her attention swept out across the wide-open field. The green expanse was laced with so many paths cut by wagon wheels, it resembled the leg of her mother's antique table, where the old family cat's claws had carved patterns. A few figures dotted the criss-crossing paths, quiet compared to the noise of the city that lay behind them. She turned an ear back the way they'd come, half expecting to hear the dogs.

She heard nothing.

Gil nodded toward the trees beyond the field. "The river is on the other side of that sugarbush. Once we're through the trees, we'll cross the water. The dogs may lose us there."

"I can't swim that well," Thea protested. "And certainly not in a dress."

"We won't swim. We'll take the ferry."

She scanned him from head to foot and snorted. "They'll never let us aboard." On her own, she might have stood a chance. But even had he agreed to remove the executioner's mask, he was still dressed all in black—an unlucky color, one the ferryman would never allow on his boat—and the assortment of knives sheathed at his waist and strapped to his thighs could have armed a dozen men.

For a moment, she thought he might protest. Instead, he glanced down at himself and evaluated his appearance. Without a word, he pulled a piece of dull green fabric from her sewing basket and wrapped it around his shoulders. He was deft, even one-handed, and a moment later, he'd fashioned a makeshift hood and a cloak that covered most of his upper half.

Thea pursed her lips.

"It will do until you make me something new. And then I won't need to worry about hiding." He removed his mask to reveal a smile so grim, she almost wished he'd kept it on.

"The ferryman will be able to identify you," she said instead.

"Choose your battles, woman. I cannot possibly satisfy all your complaints right now." The bloody mask disappeared beneath the green cloth and he nudged the back of her boot with his foot to set her in the right direction. Together, they crossed the open field.

It was more exposed than she'd first imagined. Her heart beat harder as they zigzagged across trails toward the river, its waters little more than a silver gleam in the distance. Soon, the sun would set. How would they travel in the dark?

The sawmills along the river came into view and a long, keening cry rose in the field behind them.

Thea's heart leaped into her throat.

"Remain calm." Gil's hand closed on her upper arm, keeping her from jumping or running ahead. "Nothing has gone wrong. All we have to do is reach the ferry."

And the dogs would follow them right across the river.

The moment she opened her mouth to ask his plan for when that happened, he cursed under his breath.

As the ferryman's shack came into view, so did a dozen armored guards.

"Our little detour was costly," Gil murmured.

A prickle of irritation crawled up her neck. Surely he didn't mean to imply it was her fault. He was the one who demanded her magic.

He didn't give her time to protest. Instead, he grasped her by the wrist and pushed the basket's handle into her hold. "Board the ferry at the first opportunity you get. No matter what happens, you must cross the river."

Her fingers closed and he released the basket so swiftly that her arms dropped with the sudden weight. "What do you mean?"

Gil put a hand against the middle of her back and steered her through the grove and straight for the ferry.

A guard stepped into their path with a hand raised, palm out. "Ferry's not running. You'll have to turn back."

"Not running?" Gil sounded convincingly dismayed. "You can't possibly mean to divert us to the bridge this close to nightfall."

The guard's voice turned gruff. "Bridge is closed. Head back for Samara." He pointed toward the city.

At the same time, another guard spoke. "Take down your hood."

Gil pressed more firmly against Thea's back, aiming her toward the ferry behind the guards. "I would rather not."

The guard frowned and stepped forward, hand out to seize his hood.

Gil caught his wrist and wrenched his arm.

A wave of shouts went up from the guards. They sprang forward as Gil struck his captive twice in the chest and sent him to the ground. Two went for Thea.

He targeted them first. "Go!" Gil snarled as he intercepted them. The dagger he drew to deflect their swords seemed woefully inadequate.

Thea yelped and scrambled around the guards. More came at her and she ducked under a blade with her hands over her head.

Gil kicked a man's knee out from under him and the guard collapsed with a cry. He darted closer, striking a new enemy, drawing attention instead of coming to her rescue. The guards centered on him as he took another down. "Move!"

"I'm trying!" Thea scrambled forward and squeaked when a guard caught her by the hair. She stumbled and gripped her temples as pain shot across her scalp.

An instant later, Gil's open palm impacted the guard's jaw and sent him reeling. A dozen guards, and he'd already taken down five.

Gulping back fear, Thea cradled her sewing basket in both arms and dove for the ferry. It rocked beneath her, water sloshing across its stained planks. Gil was right behind her, and the guards behind him.

"Stay down," he barked as he seized the guide chain and pulled hard. The ferry lurched and jerked to a halt. His breath hissed between his teeth as a guard leaped the gap between the dock and ferry.

Thea disobeyed. She dragged herself across the ferry's deck as Gil parried a slash, her basket looped over her arm. Another guard prepared to jump. She reached up and snagged the hilt of a dagger on Gil's thigh.

He glanced down at her, startled, and the distraction let the guard's sword sweep dangerously close to his ear. It speared the fabric of his makeshift hood and snagged instead of slicing, leaving the man wide open for attack.

Thea jerked the dagger free as Gil took advantage of the opening. Two blows sent the guard crashing backwards into the water without his sword. She grimaced as the murky river water spattered her face, but leaned farther over the side anyway. The rope that bound the ferry to the dock resisted as she dragged the dagger across it. Why had she thought it would be easy to cut?

The second guard made the leap and was greeted with a fist to the face.

"Come on, you," Thea growled as she sawed faster.

The rope snapped without warning and she almost fell over the edge. A strong hand closed on the back of her dress and hauled her up just far enough to drop her on the deck. It wasn't far to fall, but her breath left her in a whoosh when she struck.

Then the ferry lurched into motion again. The gap grew and the guards clustered at the end of the dock as the baying of search dogs rose among the trees. Already, some of the guards raced to meet the newcomers, while others shouted for boats or watched helplessly from the shore.

Gil set his jaw as he heaved them along the guide chain. The torn fabric slipped from his shoulders as he pulled, every tendon standing out in the backs of his hands.

Thea caught the fabric and gathered it close as she looked back. The river was wide and dark, but the light of the setting sun hit the city of Samara and set its trees aflame. A lump rose in her throat as she watched her home shrink away behind them.

"Look forward," Gil said softly as he repositioned his hands. He kept them moving at a steady pace, faster than the ferryman would have done. "There's nothing for you there now."

She stared a moment longer, then lowered her eyes. His dagger was still in her hand. She tilted it and studied her distorted reflection in its polished surface. "There was nothing for me there to begin with." He was too busy to take it, so she leaned forward to return it to its sheath.

He watched until he deemed her no threat. For a time, they rode in silence, but as they neared the far side of the river, he spoke. "I committed an error."

"You didn't check the rope."

"I allowed myself to be distracted."

"But you rescued me, so I suppose I should be grateful for that." An absurd notion, she mused. Gratitude toward the man who'd put her in this situation to begin with. She gave her head the slightest of shakes, determined to dislodge any appreciation before it could take root. She would sew clothing to hide them in exchange for her life. She would escape Kentoria. And then she'd start over, and the two of them would never cross paths again.

"I had little choice," Gil replied, shattering what little respect she might have grudgingly offered. "We still have need of each other, don't we?"

Unfortunately so. Thea turned in place to stare at the shore, where the guards in their glinting armor converged on tiny boats in preparation for pursuit. "How are we escaping when we land?"

He didn't look back, wholly focused on dragging the ferry along the chain. A mist of sweat speckled his forehead, betraying the effort it took. "That part's easy."

"How so?"

Gil's answer came with a grim smile. "We run."

CHAPTER FOUR

THEA HAD NEVER BEEN ATHLETIC. It did not take long to conclude her accidental association with Gil would change that. From how easily he loped across the hills and hollows that formed the countryside north of the capital, she suspected he could run for days. She, on the other hand, had tripped seventeen times, and was uncertain whether or not the time she'd stumbled as he lifted her from the hole of a rabbit's warren counted as an eighteenth. It did not, she decided on the spot. She wouldn't have stumbled if he hadn't caught her ankle and held it for inspection.

That sort of gentleness had been entirely unwelcome. He was dangerous, a savage brute who killed without remorse, who had ruined her life and was responsible for her needing to run in the first place. That he would look after her well-being now was the least that he owed her, but he could do that without daring to touch her without permission. They would have to establish ground rules for the rest of their travels. When they stopped to rest, that was. It took all her breath just to make it up the next hill.

He paused at the top and turned back to face her, poised to

offer a hand. He'd done that far too many times, and with genuine concern on his face.

She averted her eyes before he could extend his hand, rejecting help before he gave it. "Surely we've lost them by now," she panted, unsure what to say. Night had long since fallen. By blessing or perhaps design, a hunter's moon hung in the sky, providing more than enough light by which to flee. But not, she thought ruefully, enough to avoid the burrows and holes animals left in the hillsides. It was a miracle her ankle hadn't been twisted. If it had, Gil might have tried to carry her.

"Unlikely." His eyes swept from her to the southern horizon, where Samara and its lights remained only a faint glow against the sky. Before long, that too would pass beyond sight. "You must consider why they chase us. They will not halt their pursuit."

"We shouldn't have taken the ferry, then. They were waiting for us."

"As they would have been at any other crossing point. My original plan involved swimming across, at the narrow point just before the lake."

Thea braced her hands against her hips and tried to catch her breath. She'd come to regret her choice of attire, but at least it would be short-lived. The sooner she had a chance to sit and sew, the better. "When will we stop?"

"Soon. We can run forever and die of exhaustion, or we can count on our headway to provide time to work." Gil started down the hill without indication he expected her to come along. She supposed by now, the assumption she would follow was sound.

"Surely the dogs will pursue us anywhere. They saw us cross the river, the water was no aid."

He nodded. "Indeed they will. Which is why we must take advantage of the distance we've gained. Approximately two miles from here, there's a sugar shack where we can stop. I suspect you are eager for rest?"

"An astute observation," she grumbled.

"I am given to those." The smile he sent over his shoulder was disarming.

Thea refused to be charmed. "An assassin shouldn't try to be so personable."

His brows arched, the expression less distinct than his teeth had been in the moonlight. "Do you know many?"

"Do I seem like the sort of person who would want to associate with killers?"

"You seem like the sort of person who wouldn't want to associate with anyone at all. I've met scholars with fewer books on their shelves."

She didn't know whether to be offended or disturbed. "How would you know anything about my books?"

"I was on the stairs while you packed."

If that was true, then he'd also been there while she'd changed clothing. Heat blossomed in her cheeks and she was grateful for the cover of night.

Gil returned to the original subject unprompted, sparing her the embarrassment of discovering whether or not he'd stayed to watch her dress. "For the record, a cordial killer is often more effective than one who makes himself standoffish. Charm engenders trust, and trust gives rise to vulnerability. There's a reason kings keep few friends."

"While assassins have many?" She was short of breath again, trying to keep up with him. Her words were ragged.

"Assassins have none." He spread his hands as if in lament. "But they're the only ones who know it. Look. Our destination is there, at the edge of that grove."

Thea could barely make out the shape of the sugar shack against the dark trunks of the trees, its roof shaded by leaves that lacked vibrance in the moonlight. Instead of replying, she hefted her sewing basket from one hand to the other and walked with a more deliberate stride.

By the time they reached the shack and Gil undid the lock,

she was ready to collapse. He ushered her inside and lingered at the door for a time, watching the countryside for any sign their pursuers might be closer than anticipated. The night was still, save the song of crickets, and he shut the door when he was satisfied. Darkness swallowed them, but the sound of his footsteps made it easy to track him across the shack. "Give me a moment. I'll ensure the windows are covered, then I'll start a fire."

A fire sounded pleasant, but she still shook her head as she sank to the floor, despite knowing he wouldn't see. "They'll see the smoke. No one should be in here this time of year. It'll be suspicious."

"If you believe yourself capable of working in the dark, I won't dissuade you." He shifted something and what little moonlight had reached the inside of the shack disappeared.

Whoever owned the place, they'd already boarded over most of the windows, from what Thea could tell. Preparation for winter. More proof their presence would be obvious and out of place. "A lantern would suffice."

Gil continued without acknowledging her again, but when a light flared to life, it was trapped within the glass panes of a square lantern. He sat the lantern on the floor beside her. "Begin sewing."

"Now?" She was so weary she could hardly lift her arms. How could she so much as thread a needle at a time like this?

"We both have work to do. The sooner we both start, the sooner we can continue our journey in safety." He sat cross legged on the floor and moved his bag before him.

The bag with the head. Thea's stomach lurched.

Her expression must have changed, for Gil paused with the satchel's top only partway open. "If you are squeamish, I will turn so you have the ability to look away. But my work requires light as much as yours, and this cannot be put off, or the royal dogs will follow us to the ends of the earth."

"Turn, then." She put her chin down and opened her own

things. Not the sewing basket, as he'd ordered, but her personal belongings. At the very top, the cake from Elia waited in its wrappings. A consolation indeed. Thea pulled it out, her stomach more hollow than ever before. She would need water, too, but something to eat was a start.

Gil's brow furrowed at the sight of the package, but he didn't look for long. As he'd said, he turned before he removed the head from his satchel. The stench of hours-old blood hit her like a slap in the face and made her reconsider her meal.

"I know," he remarked as he positioned the dark leather bag to hide whatever it was he meant to do. "But try to eat. You'll need to keep up your strength."

"I didn't say anything." Thea tugged at the strings that held the paper closed, though she was unsure she'd be able to eat now.

"Your face said plenty."

The cake inside the paper was dense and smelled heavenly. She scooted farther away and lifted it to her nose, hoping it would remain enticing if she focused on it. "What do you mean to do with that, anyway?"

"Preserve it. I won't disturb you with details, lest I harm your appetite. But he must remain recognizable, and we have a long way to go." He removed something else from his satchel. Tools, she assumed. Perhaps herbs or oils. As if to confirm her suspicion, a cork popped and a spicy aroma touched the air. That addressed one problem, at least. If she turned away, maybe she could pretend he was doing something innocent. Wood carving, or something equally mundane.

She turned to face the wall as she ate. "I'd think recognizability would hinder our travels, the first time someone catches a glimpse of what you're carrying. Perhaps you could make him wear that atrocious mask and protect his identity."

Gil snorted in amusement. "I'll consider it."

For a time, she chewed in silence and stared at the walls. The shack was more solid than she'd first assumed, every gap between boards filled. Whoever had prepared it for winter, they'd done a good job. Or maybe it had been constructed well to begin with. Kentorian craftsmen excelled in a number of ways; those without magic were forced to perform at a level few others could. From what she understood, other countries were not as accepting of artisan magics. Her abilities would not be appreciated everywhere. A seamstress could still make a good living without being a Threadmancer, but she would never likely know comfort again on the level she once had.

Some tool he wielded made an unpleasant sound.

She decided to cover it with conversation. "Do you know if mages are welcome in Ranor?"

"Is that where you intend to go?"

"Perhaps. If I have to settle somewhere new, I want it to be where I can earn the most from my work." Selfish, she knew, but after all this, wasn't she allowed to be a little selfish? If the world was open to her, she'd settle in the best place.

He made a thoughtful sound. "They face tighter regulations than mages here. Most artisan mages who ply their craft in Ranor do so in service to the crown."

"Does Ranor change rulers as often as Kentoria?"

"No one changes rulers as often as Kentoria. When Ranor crowns a new ruler, it's with much deliberation and ceremony, and it's never anyone so young as the Kentorian kings."

Hungry as she was, Thea's appetite evaporated after only a quarter of the cake. It was too rich, she told herself. Not proper to eat on an empty stomach, better saved for a treat after a savory meal. She folded the paper closed. "And now Kentoria won't have a king at all."

"I doubt that. There's no shortage of nobles to set upon a throne. The more likely scenario is a great deal of infighting while they try to determine who is best equipped to take over, now that the throne is vacant. Though I suppose it's always possible you might end up with a queen." His nonchalance shouldn't have been surprising, but Thea found herself glaring over her shoulder all the same.

"Do you truly care so little for the turmoil you've caused? For the trouble you've caused my country?"

"On the contrary, I've done what I've done because of how it will aid Kentoria."

Thea snorted. "How is killing our leader supposed to help us?"

"I don't expect you to understand." He paused in the midst of whatever it was he was doing, a pensive sort of look claiming his face. "Though I... I admit that I wonder what sort of person he was. If perhaps he thought he was helping the kingdom, too."

She crossed her arms and lowered her eyes to her sewing basket. Tired as she was, she knew she needed to begin. There wouldn't be many quiet moments in which she could sit and sew. She could hardly afford to waste one now. "He was awful."

Gil looked up. "What makes you say this?"

"He was a Rothalan king. The first was all right, but the rest of them weren't, and everyone said Gaius was the worst. Heartless, merciless, and cruel. A hard and hateful man who cared nothing for his people." Yet he hadn't been the one to take her brother's head. She tried not to let the opinions of others color her own perceptions, but no one in Samara had liked Gaius. It seemed unlikely he might have defied her expectations.

"Hm." He regarded his work with a deep frown. "Then perhaps I've done Kentoria a greater favor than I thought."

"Kentoria, maybe, but you certainly haven't helped me." Thea dragged a piece of cloth from her basket, evaluated the weight, then chose another. It would do.

"Oh, yes," he intoned dramatically. "Your taxes. I suppose an argument could be made that I did help you. It's not as if you'll have to worry about paying them now."

Instead of arguing, she scowled and set to work. She knew her own measurements by heart and could mark a perfect seam allowance freehand, though she now regretted that she hadn't packed any yardsticks by which she might draw a straight line. A few sweeps of her hand smoothed wrinkles from the folded fabric on the ground, then she found her measuring tape. A few swipes of the chalk blocked out the length of her legs and the width of her hips. She'd want something comfortable, something that gave her plenty of room to flex. Yet she'd want a close ankle, something that would fit inside her boots to deter pests without bunching or chafing. She added extra space for ease and drew a waistband that wouldn't restrict or rub if she had to bend or sit in awkward positions.

"Add more pockets," Gil said. "They're always useful."

"I put pockets in all my garments. I wouldn't dare short myself." She'd already drawn the opening and marked pieces for the lining.

He paused then, studying the shapes she'd drawn. "What are you making?"

"Trousers. For myself," she added firmly before he could ask.

"Yourself? It's far more urgent that you make something for me."

"And I'll make you something soon enough, but I'll travel much faster if I don't keep tripping over this Light-blasted skirt." She double-checked each measurement before she drew her shears from the basket and cut out her fabric. Front, back, pockets, and waistband. They would be simple and utilitarian, but they would do.

Gil made no argument, so she pulled out her thread and the packet of needles. Now was when the hard part began.

She passed the thread through the needle and wrapped the end around her forefinger and thumb. *Bind,* she told it as she rolled the thread between her fingers and tightened the knot. Her fingertips tingled with the first blush of power. She gathered the first piece in her hands and began the tidy row of stitches that would fuse the pocket to its opening.

Pockets deeper than they seem, she thought. She willed the concept to swell in her chest, to travel down her arm and sink into the needle. It twisted itself into the fabric alongside the thread as the tingle in her skin became a pins-and-needles prickle. Fitting for a Threadmancer, she'd always thought; whether it felt the same for other artisans, she could not know.

Stitch by stitch, she secured the pockets and began the seam down the outer leg, pausing now and then to shake her hands. After a time, she grew aware of Gil's eyes on her as she worked.

"Do you feel it?" she asked. She'd wondered, considering how easily he'd pegged her as a Threadmancer. Artisan mages didn't often sense one another, but an artificer might, and she supposed that could be a useful skill for an assassin to bear.

"No," he said. "And I wouldn't know what you were doing, save for such concentration on your face. I cannot say I've seen such focus before."

She allowed herself a smirk. This was nothing yet. Embroidered magic always took the most out of her. Whenever she embroidered, it was up to Elia to watch the shop, for nothing could steal her attention then.

"Long seams," she said as she ran a finger down the unfinished side. "For endurance. Stamina. A long and stable stride." She didn't often voice the intentions she stitched in, focused instead on pressing them into the fabric with thought and will. But he'd paused whatever work occupied him and watched with fascination. She couldn't help but explain.

So she repeated the same intention for the other pant leg as she pushed the magic down the needle and drew it tight with thread. Whenever she fell silent, traveling down the length of those seams, he returned his attention to preservation of the severed head. But every time she spoke, he looked her way again.

"A curve, to capture change," she said as she stitched shut the rounded seam up the back. "To bend my appearance, ever so slightly." A forbidden talent, but no harder to embed in the seams than any other enchantment. She hesitated before moving on to the front, where buttons would fasten the trousers and extra magic could be woven into the buttonholes. "A closure. For security, and secrecy."

Gil fought back a snicker.

Everyone always snickered at that. Thea rolled her eyes. "Oh, would you prefer your pants not hold secrets?"

That earned a full laugh. "Forgive me. Continue."

She settled back to work, but her fingers had already begun to ache. "I won't be able to do much more tonight. The needle is harder to push when there's magic sitting in it."

"Have you not imbued them enough already? I can hardly imagine something as mundane as pants containing magic at all."

"Every inch of thread necessary is an inch of power that can be put in. I should put increased durability around the knees and rear pockets to make them less likely to tear. And the waistband is one long curve. Another opportunity to work in some illusions." Not that she'd decided what the illusion should be. To make her appear a little taller or shorter, she supposed. Illusion magic worked best when it was applied to a garment worn on the part of the body one wished to change. Aside from altering her height, what could be done with her legs?

Gil wiped his hands clean. The sharp scent of blood had returned, though they'd been sitting in its presence so long that she only just detected it beneath the fragrance of herbed oils. "You need to finish them tonight. Tomorrow, you're going to begin work on mine."

"I can't possibly work that fast," she protested.

"Then you'll have to sacrifice some of the magic you want and settle for ordinary trousers. Can't you imbue them with more power later?"

If she could get her hands on things for embroidery, it was possible. Thea pursed her lips and let her hand hover, needle poised between her fingers. "Will we pass markets on the way to Ranor?"

He paused with his hands full of peculiar blades and picks

whose purposes she didn't dare imagine. "What makes you think we're going to Ranor?"

She shrugged. "We've been going north, haven't we?"

Gil started to answer, then paused with his head canted to one side. Listening. Was something out there in the night? The guards pursuing them, perhaps? If they were, she couldn't hear them.

Abruptly, he jammed his tools into his bag and stuffed the king's head in after them. "We must go."

"What? Now?" Despite the questions that leaped from her tongue, she was quick to tuck her needle into her project and fold her sewing into the basket.

"There's a small tributary river not far from here. We'll finish there and the water will help hide our presence. Come." He offered a hand to help her rise. Though he'd wiped them well, his hands were still stained.

Thea's lip curled and she stood on her own.

"Suit yourself." He scanned the shack once, then extinguished the lantern. For a moment, she considered asking if they could bring it. Then she heard what must have caught his ear. The distant howl of hounds on their trail, all but lost in the cold winds of night.

"To the ends of the earth," she sighed.

Gil chuckled as he pulled open the door. "Let's hope we don't have to run that far."

"Just to Ranor, then."

"Indeed." He shut the shack as they stepped into the night, but there was no undoing the shattered lock. "To Ranor."

CHAPTER FIVE

GIL HAD NOT LIED. The narrow river was not far from the shack, but Thea still ached with exhaustion when they finally reached its banks. The sounds of the royal hounds never came closer, but they were always there, soft and haunting.

"We must cross," Gil announced at the river's edge. "It isn't deep, but the water will mask our passage."

Thea observed the current with a frown. It was sluggish to the eye, at least in the dark, but she did not doubt it would be enough to pull her off her feet. "I don't think I can make it in a skirt."

"Unfortunate that you didn't finish your trousers, then. Shall I have to carry you?" The question was light, teasing, but a hint of reservation in the way he smiled told her he would not object to helping her across.

Thea objected enough on her own. She sat on the bank and reached into her basket. "I'll finish them now." Whatever she did in the dark wouldn't be perfect, but it would hold together well enough for her to cross the river. Rough stitches could be picked out in the morning, when she could see to do a proper job.

She expected a protest, or at the very least a complaint. Instead, Gil merely turned to the river and crouched. The moon had risen high and the trees here were thick, but they had shed enough leaves that she could still make out shapes as he emptied his bag. The lack of visibility was a blessing, she decided when he sat a particularly large something aside. She didn't want to see. She would have been happier to pretend it didn't exist at all.

He leaned down to submerge his satchel in the river. "I'll carry your basket when you're finished. That way, your cloth will stay dry."

"And my chalk won't melt."

"And your books will remain unwrinkled."

Thea shook her head. "My books are in my bag."

"Then you'd best put them in the basket, if you want them to stay dry." He scrubbed his hands and arms with handfuls of sandy soil from the riverbank, then scrubbed the inside of his bag, too.

She worked her needle through the remaining pieces of her unfinished trousers as fast as she could. Magic would have to wait. Anything she worked into the cloth now would stay there and could interfere with anything else she tried to add later. "I don't think you'll be able to save that bag."

"No, but this will make it harder to track us. The dogs rely on scent, and this has been dripping since we left the palace." When the leather satchel met his expectations, he cleaned his tools and... the other thing he carried. From now on, Thea thought it might be easier if she pretended she didn't know it accompanied them.

By the time he put everything away, she was tying a loose knot at the end of her messy stitches. "Don't look while I'm changing."

"I wouldn't be able to see anything, anyway."

She untied her boots and wiggled her feet out of them. Once free, she waited to be sure he wasn't looking, then slid her improperly-made pants on beneath her skirt. She had them halfway up her thighs before a realization made her stomach sink.

She hadn't chosen a separate skirt. She wore a dress, and she had no shirts among her things.

Well, there was only one solution for that. She squinted at him in the dark to be sure he still faced the other direction, then hiked up her pants the rest of her way. "Give me a knife."

He raised both hands to show they were empty. "I understand your concerns, but I promise, you have nothing to fear from me."

"I could probably argue, but I assure you that you misunderstand. My dressmaker's shears would be too awkward for me to use behind my back. Give me a knife. The sharpest you have." She gathered her skirt in one hand and tugged the fabric away from her body. Her other hand, she held out in clear expectation.

Gil finally glanced her way, examined the situation, and understood. He unsheathed a blade and stepped toward her. "Hold still."

The dagger glinted in the moonlight and her heart skipped a beat. "I can do it myself."

"A knife would be no easier to wield behind your back. I told you I mean you no harm, and I don't intend to see you harm yourself, either. Whether or not you mean it." He seized her skirt from her hand and plunged the knife through the fabric. The sound it made as it tore made her stomach lurch.

One step at a time, he circled around her, severing the skirt from the bodice of her dress. The fabric fell away in a heap at her feet.

"It's as straight as I can cut it, though I doubt it will meet your expectations," he said as he sliced the last few threads and stopped before her.

Her legs felt bare in her skirt's absence and she crossed her ankles as if it might help her hide. "I'll fix it. Somehow. But not tonight."

He flipped the dagger in his hand and returned it to its

sheath. "No. Tonight, we run for as long as we can. If we can wade along the river's far edge for a time, it will help."

"By hiding our scent?" She stepped out of the ring of fabric and bent to gather it. There was just enough space in her sewing basket to stuff it inside.

"By hiding signs of our passage. The hounds' noses are too keen to be fooled by water. But the handlers, those are the weak point. If a handler cannot see where to guide their dogs, they'll tire themselves out looking for somewhere to resume." Gil took the basket from her hands before she was ready. She motioned for him to wait while she took her books and the paper-wrapped cake from her cloth satchel and added them to the basket's load. Then she donned her boots.

"So that's all we're doing? Hoping to tire out the dogs?"

"For now, it's all we can do. It should be easier for them to lose interest now that the path will not be so clear to the handlers, but it will only gain us so much time. The best way to escape is to finish preservation so we leave no blood trail, then find a city with a dense population where the dogs' senses will be overwhelmed." He checked his things to make sure all was in place, then raised the basket to shoulder level and stepped backwards into the river.

Thea hesitated at the edge. "I trust you know where that is."

"I have a clear plan, yes. You were not a part of it, but the skills you bring are most welcome." He offered his hand.

For a long moment, Thea considered telling him to continue on his own. If the hounds were after the scent of his bag, then perhaps she could escape by herself. But to where? It wasn't as if she could turn around and make her way back to Samara. He was going to Ranor, and no matter how she turned the situation over in her head, escaping to the one country that did not like her kingdom seemed like the only chance she had.

She slid her hand into his and let him guide her into the water.

Bit by bit, he led her into the center of the river. It was no more than waist deep. "Move slowly. Search each step before you take it. Lean on me for balance if you must." As if it weighed nothing, he kept the basket suspended beside his head. The same basket had planted what might be a permanent ache in her back and shoulders. How could she have ever thought to escape a man so strong?

"That's it," he reassured her as they crept up the riverbed. It was shallower in some places and deeper in others, but he guided her steadily north.

"Light's mercy, but the water's freezing." She didn't know what else to say, but she thought remaining silent would let fear get the best of her.

"You'd best get used to the cold, if you plan to settle in Ranor. The winters we know in Samara are mild compared to what they have each year."

Her brow furrowed. "We?"

Gil answered first with a soft chuckle. "Does it surprise you that I'm Kentorian?"

Yes, she thought, but she kept her response more reserved. "I thought assassins most often came from enemies. And that might be why we move north."

"You'd be surprised where assassins come from. And while Ranor may be a political antagonist, they're a tiny, land-locked country. They wouldn't dare challenge Kentoria. Not truly."

Thea couldn't help but sigh.

"Had you hoped for a different answer?" He sounded intrigued.

"No. Or, perhaps. I don't know. By the Light, it shouldn't be so easy to speak with you."

"Is that so? Personally, I'd think it a good thing you find conversation easy. Imagine traveling all the way to another country with someone you found abhorrent."

She should have found him abhorrent. He should have struck her as a monster. Instead, he was effortlessly charming, his words and voice both pleasant to the ear. Was this what he'd meant, about cordial assassins being more effective? Even knowing what he was, what he'd done, she found herself unconcerned about traipsing through a river with her hand in his.

"Ah," he said.

Thea craned her neck to look at him, though his features were nothing but shadow. "What?"

"You do find me abhorrent."

"No," she said slowly. And perhaps that was the most abhorrent thing of all.

"Ah, don't feel as if you must protect my feelings. No one could fault you." He paused to guide her around a dip in the riverbed before he went on. "Selfishly, I'll admit travel is easier with someone whose company you enjoy, but you are under no obligation to be polite."

She considered correcting him, perhaps even sharing the strange revelation that she didn't despise him, then chose to keep the thought to herself. It was too soon to reach such a conclusion. Not even a day had passed since their ill-fated meeting. Far too little time to decide what she thought of him, much less what she thought of the whole situation. At this point, none of it felt real, and she owed him nothing.

They traveled by river until it veered too far east to be of any use. Ranor was northwest, and they'd gone several miles before Gil snagged a tree branch and used it to drag both of them up the steep river bank. "That'll leave a clear mark, but there are deer prints about. Maybe we'll get lucky and they'll assume one of the deer fell in."

"Will the deer confuse the dogs?" Thea asked.

All he did was grin.

The sound of the animals had long since disappeared, though she doubted they'd left them behind for good. The stars had begun to fade from the sky, and dogs could not work forever. At this point, it seemed a miracle the two of them were still standing. Going against the river's current had been slow and difficult, even when its path widened and the water grew more shallow. Thea's feet were numb when she stumbled into the grass. After two sloshing, squishing steps, she sat and undid her boots so she could dump out the water.

"Are we going to have to sleep in the open?" She hadn't considered sleeping arrangements when she decided to go with him. There were worse things than sleeping under the stars, but they were near the end of autumn. The first snows would soon fall and there would be no comfort in camping then.

Gil emptied his boots, too. Even his socks were black. "There's a city ahead. Not close, I'm afraid, but three or so hours of walking at a good pace. I have a contact there. We'll be able to rest in his home."

"Three hours?" Thea could have cried. She was bone-tired, cold, hungry, and the sun was already rising. How was she to trudge on for another three hours?

"Yes. Eight or nine miles." He replaced his boots and stood with the sewing basket on his arm. It had never so much as brushed the water. Even now, he behaved as if it were empty instead of being packed with heavy fabrics. "But we should reach the city long before any search party does, even if we're on foot. Kentoria has never been much for cavalry. The best they'll muster is a few scouts who will carry word to whatever guard force may be waiting elsewhere. They will not linger."

"And they won't know our faces." It was a small consolation. She waved him closer and pointed to the basket when he approached.

He lowered it with a frown, but his confusion shifted to intrigue when she retrieved and unwrapped the cake. "What is that?"

"My consolation cake." Thea broke it in half and raised a piece in mock tribute. "To the headless king of Kentoria." The other piece, she extended toward him. He'd eaten nothing along the way either. If she was starved, he had to be, too.

Gil regarded it with suspicion.

She pushed it toward his hand. "I highly doubt my cousin had the foresight to poison you with a cake she purchased for me." As if to emphasize her point, she took as big a bite as her mouth could hold.

Slowly, he opened his hand to accept it. "This is what you were eating?"

"Made with the finest maple sugar last year's sap run had to offer." The sticky sweetness meant it was hard to swallow without something to drink, too. She licked her lips several times. "I don't suppose you know of a water source cleaner than the river? I feel as if I'll die if I don't get a drink."

Without a word, he unfastened something from his belt and passed it to her.

A water skin.

She stared at it in the growing light. Had he carried that the whole time?

"You could have asked," he said simply as he bit into his half of the cake.

Half of her wanted to chastise him, but the promise of water was too much to ignore. She crammed the rest of her cake into her mouth to free up her hands, then unfastened the stopper and drank. It was as cold as the river had been, but blessedly clean. She gulped down what had to be half its contents before she shoved it back into his grasp and glared. "How was I to know you had that all night? Were you hiding it?"

"Saving it, more like."

"Weren't you thirsty?"

He raised the water skin in salute and then drank his share. "I've trained a long time in preparation for this night. Mere thirst is unlikely to stop me." Then his face softened. "But I failed to consider the same was not true of you. I am sorry."

The gentle, earnest statement took her off guard and for a moment, she could do nothing but stare.

If he noticed, he didn't show it. In a few bites, his portion of the cake was gone, and then so was his water. "Come. We've dallied long enough. Our clothes will have to dry as we walk."

Thea wasn't sure her hasty stitches would last a whole nine miles, but there were few other options. Her bag held clean undergarments, but no other dresses or skirts. "Will we have time for me to stop and sew?"

"You can resume threadmancy when we reach our destination." There was no road, nor even a path, but he headed northwest with absolute certainty.

Seeing an argument would get her nowhere, Thea chose to remain silent.

That silence persisted for what became most of the journey.

Eventually, the grassy hills and scattered groves gave way to tidy farm plots and a well-maintained road. Travel was easier on the packed earth, but Thea glanced over her shoulder every so often, unable to relax, and Gil said nothing to settle her.

The transition from farms to city was so gradual that she didn't realize they'd made it until rows of storefronts rose before her.

"There's no wall?" She looked back twice, afraid she might have missed it. Only farmsteads and scattered houses lay behind them.

"Few cities wall off more than the resident lord's home." Gil had pulled the green fabric from the basket and draped it around himself again. The cut part of it dangled down his back like a cape and she frowned every time it caught her eye. It would serve him right if she turned that into his cloak and made him wear it with that slice visible forever. Perhaps she would.

The streets were not crowded, but they were busy enough that the two of them were not out of place. The sewing basket on Gil's arm made him less threatening, and the makeshift cloak hung down far enough to hide most of his knives. By comparison, Thea felt naked. She tugged the bodice of her severed dress down around her hips, but there was no hiding their curves.

"Where did you say we were heading?" she asked. Few people looked at her, but the sooner she had a chance to sew herself a proper tunic, the better.

He did not answer. Instead, he crossed the wide street toward a tall stone building. A hanging plaque declared it an inn.

"I thought we were going to your friend's house," Thea said.

Gil adjusted his temporary hood before he opened the door and pointed inside. His silence was irritating, but perhaps there was a reason. She hadn't seen any guards, but that didn't mean they weren't there. Maybe the less said, the better.

"You're too late for breakfast," a man called from across the sunny room. "And noon's not for a few hours yet."

"But it's never too early for bed," Gil replied.

The man swore and hurried out from behind the reception counter. "You made it. I didn't think—who's this?"

Thea drew back a step, but Gil shut the door firmly behind them so she couldn't escape.

"A complication." His voice held none of the amicable nonchalance it had through the rest of their travels, but it wasn't threatening, either. Just flat.

The innkeeper swore again.

"Mind your tongue, Jaret. We are in a lady's presence." Gil motioned toward her, as if she could have been missed. As if they hadn't just spoken of her.

The displeasure that twisted Jaret's mouth indicated he didn't appreciate the prompt. "Light scorch your chivalry, G—ah, does she...?" His eyes flicked to Thea's face.

She raised an eyebrow. "Gil has introduced himself."

For an instant, Jaret looked surprised. Then his scowl grew deeper and his attention swept back to Gil. "You're a madman. You know you are. I never should have let you tangle me in this."

"But you owed me, and after this, your debt will be repaid." A broad smile cracked Gil's face. "Give us a room. We need rest, and my Threadmancer here has a task to complete."

Jaret's brows shot halfway up his forehead. "A Threadmancer? You don't mean—"

"I do, and I would appreciate a room so we can complete the project in peace."

Thea tried to offer a smile of her own, but it was tight, strained.

The innkeeper considered her for no more than a second, speculation thick in his dark eyes. "One?"

"Do not question me," Gil said, the edge in his voice a harsh reminder of the way he'd spoken to Thea as they fled the palace. How had that contrast already become jarring?

Jaret made a noise that was either dismissal or disagreement, but he strode around them to lock the door and then jerked his head toward the back. "Come with me."

They followed him to the stairwell nestled between the front room and a private dining area. Upstairs, most doors in the long hallway stood partway open. The innkeeper gestured for them to go ahead. "Pick one."

Gil swept ahead, his boots strangely silent on the hardwood floor. He stopped halfway down the hall and slid into a room. "Thea."

She twitched at her name and shuffled along behind him. The room he'd chosen was airy and bright, with a small table and a cozy-looking narrow bed. She eyed that for a long time.

"You may leave us," Gil said to Jaret as he unwound the green fabric from his shoulders. He put down the sewing basket and draped the cloth across it. "I will be down to speak with you after we've had a chance to rest."

"And when Samara's finest guards come knocking at my door?" Jaret asked flatly.

"Then you greet them with surprise and disbelief and answer them as honestly as you dare." Gil smirked and shut the door in the man's face. The moment it was closed, he exhaled and seemed to deflate. For the first time since their escape began, he struck Thea as weary.

She glanced toward her basket of sewing supplies. "Should I—"

"You should rest. We cannot stay here more than a day. By the time the sun rises tomorrow, we must be moving again." He plucked a dagger from its sheath at his waist and wedged its tip between the window and its sill, then closed the curtains.

Slowly, Thea sank onto the bed. It was worn, but as soft as her mattress back home. She willed herself not to think of the large bed she'd never sleep in again as she wiggled her feet out of her boots. Her socks were still wet, her toes shriveled. She peeled the woolen socks off her feet and draped them across the footboard of the bed.

Gil pulled the lone chair from the table and spun it to wedge the back beneath the doorknob. Then he shed his own boots and lowered himself to the floor.

She leaned forward, peering at him. "What are you doing?"

"Sleeping. As I suggest you do."

"On the floor?"

"That Jaret gave us a room here, where they all hold one bed fit for a single sleeper, was a statement on his part. We are not welcome, and we will leave as soon as we are able." He settled on his side with his bent arm as a pillow.

"Isn't that uncomfortable?" She didn't know why she asked. If he was willing to give her the bed, she wasn't about to trade.

He chuckled. "I've slept in worse conditions. But also far better. Right now, all that matters is sleep."

Thea stared at his back until the pattern of his breathing changed. She sank into the bed and pulled the blanket over her shoulders and hips, leaving the damp lower legs of her shoddily-sewn trousers exposed.

There he was, a murderer who should have terrified her, a man on the run after shattering her life and dragging her down with him. He was a monster, but one who feared little, for he lay with his back turned to her and slept soundly despite all he'd done. Yet in the face of all those things, all she could think about was the richness of his voice and the strange kindness in his smile. She'd heard stories of assassins and met cruel men, and when she compared thoughts of them to the man on the floor beside her, she realized there was something wrong—though she could hardly imagine what.

Unsettled, she shut her eyes and tried to sleep.

CHAPTER SIX

WHEN THEA WOKE, she was alone. Her sewing basket remained, as did Gil's dagger wedged at the window, but the chair that had pinned the door shut was back beside the table. His boots were gone.

Afternoon sunshine peeked between the curtains, promising to aid with her grogginess, so she pulled them back and let the light spill in. A few voices carried from somewhere downstairs, or perhaps elsewhere in the rooms nearby, but she recognized none of them and couldn't make out what they said.

For a time, she lay listening and did nothing at all. Wasting precious time, she told herself grudgingly when she finally pushed herself upright. If Gil was out, it was the best time to work on her trousers. While she was still tired, she was no longer exhausted, and magic felt within reach once more. She stripped off her trousers and dragged her sewing basket onto the bed, then sat cross-legged on the mattress and wrapped the blankets around her bare legs. The fabric of her trousers was stiff and dirty after their slog through the river, but there was nothing to be done about it now. Eventually, she'd reach somewhere she might be able to wash them.

Despite having sewn them in the dark, she congratulated

herself on a job not terribly done as she picked out the stitches and settled to working more magic into new, proper seams. She worked faster when she was alone and undistracted and it didn't take long to finish. She considered trying to do something with the raw edges at the bottom of the cut bodice she still wore, then discarded the idea. There was no sense in wasting time repairing something old that couldn't hold much new magic.

Instead, she pulled a piece of cream-colored fabric from the basket and measured out simple blocks to shape into a tunic. It would be practice, she told herself; something to refresh her skills and determine the best way to craft their disguises. It mattered less if her illusions weren't perfect. She could make new garments to redo them later if she chose. For Gil, she only had one chance to craft something good enough that he'd leave her be and never return.

"And any artificer worth their salt will someday trace that right back to you," she murmured as she double-checked her measurements and made the first cut. Everyone's power bore a unique signature. The more potent the magic, the clearer that signature grew. Yet there was little she could do about that. Illusions were always potent, and dulling it down would only fail to meet his request.

His demand, she told herself. He hadn't needed to say much for it to be clear there was no room to turn him down. She could tell herself she'd chosen this path, but it didn't make it true. Choosing to help was no choice at all when the alternative was the gallows—or the headsman's axe.

By the time the door creaked open, she'd finished her tunic and had just slid it on. Her fingers were cramped, as were her shoulders, but she knew her illusion was effective the moment Gil stepped inside and froze.

"You've changed your hair." A strange note colored his voice. Disappointment? Thea couldn't fathom why. Her curls shimmered like the brown-black of a starling's wing. She'd always wanted darker hair. Why shouldn't she have it?

Instead of replying, she stuck out one leg. "I finished my pants, as well. I'll be shorter now. At least, at a glance." Most people could see through an illusion if they knew it wasn't real; it took momentous effort to create an illusion so strong that its power overtook reason. Glamours were weakest when one didn't believe, or when they suspected what they saw was false. In an ironic way, that had made her illusions stronger. If illusions were forbidden in Kentoria, no one had any reason to doubt their eyes.

He was less interested in her pants. "I see." He shifted to display a plate he balanced on one hand as he closed the door with the other. "I've brought you breakfast. I'm afraid it's cold. And left over after middays, but Jaret's sister prepares a fine meal."

Thea gathered her supplies and stuffed them into the basket. "Thank you. I'm ravenous, but I didn't want to set foot downstairs until..." She motioned to her outfit.

"Wise. I'm afraid the news has already spread." He passed her the plate and then pulled out the chair so he could sit. He'd slept less than she had, yet he appeared fresh and vital. At some point, she'd have to ask what sort of conditioning he underwent to achieve that. For now, all she did was tuck into her food.

The meal was nothing special, just roasted vegetables and meat from some sort of fowl, but Thea devoured it before she had time to decide it didn't taste all that good once cold. It must have been delightful when it was warm. She cleaned every bit from her plate before Gil spoke again.

"We will sleep here tonight, and then we will have exhausted Jaret's hospitality. We must resume travel before the sun rises tomorrow morning." He rubbed his palms against his thighs. "In the meantime..."

"You expect me to sew," she finished for him.

His shoulders relaxed. "Yes." Had he feared she might refuse or resist? It wasn't as if she had any other options.

61

She pushed herself from the bed and sat her empty plate on the table. "We'll start with something simple, then. Stand up."

He rose before she could move back and she found herself only inches from his chest, looking up at him. Her heart leaped into her throat at the same time her stomach dropped. She'd known he was tall, but to be so close made him loom over her like the red granite walls of Samara's palace. He was giant, and every inch of him exuded the sort of violent strength she could only pray she'd never see. Her pulse soared as fear gripped her chest and threatened to tear her apart. Her knees wobbled and she stumbled back a step before his hand shot out to stop her.

No, not to stop her. His fingers curled around her elbow and rebalanced her as his other hand came forward to seize her other arm and keep her from tipping over. His grip was firm, but gentle, and he averted his eyes with a sheepish bite of his lip. "Sorry."

The ridiculousness of it all—his speed and her reaction—tore a laugh from her throat. She stepped backwards, more steady now, and drew her arms out of his grasp. "Maybe not so fast, next time."

"Of course." He didn't look her way again as she retrieved her measuring tape from her basket, but she found herself fixated on his eyes anyway. Not storm-gray, not steel. Now they were soft, the comforting gray of the family cat's coat. She tilted her head and watched him until he finally glanced in her direction. For a moment, she saw uncertainty. Then it hardened, and the storm came back.

She unrolled her tape. "Put out your arms, spread as wide as you can reach."

Gil brought his feet together and stood straight with his arms to either side. She ducked under one of his arms to stand behind him and measure from the center of his spine to his fingertips and down the length of his back. Then she slipped to the front again and draped her measuring tape around his neck. He twitched as she drew it close.

"Sorry," she murmured. Few people liked having the tape around their necks. She supposed an assassin might like it least of all. She checked the markings, then gave him the tape's end. "Here, hold this against that bone in your spine at the base of your neck."

He did as he was told, his face twisting with a quizzical frown as she brought the rest of the tape up over his head.

"For the hood," Thea explained. "I'm making your cloak."

"Ah." He let go of the tape when she tugged on it and then lowered his arms. "The simplest to make, I assume."

"And the most effective, at the same time. Cloaks are ideal carriers for illusion magic. Their entire purpose is to cover someone." She returned to the bed and pulled the green fabric from the basket. "It's also probably the most useful, since the rest of your outfit won't stand out so badly with this over the top."

Gil made a thoughtful sound. "I'd prefer red. It's autumn."

"Red cloaks are unlucky. And they draw a lot of attention. Green is an auspicious color. For spring, growth, new life." She shook out the fabric and then spread it on the floor so she could fold it into a rectangle. It wasn't wide enough for a full circle, she could tell already. "Besides, I didn't pack any red."

"Unfortunate. It's my favorite." He moved his chair back to give her more space to work, then sat.

"I'm sure there's something to be said about an assassin choosing red as their favorite color, but it strikes me as distasteful, so I won't say it." Thea hooked a finger in the corner of the folded fabric to pull it out smooth.

"I never actually said I was an assassin. You made that assumption on your own."

"Is it wrong?"

"That depends on your definition of assassin." He leaned back in his chair and when she glanced up at him, there was a playful sparkle in his eyes.

Unsettled, she made herself focus on measuring out the pieces she'd need. The sense of wrongness she'd felt the night before —the sense she was missing something—returned. But she'd started this, and to change the subject now seemed ridiculous. Shouldn't she want more answers? "A person who kills others for money."

"Then I am not."

"Or," she added, her hand poised with her chalk between her fingers, "someone who kills for political gain."

Gil hesitated.

It was enough. "You don't refute that one." Though if she thought about it long enough, she'd probably question some of her own reasoning. If all it took was killing and money, then she'd have to paint Ashvin and every other soldier who'd served Kentoria with the same brush. Slowly, she shook her head. No, there was a clear difference between those who served in the kingdom's armies and those who killed innocents for their own gain. But then, could King Gaius be considered an innocent? She wasn't sure she'd label him so.

"It's complicated, sometimes," he said slowly. A response to her head-shaking, she realized; he thought she was disgusted. "And if I am to be fully honest with you, sometimes I am not sure whose benefit I'm working toward. Kentoria's, I tell myself. But there are times I am not certain even that is true."

The rasp of Thea's shears struck a cadence between his words. She finished cutting and turned to put away the shears before she spoke. "It shouldn't be that hard. Who sent you? That should tell you enough."

He gave a soft snort. "I sent myself."

She missed the basket and her shears hit the floor with a clack. He'd plotted this on his own? If that didn't put him firmly in the camp of being an assassin, she didn't know what else could. "So you seek benefit for yourself."

"I seek answers. If those are benefits, I'll take the blame."

Thea didn't know what to say. She'd already pegged him as guilty in her mind, but hearing the confirmation in his own words still caught her off guard. Yet it wasn't quite the confirmation she'd anticipated, and while curiosity prickled at the forefront of her mind, something in the back of her head warned her not to pursue it further. Knowledge was dangerous. If he lacked answers, it made his mission that much riskier. But she lacked them too, and the tingling desire to have her questions resolved won out.

"And," she began slowly as she threaded her needle and knotted the end, willing her power to bind there, "you think those answers will change things?"

Gil watched as she began the first seam, connecting the two halves of what would become a hood. "Yes."

She only finished two stitches before she paused. "Why?"

"Because four Rothalan kings are dead, and the same person wanted it every time."

Her brow furrowed. "But Gaius was the fifth king."

His eyes darkened from storm-gray to stone. "I am aware."

Thea stared at the needle in her hand. The tingle of magic brimmed in her fingertips, but she couldn't make herself sew.

She'd seen the fifth king die. Watched his crown roll across the floor as Gil cut the man's head from his shoulders. The memory of the other deaths and the simplicity of their announcements spun through her head so fast, they left her dizzy. "But that means—"

"Yes," he finished for her, his voice both rich and resigned. "A king still lives, and I intend to put him where he belongs."

A living king. A rightful leader for Kentoria. So her kingdom wouldn't be reduced to shambles after all. And if Gil achieved what he was after, it would be his hand that restored peace after the travesty that had been Gaius Rothalan's rule.

Political power like no other, right at the tips of his fingers.

She gulped and turned to face him. "Do you think that..." She trailed off as he gathered the cut fabric and pushed it into her hands.

"I think I've done the right thing by removing a wicked man from the throne. Whether or not the rest of my efforts will prove fruitful, it's still too early to say. What will be fruitful is you finishing my cloak, and it's already late afternoon. I suggest you get back to work."

Her heart sank, but she nodded.

If anything, now she had more questions than ever before.

For one, if Gil had taken this mission for himself, why did he need the dead king's head?

CHAPTER SEVEN

GIL ANSWERED NO MORE questions after he told her to work. After a time, he departed, leaving her with instructions to continue without him. Thea couldn't imagine he'd go far, so she put her head down and worked.

At first, she considered leaving the bottom edge of the cloak raw. It would soon unravel and earn a tattered look, which might help him look a little less obvious. She discarded the notion fast. She was a Threadmancer. If she couldn't shape an illusion strong enough to make him completely unworthy of notice, she could take no pride in her work at all.

So she rolled the hem and fastened it with tight, tidy stitches that were so fine, they were all but invisible. She'd already finished the hood, and she was proud of what she'd achieved. Sewing a strong mental image into the cloth took more energy than the subtle enhancements she'd secretly worked into any wedding gown she'd ever made. When he put on this cloak, he'd become someone different, and even the strongest of artificers would struggle to see through such a disguise.

Gil returned at nightfall with another plate of food. This one was warm. "Have you made progress?" he asked as he left it on the table and motioned for her to sit and eat.

"I'm nearly done." Thea was still glad to fold the cloak and set it aside so she could stretch and take a proper meal. The room was well-sealed against the changing weather outside, but there was no hearth, and it had grown cold. The bed and its blankets were a blessing, but she couldn't sew when she was tucked away under the covers.

"Good. It will be a necessity for travel tomorrow. As will your own changes." He regarded her hair with a speculative eye and the corners of his mouth drew down.

"If you're seeing through it a bit now, that's normal," she said. "You already know it's just an illusion. It makes the magic less effective on you."

When she sat in the chair, he settled on the bed. "Should that concern me?"

"Not in the slightest. Kentoria's monarchy helped with that. Illusory magic is forbidden, remember? No one has any reason to doubt their eyes."

"Aside from us."

"Aside from us," she agreed with a grin. "But yours is the strongest I've ever worked. Once we layer the cloak with more pieces, I don't think anyone will recognize you ever again. Even me." The food he'd brought this time was mouth-watering. More vegetables and fowl—she thought it might be chicken—but it was accompanied by a thick slice of bread slathered with maple butter, and the aroma was enough to make her stomach gnaw at her from the inside.

Gil ran a hand across the bed. Contemplating why he'd allowed her to have it, perhaps. "Will I be able to see through it?"

She tilted her head. "What, through your own illusion?" While he nodded a confirmation, she finished a mouthful of food. "Mirrors aren't common, and the belief they can reflect the truth and betray an illusion is a myth."

The answer surprised him, for he raised both brows. "Is that so?"

Thea allowed herself a few more bites before she replied. She hadn't been impressed with the cold noontime fare he'd brought her, but he was right. Jaret's sister produced a fine meal. "They say a mirror works by bending your image and casting it back at you. Illusions work in the same way, somewhat. It might get a little more bent as it's cast back, gaining a little distortion, but the illusion layer is what's bent first. If that makes sense."

"Not particularly, but I'm not well-versed in magic. No such talents ran in my family." He leaned back until he lay flat on the bed, then sighed.

That was little surprise. Magic wasn't all that common. Artisans who took the time to learn to manipulate their unique talents even less so.

They'd ventured down the same path of thought, because he turned onto his side to look at her. "What happens if a Threadmancer doesn't want to learn sewing? Can they apply their skill to some other trade?"

"I'm afraid not. Well, not exactly. There's always some overlap between different artisanal abilities, and different branches of magic lend themselves to different skills." She gestured with her fork as she spoke. "A Metalmancer isn't limited to making jewelry, though that's often the most lucrative path. They could become a swordsmith and create power-imbued weapons. Or they could become a locksmith, creating locks that know who owns them. Or even a farrier."

"Lucky horseshoes?" he asked.

She grinned. "Precisely."

"Huh." Gil turned onto his back again, one hand tucked behind his head on the pillow. "I fear Kentoria's mage regulations may have harmed our predilection for accomplishment."

"There are some who believe that, yes." She swiped her bread through the remnants of whatever sauce had been on her meal and allowed herself a hint of disappointment she was unlikely to have more. Or, more of Jaret's sister's cooking. She hoped there would be more food. "Will we have provisions for the second leg of our journey?"

"I've already gathered what we'll need, aside from your illusions." He nudged the sewing basket with the toe of his black boot. "From here, we wait on you."

"No pressure," she muttered.

"None at all."

There were no napkins. She licked her fingers clean and rubbed them dry instead. He'd brought no cup to drink, but she recognized his water skin on the table, so she unfastened the top and took a drink. By the time she closed it again, the shift in his breathing made her suspect he was dozing. She slid from her chair, meaning to take the cloak without disturbing him, but he still cracked open an eye to look at her when she reached for the basket.

She took it anyway. "I've discovered a problem."

He raised a sleepy brow. "With the magic?"

"With you."

His other eyebrow climbed to join the first.

Thea returned to the chair. "I'm not afraid of you."

"Nor I, you."

"Aren't you supposed to be frightening? Shouldn't I be scared? You've kidnapped me, and then—"

"Kidnapped you," he interrupted, both eyes open now. "You accused me of that before. I've thought about it since then, and I've decided I've done nothing of the sort."

She blinked. "But you agreed before."

"Before, you said *essentially*. And I understood. We were still in Samara, and you had nowhere else to go. But now? At this point, you're following me of your own accord. You spent half the day alone in this room, after you completed your own disguise. The door was never locked. You are here because you choose to be, Thea. You could have left, and I would have done nothing to stop you."

Her mouth fell open before she could stop it. She struggled to find some argument she could wage against that and turned up nothing. Eventually, she gathered the unfinished cloak in her hands and twisted the fabric in frustration. "You're taking me to Ranor. It's the only place I feel I have a chance of living out the rest of my life in peace. What else am I supposed to do?"

Gil chuckled. "Nothing. Nothing at all."

She had but a foot of hem left to finish when Gil announced it was time to sleep. After a long afternoon of pushing magic down her needle, Thea was disinclined to argue. They traded places, her on the bed and him again on the floor.

He woke her before dawn with orders to get ready.

There was little to do for preparation. Gil produced a bag of provisions seemingly from nowhere, which he carried alongside the bag she'd rather not think about. All Thea had to do was complete that last foot of hemming, pack her sewing supplies, and present him with his finished cloak.

"I think you'll be pleased," she said as she offered it on upturned palms. Folding it so neatly had been unnecessary, but she was used to presenting clients with products in a way that at least resembled professionalism.

He drew it from her hands without touching her. "You are prompt."

"This is my livelihood. I wouldn't stay in business if I were not." She busied herself with ensuring all her supplies were present before she closed the basket and took her sewn bag from the floor. The soft rustle of fabric filled the silence that followed.

"I didn't realize it was possible for something like a cloak to be a perfect fit," Gil said as he settled the cloth around his shoulders. "It feels as if I'm wearing nothing at all."

"Aside from what you've been wearing the past few days, I hope you mean." She dared a glance.

Her stomach gave an unsettled flop.

She'd created the illusion, worked it up in her mind and chased it down into the thread she drew through the fabric, yet she wasn't prepared for the difference it made or how that difference might affect her. She'd never made any illusions so strong.

The face that looked back at her was not Gil's. She'd erased everything that made him handsome. His hair, eyes, even the reddish stubble that had decorated his jaw was now a dull mud-brown. The magic resculpted his face, blunting every appealing feature into something mundane. Scars and texture sprinkled his previously smooth complexion, and when he smiled at her, even that had been softened so it wasn't quite so warm.

He ran his hands down his front. "What do you think?"

"You may be the most ordinary man I've seen in my entire life." And somehow, she wasn't sure she liked it. The look on his face when he'd seen her in her own illusory garb sprang to mind. Was this how he'd felt?

Gil's smile faltered. "Is that not a good thing?"

"It is. It's exactly what we wanted." But she was no longer sure.

When they descended to the front room with their things, Jaret stood waiting. Surprise lit his face, but he tamed it fast and settled back into a disgruntled frown. "There's news."

"I'd be amazed if there weren't," Gil murmured as Thea passed him the heavy basket.

Jaret glanced up the stairs behind them, then scanned the room. They were alone, and that he found it necessary to check left Thea unsettled. "Security along the country's borders is tightening. When you reach the edge of Kentoria, be prepared for trouble."

"We already are." Gil shifted the sewing basket to his non-dominant arm so he could offer a hand.

Jaret eyed it as if he'd offered a snake instead, but he still reached forward and clasped it. They shared the sort of grip Thea had seen soldiers like her brother use dozens of times, something that doubled as both greeting and farewell, and she tucked that bit of information away for future questions.

"Be careful," Jaret said.

Gil stepped back. "You, as well. Wish us luck. Then forget you ever saw us."

"If you come back—"

"I won't. Your debt is filled." Gil hefted the basket back to his other hand and turned Thea toward the door.

She remained silent as he led her into the predawn shadows and they found the road that ran north. Her socks and boots had dried, and her finished trousers lent comfort to her long strides. Once they passed beyond the sleeping city's edge, the sun rose over mist-filled fields.

"When the mountains come into sight, we still have three days to go before we reach them," Gil announced.

She saw no mountains for a long time.

CHAPTER EIGHT

OVER THE DAYS OF TRAVEL, there was little to do but talk. Though part of Thea longed for more information, most conversation was light, and she was delicate about what she used to probe.

"Were you a soldier?" she asked one afternoon as they waded through knee-high grasses. They tangled around her feet and hindered her passage, though they seemed to part easily for Gil.

He considered the question for a while before he answered. "I have some military experience. I would not call myself a soldier."

"What would you call yourself, then?"

"Trained."

For a role as an assassin, she had no doubt. There was more she wanted to know about that, but his hesitance to answer a question he could easily dismiss let her know any inquiries on that subject would not get far. She chose to focus on connections instead. "Is that training how you know Jaret?"

This time, he looked at her from the corner of his eye. Studying, or perhaps appraising. "What gave you that notion?"

"The way you parted." She put her hands together in a clumsy mimicry of the arm-grasp they'd shared. "I've seen that before. From soldiers."

A hint of a smile curved his lips. A genuine smile, peeking through the illusion she'd crafted—though barely. It was only clear when she looked close. "I suppose I should not be surprised by your attention to detail, given your profession."

She allowed herself to smile back. "So the two of you trained together?"

"Not so much together, but at the same time. Circumstances forced us to work together at one point. But I'm afraid that assignment was what drove him from the army, and I believe he blames me for the atrocities he suffered."

Not a story of a friend he might care to recount, then. She retreated to an earlier subject. "Did you enjoy training with the king's army?"

The corners of his eyes tightened. "No."

With that, she knew he would tell her no more. The rest of the afternoon passed with little talk, and the quiet tension that question put in him did not fade the following day.

They stopped rarely during the day, and never long enough for her to pull anything from the sewing basket to work. She'd anticipated being able to sew in the evenings, but it was dark every time they halted to make camp, and Gil never lit a fire. Better that they go undetected, he told her, even if it delayed her work. For now, he seemed satisfied with the cloak.

It would not satisfy him for long.

"We'll need to find somewhere to stay," Gil announced when a sizable city at the foot of the mountains came into view.

"No friends in this city?" she teased.

"No friends in the previous city, either," he said grimly.

The sewing basket bounced against her legs. They'd taken turns carrying it, though Gil had done most of the work. His arms never seemed to tire, but her stubborn pride demanded she share the burden. She hefted it higher, so the handle hung from her elbow. "Where are we, anyway?"

"The very edge of Kentoria. Heartroot is our largest settlement against the border. Ranor holds the mountains on the other side. The mountains have always forced a stalemate. They're why Kentoria never conquered Ranor, and also why Ranor never impressed us enough to become proper allies."

"Because we couldn't get across the mountain?" She squinted at the peaks. The range wasn't as impressive as she'd imagined, though it was pretty, covered in bright foliage.

"And neither could they. Having the mountains at their backs would give them an advantage, if they just had the strength to bring an army across them. Instead, the mountains became a stumbling block for us both. The advantage the mountain range grants the Ranorsh army keeps us from reaching the other side, but the difficulty of crossing means they aren't able to chase us away from the foothills." He shook his head with a smirk, as if it were funny.

"And then we settled and named the city Heartroot," Thea said. "A better name for Samara, don't you think?"

He shrugged. "The reason for naming Samara seems obvious enough when you consider our primary trade. Our founders could have departed from the tree concept, but most cities adhere to that convention. I suppose at this point, it's sort of our thing."

"Our thing," she repeated thoughtfully. "You always speak fondly of Kentoria. Even in discussing its shortcomings."

His good humor faded. "It's a complicated relationship between us. Kentoria and myself."

"The country trained you." It wasn't a question.

"For better or worse, Kentoria made me what I am. Now she'll learn which it is. Better, or worse."

Thea cleared her throat. "Do you want my opinion on that?"

The glance he sent her was startled, but followed by a laugh. "No," he said. "I don't believe I do."

With some sense of amicable comfort restored, they continued to the city. It was small, smaller than whatever city held Jaret's inn, but it struck her as better suited for receiving travelers. There were houses, but shops belonging to merchants and craftsmen and women of every sort lined the streets.

"This is the only point of trade between Ranor and Kentoria," Gil told her as they passed shop after shop. "All goods imported from Ranor pass through this city. Virtually anything you could want, you can find here."

"You've been here before?"

"I've been to every city in Kentoria. And many outside Kentoria, too. Heartroot hosts an office for imports and taxes, and one for passports as well. My contact in Ranor provided mine during a previous expedition, but we still need to do something about yours." Gil adjusted his cloak, a tiny gesture that might have meant nothing, but she suspected it betrayed uncertainty. Over finding his contact when he was in disguise? Or over seeking a passport for a woman who was now a wanted criminal?

"Why don't we just go around the city and cross through the mountains?" she suggested. "From what you've told me, it's not as if either country will have guards along the border."

Gil cast her a speculative frown and for a moment, she missed the expressive gray of his natural eyes. "If your goal is to start a new life in Ranor, that's the last thing we should do. They're a small country, and that allows them to be very particular. If you're going to Ranor, you will need paperwork, and to arrive without it would guarantee your ejection from the country."

"Is the passport office where we're headed now?" Thea asked.

"Right now, we're going to stop somewhere to rest and eat. We will sleep here tonight. I need time to notify my contact in Ranor of our impending arrival."

Which meant he'd be seeking a courier. For a single, fleeting moment, Thea considered sending a letter to her cousin. An apology for vanishing, for leaving her home and responsibilities behind. There would be garments due. Elia was a capable seamstress, but she was no Threadmancer, and the clientele expecting magic-imbued garments would not settle for less. There was not enough money in her store's till to reimburse every disappointed client. A problem Elia would have to solve alone.

"You're worried about something," Gil said.

"My cousin. I've left her a large burden."

"If she's as determined as you, I suspect she'll be fine." He offered a slight smile.

The sewing basket bumped her knees. She hadn't realized she'd let it drop. "I'm not sure I'd describe myself that way."

"Are you not? I know very few women who would trek halfway across a country with nothing but clean undergarments in their bag, on the way to start a new life in a completely foreign place when something outside their power goes wrong."

Heat rose in her cheeks. "I also have books."

"Ah, how foolish of me. The fact you're accompanied by literature changes everything." For a single instant, a sparkle lit his eyes through the illusion.

Her chest tightened. After so many days with him traveling under his new disguise, why should she wish to see the face she'd been so willing to help him cover?

"My lady, our destination." He pushed open the door to an inn and motioned for her to enter.

Unlike Jaret's establishment when they'd visited, this one was busy. Travelers sat about numerous tables, drinking from dark wooden mugs and gesturing over wide maps. The reception counter just inside the door, and a tired-looking man lounged against it.

"Meal or drinks?" the innkeeper asked.

Gil shut the door behind them, dulling the light. "A room, if you have it to spare. Two beds."

The innkeeper frowned. "Two beds?"

Was that suspicious? Thea supposed they didn't look alike

enough to claim relation. Perhaps two rooms would have been better, but she had no way to pay for her own.

Gil raised his brows and leaned against the counter to share a conspiratorial but optimistic whisper. "Do you think she'd let me get away with one?"

The man snorted. He scratched something into his ledger, marked a diagram on a wax slate, and reached for something beneath the counter. "Best hope she will, if the two of you are headed north."

A sense of uneasiness washed through Thea's limbs, prickling like her magic. "What do you mean?"

"Problems in Samara. Surprised you haven't heard. Ranor's already caught wind of it. They don't want trouble, so they're only allowing citizens and their immediate family." He gave Gil a strange look and raised both eyebrows. A hint?

"This is the first I've heard of this," Gil lied smoothly. "Kentoria isn't staging another attack against Ranor?"

The innkeeper shook his head. "People have been headed north for weeks. Didn't know why before now. Ranor started turning them back after the news. But I've said enough. I don't care about your business, but she's obviously Kentorian. Best have all your paperwork ready when you head through, or they'll send her packing for home." He slid a key across the counter, then pointed toward the stairs.

Gil took it with a frown. "Thank you. I suspect we'll be fine."

Thea held her tongue until they'd climbed the stairs and passed safely out of earshot. "What's he talking about?"

"A problem," he grumbled.

She leaned close as he unlocked their assigned door. "Why doesn't he think you're Kentorian? Your accent is the same as mine."

"Because you gave me Ranorsh coloration, and I'm wearing Ranorsh boots." This time, he entered the room first. It was dark, and he slid in with one hand on a dagger.

Thea hadn't even considered coloration when she stitched her illusions. "Boots are enough to convince someone you're from another country?"

He deemed the room safe, for he returned to the door to close it behind her. "They are when they're Ranorsh. Everyone knows Kentoria's leatherworkers are superior. We have more fields, more livestock, and therefore more practice with the material. But we first learned the skills from Ranorsh immigrants, and they're bitter that we surpassed them. People born and raised in Ranor refuse to wear anything but work by their own craftsmen."

"Why do you wear Ranorsh boots, then?"

"Because they're comfortable." He opened the curtains. "Now, we have a problem to solve."

Because Ranorsh officials would let him in, but she had no reason to enter their country. "Maybe when we get my passport—"

"This goes beyond a passport, Thea. I am not exaggerating when I say you cannot start there without documentation. I fully believe my contact has the authority needed to help a Kentorian woman settle in Ranor, but we need documentation to even reach him. If they'll turn us back, then what?" Gil shook his head and paced, the restless way he'd paced the tiny wood shed where she'd first agreed to accompany him.

She felt just as trapped now. Already, she saw the ways this could spiral out of control. To be deported from Ranor meant she'd be handed over to Kentorian officials. How hard would it be for them to discover her identity and connect her to the king's death? She'd had an appointment that day, at that exact time, and that she'd lost the letter with that information during the skirmish in the castle proved she'd been there. There was no way Samara's capital didn't know she was involved. Her throat tightened and she sank to sit on a bed. "Then what do we do?"

Gil raked his fingers through his hair. The illusion faltered around his hand, leaving an odd shimmer behind. "I don't know. We could—" He stopped short and turned to look at her.

The intensity in his eyes made her cold.

"What?" She fought an unexpected surge of panic. "We could what?"

He raised a finger. "Wait here."

Before she had a chance to protest, he slid from the room and left her alone.

This time, the lock snapped shut.

CHAPTER NINE

IT WAS LATE when Gil returned.

"I hope you've brought something to eat with you," Thea grumbled, though she'd already satisfied her stomach with provisions pulled from her bags. Being trapped inside was far from a welcome reprieve, but she'd taken advantage of the quiet anyway, drawing patterns and plans for embroidery and dozing in between ideas. The beds here were not as comfortable as the one in the room Jaret had given them. She doubted Gil would mind.

"What I've brought is far better, I assure you." He locked the door after him and drew something out from underneath his cloak. A small box and a stack of papers.

She was less than impressed. "How is that better?"

"Because of what they can achieve." There was no table here, so Gil sat on the floor and brushed a hand over the wood to ensure it was clean. Then he spread out the papers and opened the box. Inside, a wooden pen with a shiny steel nib lay on a bed of wool. Small bottles of ink rested at one end.

Thea's brow furrowed, but she kept her skepticism to herself as she leaned forward to inspect the papers. Half were blank.

Half bore writing, some of it embellished with decorative swirls and frames. "What are those?"

"Examples. My memory is accurate enough for some things, but not accurate enough to fool officials who make comfortable livings from finding mistakes." He chose a bottle of ink and scanned the room as he shook it. "That lantern in the corner. Bring it. It's growing dim outside and I'll need the light."

She slid from the bed and retrieved it for him, along with the little chest of matches left beside it. Those were a commodity; even in Samara, the artisan mages who made them charged a fortune. To find them in a place as common as an inn struck her as curious. Perhaps the extent of trade in Heartroot made some things easier to get.

Gil lit the lantern and closed its glass door, then set to work. "First, your passport."

"Are we not going to the passport office?"

"No. I've been in the streets and heard whispers of what happened in Samara. We have no way of knowing what the people here know. If the royal guard has already ordered your capture, then making an appearance in such an office would be no better than handing you to the..." He trailed off strangely, interrupted by some thought that made his face fall. He caught himself and gave his head a shake. "To the headsman."

Thea tilted her head to one side. "What's wrong?"

He held the pen above a blank paper and frowned. "For a moment, I found myself thinking that I don't know what to put on your passport, because I don't know your full name."

"But we can't use my name," she concluded.

"No," Gil said. "We can't."

She quirked a brow. "I suppose we'd best make something up, then."

"That's a task for you. This is who you're to be for the rest of your life, after all."

"What does yours say?"

The smile he gave her was nothing shy of mysterious. "Wouldn't you like to know?"

Thea stuck out her lower lip. "You can't expect me to think Gil is your real name." Though Jaret had relaxed when she'd given it. If not his real name, maybe it was the alias he used with everyone.

"Well, it is. That's what makes it easy to recall. I suggest if you mean to lie about your identity, do it by bending the truth. Put Thea in your new name, as well. That way, if you slip, you won't be wrong." He dipped his pen into a bottle of ink and began to copy the decorative framing.

She considered asking where he'd gotten his examples. They were official documents, with other people's names on them. The passport document did not appear to be his.

"It's a woman's passport," he said, as if he'd read her mind. "Kentoria produces them in different colors. Brown for men, blue for women, and black for children. The frame motifs differ somewhat between each version."

Which only provided another excuse to hide his own. "Put my first name down as Theadora."

He paused. "How close is that to the truth?"

"Wouldn't you like to know?" she replied with a smirk.

Gil cast her a long-suffering look.

Sense got the better of her, and she relented. "My given name is Arathea."

"Arathea," he repeated in a murmur, his voice like a caress. It sent a shiver down her spine and she caught herself. He was helping her, but he was no savior. All he was doing was righting his mistakes.

His pen swept across the paper, neat and precise. He replicated the image from left to right, ensuring his hand never touched the ink.

Thea settled back on her bed and drew the blankets around her shoulders. "Should I be concerned about how good you are at that?"

"Forgery is one of many things for which I was trained. I don't need to explain why I might need to falsify passports. You know what I do." When he looked at her, a hint of gray showed through the illusory brown of his eyes.

She reached for her sewing basket. "I need to make you more clothing. I'll do trousers next."

"I prefer a closer fit than what's popular in Kentoria these days."

"I can do that. I can make them fit like a second skin."

He snorted in amusement. "Perhaps not that close."

"You'll have to stand up so I can take measurements." She tilted her hand to display the rolled measuring tape.

The sheer inconvenience that drew across his face made her second-guess the idea, but he cleaned his pen, put it aside, and stood.

"I'll be quick," Thea promised. She left the blankets behind and ran the tape down the side of his leg first. "Light, but you're tall."

"Had you not noticed by now?" He rotated in place when she twirled her finger.

"I suppose my powers of observation are lacking when it comes to everything but fit and fashion." She looped the tape around his waist and tightened it, then let it slack and slid it down to his hips. "You want it close at the ankle and thigh?"

"With enough space to let me move freely."

"How comfortable are these?"

"Quite."

She passed the tape between his knees and drew it up to his thigh, then paused. "Move your dagger, it's in the way."

Gil glanced down as if he'd forgotten it existed, then undid the buckle that strapped the sheath to his leg so he could swing it out of the way. "Sorry."

"It's fine." It was a first, anyway. She'd never tailored anything to an assassin before. The possibility for unique designs that were both attractive and functional flitted through her head before she could stop them, and a tiny frown drew lines in her face. She would *not* fantasize about the intimidating garb she could create for a killer. Not even for Gil.

"Ankle," she said.

He twisted his foot free of his boot.

She measured and stood. "I need one more. Would you hold the tape like this?" She demonstrated against herself, holding the end against her stomach and letting the rest fall so it could be drawn back between her legs. "For the seat depth."

Gil took the tape and obliged without a word. Everything he did and said was professional, polite. She'd gotten more than her share of rude comments from men she'd sewn for as she took their sizing before. Why was a man like him, of all people, the only one she'd met who had manners?

She pressed the tape to his lower back and checked the length, then pulled it from his hand and wound it around her fingers. "That should do."

"I'll leave you to it, then." He removed his other boot and pushed them both under the edge of his bed, then sat cross-legged on the floor to resume his work.

Thea would have preferred to draw the pattern on something other than fine fabric first, but her options were limited. She was less confident in her familiarity with his size, even after she wrote down his measurements and worked their calculations in her head. It was just as well, she decided after she finished her planning and preparation. She wouldn't be able to lay out the fabric to mark or cut until he was finished, anyway.

After a time, Gil collected a few papers. "Behold, your passport. Miss Theadora Emroth. It just needs one more thing, and I think that's a job for you."

She took the papers when he offered them, blinking in confusion. "What can I do?"

"It's supposed to be a booklet." He indicated the sides of the papers, which he'd already folded together. "Women's passports are sewn with black thread at the spine."

"Oh," she said.

He produced his example and turned it for her to study. His work was remarkable; she could distinguish no differences between the official document in his hands and the forgery she held.

After she'd examined the thickness and spacing, she nodded. "I can do this."

"Then do it, and I'll begin work on the next thing we'll need." He returned to the floor and prepared a new piece of paper, larger than what he'd used for the passport.

"What's that one going to be?"

He drew a breath to speak, then stopped.

Uncertainty made the fine hairs on her arms prickle in chill. "Gil,"

"A forgery," he said quickly. "Nothing to be concerned about. But it may require... ah, some acting."

Uncertainty morphed to unease. "What do you mean?"

He put his head down and dipped his pen. "Think carefully, Thea. How might a man get a foreign woman into his home country without question?"

Her stomach dropped. "No."

"I suppose it is time," he said, the faintest hint of a playful smile curling the corners of his mouth. "Past time, even. I'll be thirty-two in the spring. My mother, Light rest her, would have been disappointed that I took so long."

"You cannot be serious," she protested.

"I am, and if you truly intend to settle in Ranor, you'd best be serious, too. I'll be gone to tend business long before you're settled, and word of my untimely demise will follow to satisfy Ranor's insatiable hunger for paperwork. You'll be free within a year."

Free to establish herself, to start her new life. Safely, after she'd settled, after his forgeries ensured she'd be welcome and secure. "But I—I can't—"

Before she had time to think of some reasonable protest, he

turned the half-finished document. "Sign here, Miss Emroth, and I'll finish the rest."

"Gil—" she choked.

He presented her with the pen. "Remember, it's only a forgery. This isn't even your name."

Thea's heart quickened as she stared. Slowly, she reached for the pen.

Just a forgery, she told herself, as if it would still the trembling of her hands. It wasn't *real.*

She pressed so firmly, ink bled and feathered across the paper as she spelled out her false name.

With the last letter, Gil snatched the paper away and took the pen from her hand. "Congratulations," he said, a deep rumble of humor in his voice as he swept his own signature across the proper line. "We're married."

CHAPTER TEN

THEA DID NOT SLEEP, nor did she sew. After she signed the marriage license, Gil left her alone; he busied himself with completing the fine intricacies of the license. He worked on something else, too, and while she suspected it was a revision of his own passport, she never got a proper look, and he didn't ask her to sew it like she'd done for her own.

Even when Gil slept on the other side of the room, she didn't dare try to get up to look. He'd strapped his dagger back onto his thigh when she'd finished taking measurements, and somehow, he felt more dangerous now than ever before.

Why did he think it was funny? Why had he teased her? And Light above, why had he smiled at her that way? Like a cat in the cream, licking his whiskers in satisfaction. Like a spider who'd caught a lacy-winged moth.

Or an assassin who'd stolen a bride.

She squeezed her eyes shut. It was a lie. A forgery. Nothing real. Yet she'd caught him looking at her afterward, too, a shadowed and speculative light in his illusion-covered eyes. Acting, he'd said. Just how well did he expect her to play the part?

Not too well, she decided.

He kept to his own bed.

Thea set her jaw and covered her face with both hands. Light's mercy, why did that even cross her mind? They'd traveled together more than a dozen days, all hours of the day and night, and he'd scarcely touched her, save to help. He spoke to her kindly, considerately. She'd even go so far as to call him a friend. Yet a budding friendship felt little like protection. If anything, it tangled her up more. Because for one fleeting moment, she'd considered the thought of being married to Gil and decided it wouldn't be that bad.

Murder of the king and all.

And why should it be bad? She stared at the ceiling in the dark and bit back a laugh, lest she wake him with her bitter musings. He'd been decent. He'd offered to help her, to save her, when his plan went wrong. He'd shared secrets, small as they'd been. And even when she considered the treacherous act that had forced them together, it was hard to consider it terrible when Gaius had been a terrible king.

Whatever truth and mystery could lay behind Gil's quest swirled through her thoughts with all manner of confusion until near dawn, and she still had not slept.

"You're angry at me," Gil said as the first sliver of light showed in the sky beyond their window.

She startled. He hadn't moved, hadn't opened his eyes. He did when she didn't answer, and their soft gray startled her more. When had he removed his cloak? She must have fallen asleep at some point, then. At least for a while. She'd never heard him move.

"No," she said at last, when it became clear he desired an answer.

"Perhaps not angry, then. Unhappy." He searched her face, his eyes thoughtful, gentle. How could he lay there and be so calm?

Thea pushed herself upright and scrubbed her eyes with the side of her hand. They burned, but there was little to be done for it. Today, they would climb the mountains to cross into Ranor. "What you did was a dirty surprise. You could have told me your plan at any point, and you didn't."

He studied her for a time, but did not rise. When he spoke, he sounded resigned. "My plan is to take you somewhere safe and hope it serves as penance for how I've wronged you. How I was going to do that didn't come to me until I gained access to that office in the middle of the city and saw the marriage licenses were on a sort of paper I could obtain locally and without fuss. Originally, I'd hoped to find what sort of documentation might be used to prove Ranorsh heritage."

"You're lying," she said.

The way his smile twisted told her she was right.

She scowled.

"Imagine, if you would, what your face might have been like if I told you we had to be married. You would have fought me tooth and nail. Even knowing it's all a sham." He shifted on his side, propping an elbow against his pillow and resting his head against his fist. "We've been traveling together for some time now, and I'd begun to suspect something."

She couldn't fathom what. "That I can't escape without you, and that gives you the authority to do whatever you please?"

"That you're the sort of person who crumbles under pressure. All the fight goes out of you. You give up before you try."

Thea opened her mouth to protest, but the observation cut so deep that she stopped to check the wound to her spirit first. She did crumble. She'd hardly fought when he first told her to run, when he told her to flee alongside him, when he'd decided she would make his illusions. It was no different than any other part of her life. She'd crumbled when her father gave orders that broke her heart. When clients demanded work for which they hadn't paid. When Ashvin had been taken away.

Gil continued before she thought of what to say. "Part of what I do involves learning how to manipulate people. You're free to think of me what you will because of it. But in this case, testing that suspicion was important for two reasons. For one, it allows us to continue with what I've promised will be done. And it confirms what I suspected, so that we can address that and ensure that no one will manipulate you ever again."

She knew he probably meant it to be reassuring. Instead, it pricked her like a hundred pins and needles. "Well, maybe I'll address it now and refuse to help you any longer. You've got your cloak and I've got my passport and papers. We can go our separate ways."

"I don't think that's likely."

Her hands curled to fists in the blanket. "Why not?"

A hint of a smile returned to his lips. "Because you might have the paperwork, but you still need the Ranorsh husband to be allowed to lease a building."

Thea froze. In Kentoria, women were allowed the same opportunities as men. The same education, the ability to own property, the right to own a business. That it could be different in Ranor had never crossed her mind. As she entertained the possibility, another, more immediate problem struck her.

She hadn't brought any money, nor did she have enough fabric with her to make anything to sell. How was she to lease a building? She licked her lips. "And... this Ranorsh husband will be paying that lease, yes?"

His brows climbed. "A bold question."

"One you ought to answer."

"You need not worry. I've promised to help you start over, and I know what that entails. But that also means we must go. I suggest you gather your things. Crossing the mountains will be a demanding hike." He slid from the bed. His feet made no sound when they met the floor.

"I'll need supplies, in addition to a building. Fabrics, tools, furnishings." In time, those things would let her earn enough to purchase property of her own. Or would they? The possibility a Ranorsh husband could be required for something so simple as a lease made her question that plan. She considered it as she gathered what few belongings she still had, then dismissed the problem as nonexistent. Widows existed everywhere. If nothing else, she'd be able to continue whatever lease he established on her own. She had no intention of marrying again.

Again? She chastised herself with a quiet snort. She wasn't married in the first place!

"Was that sound because you doubt my ability to provide for you, or indignation over the fact I must?" The amusement that colored Gil's tone struck her as inappropriate.

A hint of color rose in her cheeks to accompany her irritation. "You make it sound like this is all on me. You were the one who volunteered to, as you said, *provide.*"

Though she meant it to be scathing, he responded with a thoughtful nod. "Indeed. And I suppose since I volunteered, you'll just have to trust that I know how to manage it."

Thea scowled as she donned her footwear. By the time they trekked across the mountain, she'd need new boots. Perhaps she'd make him feel responsible for those, too. Good boots, expensive ones. The finest Ranor had to offer. Maybe then she'd understand why he liked them. *As if that's the best reason to want them,* she griped silently. By the Light, couldn't she have a single thought anymore that didn't cycle back to the assassin in front of her?

Gil interrupted her thoughts with a hand offered to help her rise. She stared at his palm for a moment, then let her gaze sweep up to his face. He was ready to travel, bags slung over his shoulders and his cloak on, the illusion masking his features as effectively as ever. His smile, as handsome as the rest of him, was gone. In that moment, she decided she hated it. The cloak, the magic she'd made, the promise she would create more. She hated it all. The desire to meet his eyes—his real eyes, the soft cloud-gray that shifted with storms—surprised her, but it only made her resent the illusion more.

She shoved his hand aside and stood on her own.

If it bothered him, he didn't show it. Instead, he passed her a bag and let her take the sewing basket on her own.

Silence ruled their departure from the inn and then Heartroot, but as they passed the marker that declared they'd reached the trail carved into the mountain's side by hundreds of feet before theirs, warm sunshine seeped into her skin and softened the thorns of her frustration.

Once the city shrank behind them and they were accompanied by nothing but birdsong and whirring insects, Gil spoke. "We'll stick to the trade route through the mountains. There are bridges and tunnels that speed travel, and waypoints along them where we'll be required to check in. Keep your passport ready."

"Can't we just circumvent them? Go around, through the wilds?" Thea made a rolling motion with her hand, mimicking the shape of the mountains.

"Why would we need to? We've done nothing wrong. We're just newlyweds, traveling back to the land of my birth so we might settle near to my family." A hint of a smile twitched at his lips. "Besides, bypassing the waypoints doesn't mean one can gain entry to Ranor easily. There are rangers in the hills, patrolling."

"Keeping an eye out for invaders?" Or maybe assassins? She couldn't imagine they were all so bold as he, walking through a kingdom's front gate as if he belonged.

"For traders trying to avoid paying duties, more likely. Kentorian goods are taxed at a premium to discourage import."

Somehow, that didn't surprise her. "I can't say I blame them. I don't have the warmest feelings about taxes, myself."

Gil snorted a laugh. "Yes, I would imagine. That's what got you into this mess. You not wanting to pay taxes."

"Not wanting to pay *unfair* taxes," she corrected. "I've always paid what I owed. I requested an audience because of an error regarding my father's estate."

He tempered his amusement. "Ah, I see. My condolences for your loss, then."

Thea waved a hand. "It's been years since he left us, may he rest in the Light. That's part of the problem. When my father passed, my mother settled all his affairs. There were no issues for years. It was only last winter when things went wrong. An incorrectly filed bill of lading, from my understanding. Heavy duties on something my father tried to import before his passing. He was a merchant, you see. But the taxes were unfair. That shipment never arrived. That ship sank in a hurricane years ago and all cargo was lost. I had documentation to prove it, back home. I can only assume someone misfiled an old paper they found while cleaning, instead of destroying it."

"You realize, of course, that none of this matters now." He scanned the road ahead as they walked, seemingly disinterested in her story.

She couldn't bring herself to be annoyed. "Well, yes. I just thought..." What? That he might offer sympathy? Now that the words were out of her mouth, she felt foolish. Recounting her woes to an assassin made them seem petty. But it had been her livelihood on the line. They'd threatened to seize her home, her shop, the one thing left to her after her family's financial empire collapsed.

"You thought you would feel heard if you shared what misfortune put you in my path," he finished for her. He wasn't patronizing in the least. "I cannot say what might have happened, had you been seen and your story told. But were I on the throne, I would have waived your burden and let you free."

Thea gave a quiet huff. "Thank you, but you weren't." Nor was she sure how that was supposed to be a comfort. He could have been, she realized. He'd bypassed the guards and disposed of the king without raising any suspicion. Had she not walked in when she did, not alerted the guard with her screams, he likely would have escaped. Until now, she'd assumed he'd *meant* to escape. What if he hadn't?

"Did you want to be?" she asked before she caught herself. The moment he glanced her way with puzzlement in his eyes, she wished she could take the words back.

"To be what?"

What if she didn't like the answer? Then it was better to know now, she decided. Whatever comfort she felt in his presence didn't guarantee him a place in her life, and they were close to Ranor now—close to parting ways. She made herself straighten as she replied. "On the throne."

"No," Gil said, the single word a laugh of its own. He gave a rueful grin and shook his head. The simple, honest answer—and lack of hesitation—put her heart at ease. "I've never wanted anything to do with leadership or politics."

"Your profession would say otherwise." Thea couldn't resist a smile of her own as relief swept the tension from her shoulders.

"Well, it's not as if I chose it. The path I would take for myself would be different. Very different from this."

She raised a brow, invitation for him to go on.

Instead of continuing, he spat a curse. An arrow whistled past his head.

"What's happening?" Thea cried as he caught her arm and spun her out of the way. She expected another arrow. Instead, a handful of brigands spilled from the brush that crowned a ridge.

Gil tore a dagger from its sheath and met them head on. The blade was tiny compared to the notched sword the leader carried, a difference that lulled the man into a false sense of security. He swung hard and Gil flowed beneath the blade like water, slashing at the back of his arm. The man howled as the dagger struck. Gil's fist plowed into his jaw a second later.

Before the man even hit the ground, Gil was on to the next, but the new opponent brought an axe down hard. It cracked against the edge of Gil's blade and sent the dagger flying. Gil had another in his hand by the time it landed in the dust at Thea's feet.

Its hilt was still warm when she closed her hand around it.

The second man hit the ground. Thea didn't see what Gil had done, only that he swept sideways to intercept the two brigands that remained. One launched himself at Gil while the other skirted just beyond his grasp.

Thea braced herself and held the dagger ready as memories of her brother flooded back. *Feet apart,* his voice rang in her thoughts. *Don't let them take you down.*

The man surged forward to grab her.

She hooked a foot behind his ankle and kicked back as she heaved her shoulder into his chest.

Another dagger flashed in Gil's other hand as he toppled his bandit. His shoulder hitched back, ready to throw.

Before he could, Thea's opponent hit the ground and she pinned the man with a knee on his chest, the dagger in her hand hovering at his throat.

Gil remained still, poised to strike. The brigands on the ground behind him rolled over and groaned, but neither seemed eager to attack again.

Emboldened by her small victory, Thea brushed the dagger's tip beneath her attacker's chin. "What do you want?"

The man's mouth moved without making a sound.

Metal rasped. Gil planted a boot on the back of the man in the dust before him and turned to glower at the others. The first had picked up his sword, but instead of swinging, he scuttled backwards.

"Not worth it anyway," the leader sputtered as he retreated. "She ain't even pretty."

Indignation surged white-hot in Thea's chest and she shot the man a glare. The distraction proved a mistake. The brigand beneath her shoved hard, spilling her to the dirt as he scrambled free.

Before he'd made it a step, Gil slid between them, daggers ready and a warning of danger in his illusion-brown eyes.

One of the men spat, but all four stumbled over the ridge. Only when the crash of their passage through the dry growth faded did Gil return his knives to their sheaths and turn to offer his hand.

Anger and shame made Thea's cheeks heat. She scowled and ignored the offer of assistance as she pushed herself up.

"You can fight," he said as she dusted herself off. It wasn't quite a remark, but it wasn't a question, either. An observation touched with curiosity, she decided.

She smacked her thighs to shed dirt and crumbled leaves. "If I could fight, do you think I would have let you drag me out of Samara like you did?"

"There's a vast difference between fighting with a common highwayman and fighting someone like me. I think you were wise not to try it."

Thea was inclined to agree. "Just the same, I wouldn't call it fighting. But I am a woman, one who lived on my own in a large city. My brother felt it necessary that I learn to defend myself. At least, a little."

A shadow of something drifted across his face. Conjecture? She wasn't sure she liked that.

"You never tried to defend yourself against me."

"I didn't have to," she said. No matter how he'd maneuvered her around the city, he'd never done more than steer her. "You never attacked me."

His expression remained thoughtful. For a time, he said nothing. Then he sank one knee to the ground and worked to unfasten a sheath hidden within the top of his boot.

Thea's brow furrowed. "What are you doing?"

"Loaning you a knife."

She tilted her hand and the blade she still held glinted in the morning light. "I already have one."

"You can't have that one. You can have this one." He pulled the sheath free and stood. The dagger he held looked no different to her.

"What's wrong with this one?" She looked at the blade in her hand again, unsure if she'd missed something.

"That one is my favorite." Gil motioned toward the empty sheath against his thigh, then held out both hands. One to take the dagger she held, one to offer its replacement.

She resisted the urge to be stubborn and refuse to give it back. "I'm not very good with a knife. My brother showed me some things, but I never... I didn't need to be."

"Then you are fortunate." He pulled his dagger from her grasp and pushed the sheath into her hands. "Fasten it to your leg. The straps are adjustable. It should fit."

"What if it doesn't?" The straps looked long enough, but she wanted hers higher than her boot. She put it against her thigh, like how he wore his.

Gil stepped back and scanned her from head to foot. "Then we'll figure out how to tie it at your waist. It would be easier if you had a belt, but I suppose I can't blame you for not packing one when you left in a dress."

The sheath felt odd against the outside of her thigh. The lower strap buckled, but the upper one fell short of reaching the last hole.

Gil made a thoughtful sound and slid forward to kneel before her. "Perhaps the illusions you wove into your clothing made me miscalculate." He took the strap from her and produced a slender blade no longer than his finger, seemingly from nowhere. Its tip was needle-thin and he punctured the end of the strap with little effort. "You're a very shapely woman."

"Oh, is that so? Here those bandits had me convinced I'm ugly." She shifted as he buckled the strap for her. It was tight, perhaps uncomfortably so, but maybe it would stretch as she walked.

He lingered with his fingers on the buckle and when his gaze slid up to meet hers, he was so serious that it gave her pause. "You're not."

Thea's heart fluttered. An instant later, her stomach did, too. That shouldn't have pleased her. What did his opinion matter? He wasn't the sort of person she should seek attention from. Yet her pulse quickened as she searched his eyes, detecting no flattery or falsehood behind the illusion that hid their true color. Maybe she wouldn't. It was part of his job, after all. She swallowed hard. "You aren't, either, though I tried to make you."

A smile cracked across his face at the jest. "Then perhaps I should thank you for that." He stood, so close he could have put an arm around her. He still towered over her, imposing and powerful in ways she couldn't explain, yet with his eyes still fixed on hers, she no longer feared his strength.

She took a step back and touched the blade strapped against her thigh. It felt strange, too tight to be comfortable, yet she feared it would slide down. How did his blades stay up when he was moving around? She tore her eyes from his to study how his daggers attached. Maybe the straps connected to something on his trousers. There was a possibility; she could add belt loops to the seams to help hold the knife in place. "I hope you don't think me carrying this means you won't have to protect me during the rest of the trip."

"No," Gil said, a soft note of amusement back in his voice. The way it softened his tone was pleasant to the ear. "But anything I can do to ease my conscience after I leave you alone in a foreign land will help."

A tiny hint of uncertainty touched her heart. "What does that mean?"

"That means, dear Thea," he said, the sound of her name something like a caress, "you're going to learn to fight."

CHAPTER ELEVEN

THEA HAD ALWAYS assumed roads could be unsafe, but nothing had prepared her for the experience of traveling through the mountains. The waypoints were numerous; they'd traveled no more than three hours before they reached a Kentorian outpost. It was little more than a shack on the side of a slope, but a pair of bored-looking men lounged there, checking passports for those coming the other direction.

"Watch the road," one called as Gil and Thea passed.

"Too late for that," Gil replied, and the man gave a resigned nod.

"I don't understand," Thea said as they worked their way farther into the mountains and the shack slipped out of sight. "If they know there are brigands in the hills, why don't they station more guards along the road?"

Gil shrugged. "Ranor lacks the power to patrol their side, and Kentoria refuses to pick up the slack. One of many tensions between the two countries, though they aren't openly hostile. The danger makes no difference to them. Goods come through, one way or another, and it's a traveler's responsibility to hire a mercenary guard if they need it."

It was an unsatisfactory answer, but she knew he could offer nothing else. The way of things in her homeland were hardly his fault. Or, they were, she corrected herself with a wince. She just wouldn't be there to see the way things changed following the king's death. That led her thoughts in a new direction. "You could have killed those men."

"Yes."

"Probably all of them, before the one so much as touched me."

A hint of displeasure pinched the corners of his eyes. "Yes."

"But you didn't."

"I told you before, I mean to kill only once more. I won't rescind my convictions purely because a common thief caused me inconvenience. But I am sorry that he touched you. I would say I miscalculated, but that wouldn't be truthful."

Thea's brows rose. "You knew he would attack me?"

"I knew he would attempt to rob you. Thievery reaps less punishment than murder, for obvious reasons. I knew it would give me time to settle the others without causing them lasting harm." His eyes narrowed at the road ahead. "I did not expect that allowing for such as part of my combat strategy would make me feel so..." He grasped at the air, searching for a word. It was the first time she'd seen him unsure what to say.

"Reckless?" she suggested.

"Angry."

That was not the word she'd expected.

"I am your self-appointed protector," he added. "But I am not used to my work involving anyone else. I've never had to account for the safety or protection of anyone but myself. This was a failing, one I will grow from. I hope you forgive me."

The infraction had been so minor, so swiftly resolved, she hardly felt it required forgiveness. But his eyes swept toward her, dark and troubled, and she couldn't bring herself to call his concern silly. "I do," she said instead. "But you must expect it'll happen again, if you mean to teach me to fight."

"It may. Not because of any deliberate choice I make, but because the deeper we go into the mountains, the more concerning thieves will be." He pointed toward one particular peak. "I've been through this passage a dozen times. There's a bridge that spans a gap between that point and a lower one just north. Travelers refer to it as the Pinch, because that's what you're put in."

"And that's where we'll be accosted?" She couldn't see the bridge, but they were so far off that she supposed it wouldn't come into view for several days.

"Almost certainly. But by then, you'll have a better grasp on how to wield that new knife you're carrying. You'll be able to defend yourself, and while I may not kill, I will shed blood if I must."

Questions about why an assassin would refuse death as a tool rose to her tongue, but a merchant's caravan rumbled around a curve to work its way down the slope toward them, and she kept her mouth shut. Thus far, she had not pried. Something told her Gil might be receptive to her questions, but a handful of rough-looking mercenaries surrounded the wagons, and the way they eyed the two of them told her now was not the time.

They continued past two more waypoints before they halted for rest. Thea's legs and back ached and her knees were bruised from the sewing basket bumping against them during her turns. More than once, she found herself begrudging the easy way Gil threaded an arm beneath the basket's handle and braced a hand against its side, carrying it one-armed and with little visible effort. She tried to mimic the way he held it, but she lacked his strength, and in the end it only made her shoulders hurt more.

The place they settled was a well-used campsite, a flat space not far off the trail. The remnants of old campfires lay black in a ring of stone, and a stack of firewood sat near the camp's edge.

"The mountain's rangers sometimes stock good camping locations with water barrels and wood," Gil explained as he crammed handfuls of dead leaves between split logs. He'd arranged them just so within the ring of stone, and when he produced something from his pocket, the fading daylight kept her from seeing anything more than a vague shape. He caught her looking and turned his hand. "A fire starter. Have you seen one before?"

She shook her head. "Magic?" Even such simple objects were expensive, but they were useful tools. Judging by the quality of his black clothing and the many knives he carried, Gil only allowed himself the best.

"Yes. Although my understanding is the Metalmancer who makes them is working on a mechanical design, as well. Something that sparks flint and steel with a flick of a switch." His hand disappeared behind the wood and a moment later, a small flicker of orange licked up the sides of the logs.

"Remarkable what people come up with." Thea had already shed the weight of her belongings. She left them where they'd landed and inched closer to the fire with her hands out before her. The nights were growing colder everywhere. In the mountains, they were sure to be bitter.

"It is. But there are some tools that are better served by magic. This, for example, doesn't care if it gets wet." He returned the tiny object to his pocket.

"Are your knives magic?" She couldn't imagine why they would be, but she touched a finger to the one that rested against her leg, all the same. It wasn't as if she could detect any power within it, but she couldn't help the urge to try.

Gil shook his head. "Magic blades are expensive and generally pointless."

"Oh, I'm sure they're quite pointed."

He stifled a laugh. "Fine, you've got me there. They're sharp, but they don't offer much benefit to someone like me. Blades tend to hold practical magic. Enchantments like an edge that never grows dull. I'm certain that's useful for some, but my blades are often lost in my line of work."

"Thrown?" She flicked her wrist to illustrate.

"Rammed into someone's back and left there for a faster escape, more often." Gil sat back and watched as the fire rose and then settled into a steady burn that would last most of the night.

"Oh." Thea lowered her eyes. That should have been obvious.

A moment passed before Gil spoke again. "In the morning, when we can see clearly, we will practice with your knife. In the meantime, you should rest."

She wasn't about to refuse. "What about you?" It wasn't hard to guess the camp would make them vulnerable to thieves.

"We're not far from the next waypoint. Kentoria's rangers walk this area often. This spot is probably the safest place you've been since you closed shop to attend your audience."

"Am I not safe with you?" she asked.

He turned toward her as if startled.

Thea tilted her head, requesting an answer.

"Do you think you are?" Had he asked that sooner, it might have struck her as threatening. Instead, she read the curiosity in the way his chin angled to one side. A subtle shift in body language, but he was steadfast and stoic. Every softer action stood out against his usual tightly-regulated behavior.

"I feel safe. Or, now I do. I didn't at first." She drew up her knees and folded her arms atop them as she offered him a slight smile. "But I suppose that isn't a surprise."

"Hmm." He didn't sound pleased. "I may have made a mistake in choosing not to constantly threaten you."

"Do you think this trip would be easier if I were terrified?"

"I think I've damaged your sense of self-preservation. Considering I mean to abandon you in a foreign country, that may not be to your advantage." He dropped his chin and cast her an earnest look across the fire.

Thea grinned back at him, and he looked so aggrieved by her reaction that she almost laughed. "Don't misunderstand me, I don't doubt that you're dangerous. I've seen exactly what you can do." Not only because she'd seen him strike down the king. He'd refrained from doing more than cutting one of the bandits they'd faced, and there were the guards at the ferry, too. She'd watched her brother spar, sometimes; Ashvin once told her it sometimes took more skill to show restraint than to push to a merciless defeat. Everything Gil did was measured, controlled. A calculated game of risk, a constant determination of how much force was necessary for his desired result. That tempered her smile, but traces of it still lingered on her lips when she lowered her eyes. "But there was what you said earlier, too. That the path you would have chosen would be different. You can be dangerous and frightening without being a frightening person. You can use violence without being a violent man."

"And you can be nosy without ever asking a question," he replied dryly. "Remarkable, isn't it?"

She should have figured he'd guess what she was up to. "Tell me."

"Tell you what?" He didn't need to be told; he was too smart to have missed what she was angling at.

She humored him anyway. "The kind of life you'd choose for yourself."

Gil drew a breath as if to speak, then hesitated. It escaped him as a sigh. "You'd laugh," he murmured.

"Oh, now I'm more curious." She shifted closer to the fire, studying the pattern of the shadows and light that played across his face. She'd done him no kindnesses with the illusion she'd forged. He appeared too ordinary, bordering on unpleasant. It was a useful disguise, to be sure, but part of her longed to see his face—his true face—as she worked to lay some part of his thoughts bare. "I won't laugh. I promise."

He snorted. "You tell me first, then. Your most secret ambition. We'll see how honest you're being then."

"That's not fair," Thea protested.

"It's no more than you're asking of me," he said, a hint of teasing returning to his words. "Answer. You wanted to be a Threadmancer?"

"No." Her answer came easy. "I wanted to marry. To be someone's cherished wife and have a handful of children. And kittens to sit on my lap as I embroidered."

Gil raised a brow. "That hardly seems like some scandalous secret."

"It is when you're a noblewoman. If you rub elbows with nobles as often as you've tried to make me think, then you know what it's like. Everything is about the advancement of your family. Marrying for power or wealth instead of love. A family's children are bartered about in marriage, used as tools to gain as much as possible. How, then, was that supposed to earn me a husband who truly liked me?" She lifted her chin, challenging him to answer.

He raised a hand, palm out, to concede. "Fair. I take it such goals never came to fruition."

"My father wished me to marry. He made an attempt. He saw a union as something that could save the family's fortune. But nobody wants to be used. Not me, and not my betrothed, either." A hint of bitterness still coated her tongue whenever the situation crossed her mind. She rubbed her arms as if to ward off both chill and frustration.

"I'm sorry," Gil said simply.

Thea shrugged. It was more than he'd asked and more than she'd meant to share. His sympathy for her past felt like an unwelcome intrusion. At least it was easy to change the subject. "Now, your turn. What did you want?"

"What I still want." He pushed a stray log farther into the fire, gazing at the flickering flames.

"Gil," she scolded. "That tells me nothing."

"I know, I know." He spread his hands, telling her to settle. "It's only that I feel I must explain, and I'm not sure how. It's such a departure, I—"

"You're avoiding giving me an answer." That he'd evidently grown flustered in the process was amusing to no end, but she restrained herself and did not tease him.

"I wish to be a paladin." He dropped his hands and closed his eyes, as if to spare himself from witnessing her reaction. "To serve the One Light against the skulking shadow. Which, of course, I am a part of now."

He was right. It was such a departure from anything she'd imagined that for a moment, all Thea could do was stare. "A paladin?" she repeated when she found her tongue.

"I know it's absurd." Gil rubbed the knuckles on the back of his hand and avoided her eyes. "I know it's the farthest thing from where I am. But I didn't choose this life. This job, this role, it was given to me. It wasn't until the Old King Rothalan died that I realized I might have any other choice."

A piece of the puzzle snapped into place. "Did he train you?" She knew little about the old king; he had died not long before her mother had gone. Before she'd been left to navigate the world with only her brother to guide her, she'd paid little attention to politics and kings.

For a moment, his mien grew so stony that she feared he wouldn't answer at all. She'd struck too close to things she wasn't supposed to know, things he wasn't meant to tell her. But the kings he'd served were gone, all but the one he supposedly sought now, and she saw him war with himself for a time before he spoke again.

"He assigned me to this role. I was trained from an early age. Too early, for the weight of my burdens. But there was no other replacement for the crown's assassin before me. He was old, growing frail. I believe he—the king, that is—feared skill would be lost if they delayed." Still he avoided her gaze. That avoidance clawed at her heart.

"You don't speak of this with anyone," she murmured.

As if the statement had shattered his defenses, he lifted his head. "No." Something new shone in his eyes, simmering behind the illusions she'd made. Isolation. Loneliness.

Had she been closer, she would have touched him, but he was on the other side of the fire. Instead, she rested a hand against her chest. "I never would have laughed. I don't understand, but I don't think it comical."

"But do you think it's possible?" His own skepticism lay thick in his voice. "How can one leave something like this and be a man of any sort of virtue?"

"That's not for me to say." Admittedly, she spent little time thinking of the Light. Monotheism was customary in Kentoria and anyone in Samara would recite the Light's blessings or oaths, but her parents had been far from devout. They'd taught her and her brother to recite childhood prayers to the deity revered only in vague terms, but they'd never set foot in a temple while growing up. Their mother had tried to rectify that after their father's passing, but her attempts were half-hearted at best. To see more conviction in a man who killed for a living than in her noble parents was odd.

"I'm not asking you to speak on the Light's behalf. I'm asking what *you* think."

Somehow, that was even harder to answer. She brushed a hand over her thigh, her fingertips exploring the edges of the straps that held his dagger to her leg. "I think you're not at all what you seem. I think you're complicated, and I don't know what that means. But I don't think you're wicked. I don't think you ever were."

If the words meant anything, she didn't know, for there was a guard back up within him, shielding his thoughts and feelings away so nobody could see. That shield grew stronger, harder, until his face was so serious, it resembled a somber statue of some soldier she'd once seen among her father's goods.

"I've changed my mind," he announced as he pushed himself from the ground. "The fire's bright enough. We'll have your first lesson tonight."

Thea changed her mind, too.

Perhaps he was a little wicked after all.

CHAPTER TWELVE

NEAR THE PINCH, there were no more waypoints.

"Disputed territory," Gil explained, "which means no one bears any responsibility for whatever may befall travelers here." That he kept his voice low was a warning. He did not want to draw attention.

Thea matched his volume. "Which means something will befall us?"

The tight smile he answered with said enough.

Their nights had been occupied with training, rather than the sewing she'd intended. His new trousers and shirt were made to wait. He seemed unbothered by the delay; he never removed his cloak that Thea saw, and he threw himself fully into exploring what skills Ashvin had hammered into her.

Most of those skills were rusty. Her brother had challenged her now and then, testing to be sure she would remain safe when he was away with the army. How ashamed he would have been to see her now, traipsing through the mountains with an assassin at her side.

That assassin was determined to teach her new talents, however, and she supposed her brother might have approved of that. Gil refreshed her knowledge of throws and ways to break free of a hold, adding information on which vital points could be struck to disable an opponent without requiring strength. He taught her to wield her borrowed dagger—he swore it wasn't hers to keep—and pushed her to use it against him. She hated those parts of their lessons. He urged her to strike like she meant it, to slice or stab with the intent to kill him.

"You must be ready to kill anyone," he'd told her one night, with the moon high overhead and warm firelight playing tricks on her eyes. "Even me."

"But I don't want to kill you," she'd insisted. "I don't need to."

To that, he'd had no reply.

"Be focused." His voice came now as little more than a whisper, snapping her attention back to the here and now. Ahead, a long bridge swayed above the gap between two mountains. Fog lay beneath it, so thick she couldn't see the bottom.

"It's made of rope," she murmured. "Just like an adventure story."

"I hope you're prepared for an adventure story," he said as he readied his favorite knife. Thus far, Thea had seen nothing to indicate danger. The bridge was long, but clear, and no one else waited to move across.

She strained to see below. "Will they come from the fog?"

"I don't know. Just know that if we weren't days behind, I would rather traverse that pit than cross this bridge, but it's the fastest way across."

She exhaled through her nose and adjusted the bags slung over her shoulders. Her back still ached, but not as badly. When everything was over, she suspected she'd come through with new muscle in interesting places. "All right. Let's go."

"Be wary," Gil cautioned. "And be swift." He guided her onto the bridge with fingertips against her lower back.

That touch shot through her like a streak of lightning, setting her heart to thundering. He'd guided her that way before, but at the tip of a knife. It should have instilled fear, not set her awhirl with butterflies in her chest. How long ago had that been? Two weeks? Three? She hardly remembered.

The bridge swayed, not from her step, but from the wind that flowed across the mountain range. Her hair whipped against her face, the artificially darkened strands startling her. There had been no mirrors anywhere they'd stayed; she had yet to see herself in more than the gleaming surface of one of Gil's blades, and those reflections left much to be desired.

He crowded close behind her, urging her onward. "Do not hesitate."

She hadn't meant to. She freed a hand from the sewing basket and gripped the rope on one side. It was thicker than she'd imagined from her adventure novels. Her hand couldn't encircle it, and that something so heavy could sway so hard made her stomach lurch worse than the motion itself.

The farther they progressed, the worse it moved. The ropes were strong and the boards underfoot stable, but the motion made her stagger. Gil leaned close and pulled the basket from her hand. "Go."

How far was it? She fixed her eyes on the far end of the bridge and tried to ignore the way the middle bucked and heaved with each gust. The wind stirred the fog below and she dared not look down, lest she catch sight of the ground between patches of mist.

Something moved at the other end. A vile oath escaped behind her, the words too heavy for the wind to carry them away.

"I heard that," she said.

Instead of the sort of sarcastic quip she'd come to expect from him, Gil responded by gripping her arm and hurrying her along faster. She stumbled and her stomach dropped so hard, she thought she might fall with it. He didn't let her. Instead, he pushed her to run, though the way the bridge swayed and lurched made the hair on arms and every strand on her head all stand on end.

The second time she stumbled, she turned her head to beg he let her go, but her eyes fell on a shadow behind them and fear tangled her legs. She couldn't get up, yet couldn't make herself sit down.

"I know," Gil breathed as he hooked an arm around her waist and lifted her back to her feet. He lifted her as easily as the sewing basket and she braced a hand against his chest as he righted her. She'd expected the muscle, given his strength, but to feel it beneath her palm was something else entirely. It sent an unexpected wave of comfort through her body, leaving a warm tingle like the touch of magic in her hand.

He didn't give her a chance to wonder. Nor was it an ideal time for it, because the shadow behind them resolved into a bundled figure, and the shape at the other end of the bridge split into three.

Gil still urged her forward. Had he been alone, she didn't doubt he would sprint the whole way. The swaying kept her from meeting his demands and he restrained himself to stay at her side. His arm remained around her, but his hand no more than brushed her side. It felt different; she glanced down. He had a knife. There was one in his other hand, too. When had he drawn them? She hadn't felt him pull away.

"They mean to trap us near the other side. They'll demand our money and supplies and threaten to throw us off the bridge if we refuse." Gil's footing was sure, stable. No matter how his cloak snapped in the wind, he remained unruffled. Thea abandoned the idea of holding the rope sides of the bridge and clung to him, instead. His brows drew together in clear consternation. "I won't be able to fight if you do that."

"And I won't be able to stay on this Light-forsaken bridge if I let go."

The sound he made was nothing short of aggrieved, but he pressed onward.

The bandits closed in from both sides.

To Thea's relief, only two had joined them on the bridge. Their added weight kept it from swaying so hard and together, she and Gil moved faster.

"You'll go no further," the bandit ahead of them shouted.

"Farther," Gil replied.

The man's face scrunched. "Eh?"

"Further is figurative. Farther is distance. Regardless, I intend to do both, so I suggest you step out of my way."

The bandit gave no heed. "Silver-tongued nobles and your fancy words," he snarled. "Bet your purse is really fat!"

Gil sighed. "Get the other."

"What?" Thea squeaked. She wasn't ready to fight. She'd never fought, not really. Sparring against Gil, who meant her no harm, was nothing like dueling a thief on a swaying rope walkway above a foggy chasm!

She had no chance for further protest. Gil slipped past her, knives out and the sewing basket still on his arm, the aggression in his step so thick, it alone made the bandit ahead of them inch back.

Thea turned to see the man advancing on them from behind. He already had a knife out, but the way he moved was so unlike Gil that it gave her no taste of threat. She shifted her bags against her back and drew her borrowed dagger from its sheath. If she didn't lose it, it would be a miracle.

A thump and scrape shook the bridge. A cry from Gil's opponent followed. She dared not look back and braced instead, silently praying whatever was going on behind her would deter the bandit coming her way.

It didn't. He lurched toward her, arm drawn back to swing. Her feet were already planted when she parried the blow, but it was harder than anything Gil had thrown at her yet, and the force sent tremors down her arms that turned her muscles to jelly.

He came closer, stabbing instead of swinging, and she

ducked under his lunge to jab at his stomach. The tip of her knife glanced off something hard. Armor, maybe—she didn't have enough experience to know. His arm came back hard and he struck at her head with the hilt of his knife. He missed and punched her shoulder instead. It was enough to throw her off balance and she lurched against the ropes.

Idiot, she snarled at herself. What was she doing? A few nights of practice hardly meant she knew how to fight.

The bandit lunged toward her again. She dropped to the planks to escape and slashed upward, toward his thigh instead of his stomach. The blade sliced through his breeches and bit into his skin. He screamed something, the words lost beneath her concentration and the howling winds. He staggered close and she stood fast, bringing her clenched fist up into his jaw. The dagger's hilt in her hand made her knuckles crack that much harder against his chin. He howled and reeled back against the ropes on the opposite side.

Thea gasped for breath. Her hands shook and her bones ached from the impact, but the man grabbed hold of the ropes to keep from falling and did not move on her again. She dared a glance in the direction they'd been going, half expecting to see Gil locked in battle.

He stood with his arms crossed, three men sprawled on the bridge behind him and a smirk on his face. "Good."

She gaped. "You could have helped me!"

"Yes, but you're better served by learning to manage on your own." He offered a hand. His knives were already put away.

Behind his fluttering cloak, one of the men reached to grab Gil's foot.

"Look out!" she cried.

Gil barely glanced his way. He stomped once, hard, and the man rolled away with a yowl.

Thea gasped and lunged forward too late to stop him.

The bandit's legs went over the edge and panic took his face.

Gil hissed something and dropped to his knees. His hand

snapped out and latched onto the man's arm as his body scraped over the ends of the planks. The bandit's full weight jerked him down flat.

"Mercy!" the man screamed. He clutched Gil's wrist with his free hand, his legs flailing over the trench.

"Light-blasted fool," Gil growled as he wrenched his other arm free of the sewing basket and strained to lift him.

Thea scrambled backwards to get out of the way and almost tripped over the man she'd punched. He snagged her by the arms and she drove an elbow back hard. It hit whatever armor he wore beneath his coat and sent pain lancing up and down her arm.

The other two men on the bridge scrambled to aid their companion. One grabbed Gil by the shoulders and the other reached down to seize his dangling friend's arm, and the three pulled back.

Terror held the man's eyes wide as he came back from the abyss. He sprawled flat on the bridge, gasping and whispering prayers of thanks more fervent than anything Thea had ever heard.

Gil stood straight. He offered them nothing, no warning or comeuppance, just took the basket from the planks and turned to extend a hand toward Thea.

The man who held her arms didn't just release her. He inched forward, aiding her in retaining her balance as she stepped over his praying friend.

Thea slid her hand into Gil's and he gave it a squeeze, then pulled her the rest of the way across the bridge. Their silence was punctuated by the soft moans of the wind and behind them, the bandits said nothing.

When they reached solid ground again, Thea looked back. The four men remained, all of them watching, but if they spoke, their words were lost to the mountains.

"You saved him," she said.

Gil grunted. "One life. That's what I'll take. He is not worth the expense."

Her hand ached. She shook it and then wriggled it into her pocket in hopes the warmth there would ease the pain in her knuckles. "You mean to kill someone in particular, don't you?"

"That is my job."

"A job you gave yourself."

"Who ordered it doesn't matter. It will be done."

"Why?"

He paused, the look in his eyes one she hadn't seen since the beginning. Cold, threatening. The eyes of a man who would not be deterred. "You claw for answers, yet you do not consider the danger in having them." Then he looked away, and the hard edges of his expression softened. "I will discuss this no further." He strode ahead, toward a bend where the mountainside would shield them from the wind.

Thea stared at his back for a moment before she made her decision. She had one more question, and this time, she would not hold her tongue. "Is it worth it, Gil?" she asked as she jogged to catch up with his long-legged gait. "This mission you're on, this life you must take. Is it worth it?"

He raised his chin and she didn't think he would answer, but his words came, soft and somehow resigned. "We will see."

CHAPTER THIRTEEN

THE BRIDGE SHOULD HAVE BEEN the most frightening part of the journey. If not the bridge, perhaps the fact the journey had happened at all. That she'd walked in to see the king beheaded, that she'd been spirited away by his killer. Instead, the most frightening thing was standing beside that killer and holding his hand while the clerk on the other side of a simple wooden counter examined their documents.

"It'll be more convincing," she'd claimed outside the little office before they'd gone in. She still believed that was true, but it was only part of why she'd asked. In truth, her hands shook like the last wind-battered leaves before winter, and the moment Gil had obligingly twined his fingers with hers, she'd felt better.

Better, like he wasn't a monster, a murderer, a brute with the dead king's head in a bag at his hip. At least, she thought he still carried it. He'd never mentioned it again, and she preferred not to think of its existence.

He squeezed her hand.

At last, the clerk sniffed and reached for a wooden block stamp that perched atop a tray full of ink. The stamp just touched the ink before he thumped it down on both of their passports, in addition to a new document he'd drawn from a drawer. He rolled that and their fraudulent marriage license together and tied a pale yellow cord around them to hold the paper shut. "Welcome home," he announced, his smile both warm and polite as he slid the documents back across the counter.

"Thank you." Gil accepted the paperwork with only one hand. He made no move to extricate his fingers from Thea's grasp. If anything, he held her tighter now. "We will need accommodations for the night, but it's been so long since I've visited that I no longer remember where I last stayed. Would it be rude to inquire after accommodations that might serve Kentorian foods?" He tilted his head toward Thea as he spoke, indicating he meant it for her benefit. She wasn't sure if that was kind or offensive.

"There aren't many," the clerk admitted. "Harder to find Kentorian anything now, what with the mess that's befallen their crown. If your coin's Kentorian, I recommend exchanging a few for Ranorsh bits before you try and find somewhere to stay."

"Why so?" Gil asked as he put away their documents. Thea was curious, herself. Kentoria's currency was minted precious metal, while Ranor circulated notes backed by a reserve. Of the two, Kentoria's currency was regarded as more trustworthy.

The clerk shook his head. "Lots of rumors, but you know how folk are. Kentoria's coins sport the crown. Now people say it's cursed."

Gil sighed. "That's one thing I didn't miss while I was away. All the superstition. Do you have a clerk here who handles the exchange, or...?"

"Two counters down," the man said, pointing with two fingers.

"Thank you." Gil drew Thea away from the counter by their interlinked hands.

"Do people really believe money can carry a curse?" she asked in a whisper as he led her farther down the row of clerks.

"People believe many things. Kentorians are given to their

own oddities, you cannot begrudge the Ranorsh theirs." Low as it was, his voice still struck her as loud in the quiet office.

Thea chose to remain silent as he exchanged a handful of gleaming coins for the strange paper money she'd seen only once before. Her father had shown them a handful of Ranosh bills once, when he'd traveled north on business instead of sailing to less familiar lands to the east. She'd never thought much about her father's travels; they'd been an inconvenience her family was used to, nothing more. Now she thought of the bandits in the Pinch and wondered how her father's long caravan of wagons might have crossed the mountain range.

A murmur of gratitude from Gil to the money changer told her he was done. He folded the pale bills and stuffed them into his pocket, then tugged her toward the door.

Outside, the evening air was crisp and calm, though the streets still bustled. Farther up the village's central road, a handful of people worked to set up displays under colorful striped awnings. Thea gazed that way as Gil took a moment to ensure their documents were safely stored. "Is that all there is to it? Getting into Ranor?"

He pointed toward a building near what she presumed was the village center, using the same two-fingered gesture as the man inside. Ranorsh manners, perhaps. Knowing what Gil had shared about his need to fit wherever he was put, it came as no surprise that he'd pick it up so easily. "Yes and no," he said as they moved in that direction. "We must travel to Ranor's capital. Of the options, I believe that will be the best place for you to establish yourself. They will expect to see our papers there, too, but we will stay with Rilion until your affairs are settled."

"Rilion? Your contact? I thought he'd be right on the other side of the mountains."

"He would have been, had we not been delayed. By now, he will have returned to Danesse. His home is there, in the capital."

"He left?" She exclaimed. "Whatever for?"

"Because we are late," Gil said simply. "And so he will assume I am dead."

He didn't say as much, but she knew that was a problem. "It's my fault," she said. There was no point in asking. She knew.

"I don't blame you. It was my mistake, my failure. I should have accounted for all possibilities, including a strange woman bursting in while I completed my task and then requiring rescue." The tiniest hint of a smile graced the corners of his mouth and a playful spark lit his eyes.

She couldn't help but tease back. "And what if I'd been a man?"

"Then I would not be holding your hand."

She gasped and planted her other hand on his shoulder to shove him away, but he held her tight and didn't let her escape. Worse, he pulled her closer.

"Remember," he whispered, "we're newlyweds. Traversing the mountains allowed you some respite from our farce, but if we are to do all that I've promised, at least some impression must be given."

She leaned closer, her lips a hair's breadth from his ear when she responded. "Is that why you've brought me to a festival?"

"That," Gil murmured, "was wholly unintentional."

The striped awnings were only the beginning. Women with tiny flames atop poles lit colored glass lanterns along the streets, illuminating banners strung between buildings. Men stacked logs as tall as themselves in the very center of the village, while children added bundles of sticks between them. Already, people sang, though there was no stage for the few musicians present and those Thea saw clustered together still tuned their instruments.

"It reminds me of the summer-night festivals in Kentoria," she said.

"I suspect it's similar. They celebrate the pear harvest."

Thea covered her mouth to hide a giggle. "All this for pears?"

"Ranor's favorite crop. They're a staple here, as much as

maple syrups and timber are a staple for Kentoria. Come, this is where we'll be staying." He turned her toward a tall building of wood and stone. Its door was open, inviting the cold autumn air.

"I don't want to go inside," she said. "I want to dance."

"We haven't time for dancing." He gripped her hand tighter and dragged her toward the door.

She put down her heels. "What happened to impressions?"

"Thea," he breathed, exasperated.

"You'll make everyone think you despise your new bride!"

Gil clamped his jaw shut and exhaled through his nose, long and slow. The musicians had finished tuning and began a rollicking tune, eliciting a wave of cheers and shouts from the clustered villagers. He let her go, but held out his hand expectantly. "Give me your things."

She stared at his hand as if it posed danger, now that he'd released her fingers. "What for?"

"There is little threat to you here. You're free to walk around as you wish." His frown was stern, though his demeanor softened a moment later. "I will secure a room for us. We have little time to spare, so use it wisely. I will return after I've put away our things."

She didn't believe for a moment that he would. Nonetheless, the brush with independence was welcome, and she turned toward the nearest stand to see what the event had to offer.

Beneath the striped awnings, people sold handicrafts of every variety. Some offered fresh foods, while others sold jars of preserves and boxes of dried fruits to last the winter. Judging by how well-stocked they were, setup for the festivities had started earlier in the day. It was more like the events in Kentoria than she'd suspected, then; most folk worked through the daylight hours and didn't walk the festival market or participate in activities until it had grown too dark to continue labor.

With no money in her pockets, shopping was unappealing, so she turned her attention to something better suited to her needs. She knew little of popular fashion beyond Kentoria's borders.

Most of her clientele had been wealthy. People who had known or worked with her father spread her name in their social circles, his reputation offering a security his career had not. Those sort of nobles sought only to compete with each other, never looking to trends outside the capital, never thinking to introduce foreign designs. This close to Kentoria's border, she'd expected to see more of her homeland's fashion. Instead, she saw the pride in Ranorsh craftsmanship Gil had already explained. A problem, if she didn't adapt.

The coarse-spun woolen fabrics and drab dyes didn't surprise her, but the shape of most garments did. The weather here was colder than what she was used to, and instead of cloaks, everyone she saw wore thick coats lined with feathers or fur. The cut of them was square and tidy, with straight sleeves and tall collars that folded down to display linings of wool dyed a brighter shade than the rest of the garb. That would be easy to replicate, she reassured herself. Already, thoughts of making her own quality dyes and introducing colors that may not be readily available in Ranor spun through her head.

She was less certain about the trousers. None of the women wore dresses or skirts that she saw. Instead, both men and women wore the same strange, loose-fitting pants formed of a multitude of gathers. Or were they pleats? The shape made little sense, hanging low and full around the thighs and then drawing in snug at the knee so they would fit inside the tall riding boots that matched what Gil wore. Those would take more experimentation. Then again, maybe there would be some who were open to a different style. Something similar in shape but less bulky, maybe made with heavier fabrics or even leather, guaranteed to hold warmth better than what she saw. The density of those gathers meant the fabrics were thin, and just thinking of something so loose and lightweight in the winter made her want to clench her thighs together.

Children's clothing was much the same. The coats could be a little roomier, the colors a little bolder. Children often preferred bright colors, and everything here was drab. Only the striped awnings and colorful coat colors sported any sort of vibrancy. Dyes were a luxury, then. Used only for drawing attention to the most important things. Collars framed faces, and the awnings represented a livelihood for the families who sold goods beneath them.

After her circuit of the stalls spent looking at shoppers rather than goods, she went around again to confirm her suspicion. There was no dyemaker here; those bright fabrics had to be brought from elsewhere. The capital, she presumed. Danesse.

By the time she was certain there was no one selling dyes, the great fire in the middle of the village was blazing and the musicians had moved farther away, to where they could play without discomfort. People danced in an open field, where the low stone walls that separated the space from the village roads cast long shadows in the firelight.

Small clusters of village folk stood around the gates and near the walls, clapping along with music or chatting amongst themselves as they watched the dancers move. Thea lingered near one such group, observing the steps. The dances were unfamiliar, nothing like the slow, swanning motions in the usual Kentorian three-step. Before long, she found herself nodding along with the rhythm, and it was not much longer than that before a gentleman split away from the dancers to offer her a hand. It wasn't until then that she noticed the dancers were segmented into groups. There were those who danced as families, a mix of all ages that bounced along in time with the melody, and those who danced in pairs. The movements were similar, but more focused.

She smiled and touched her fingertips to the stranger's palm, as she'd seen other young women do. He led her into the field and raised her hand high overhead to lead her in the first few steps.

At first, he went slow, giving her time to learn the pattern. By the third revolution, she was confident enough to tear her eyes from her feet. She raised her head to offer a smile to her partner, but her gaze slid past his face to land on the people near the gate.

Gil stood among them, his arms crossed and his face so fraught with anger, she saw his stormcloud eyes through the illusion she'd sewn.

Thea set her jaw and stared back as she went around again. He had no right to look at her that way. She'd done nothing wrong. Yet by the time she completed the circle with her partner and looked toward the gate again, he was gone, and the sudden disappearance made her heart skip and then flutter with uncertainty.

Had she done something wrong? She'd told him she wanted to dance, he told her she was free to explore. That he might tell her she could and then rescind the offer sat poorly with her.

A shadow moved to her right and her partner halted their dance. Her head snapped around as an arm reached past her shoulder to take her hand from her companion's. Gil. How had he moved so quickly?

"It's unbecoming for a woman to dance with a man other than her husband," he said as he turned her toward him and raised their hands together, his hand cupped, her fingertips in his palm.

"Then I'll be unbecoming." Despite the anger that still furrowed his brow and set his mouth hard, she stared up into his dark eyes, challenging him to scold her.

"Not of you," he replied through clenched teeth. "Of me." He led her through the first turn, his steps more graceful than the first man's had been.

"You didn't want to dance." Four steps right. Two left. Four more right. She looked to her feet again, to Gil's feet, to his Ranorsh boots that made him a blend of her homeland and here. He fit in everywhere, truly. Even the unfamiliar dance came naturally to him. Or was it unfamiliar? She tried to picture him here before, twirling some unknown woman in the same field. The thought lodged a strange discomfort in her chest.

"I still don't." He added a new step, one the other dancers had incorporated when the music changed. Four steps. Two. Four more, and a tap of his heel against hers. The motion brought him closer and instead of resisting, she savored when his other hand came to rest on her hip.

"You're good at dancing." Was this what she'd wanted? What she'd hoped for when she tried to get him to dance? She rested her free hand atop his, tracing the tendons from his knuckles to his wrist, sliding her hand up his arm. Four steps, two. Something firm beneath his sleeve greeted her exploring fingers. A sheathed dagger. She shouldn't have been surprised.

He never tore his eyes from hers. "I'm good at many things."

"Perhaps you should show me more." Light's mercy, she shouldn't goad him. Her hand lay atop what had to be one of a dozen knives hidden on his person. What more did she need to remind her what sort of man he was?

Without warning, he stopped, staring down at her with a fire in his eyes that threatened to consume her whole.

Her breath caught and her gaze slipped to his mouth. He was right there, so close. All she had to do was rise on tip-toe, to lift her face, to meet his lips—

"You have put off your end of this bargain long enough," he growled, shattering the moment.

Her heart shattered with it.

"You will finish sewing. Tonight." He released her and spun back toward the gate to stalk toward the inn he'd chosen.

It was all Thea could do to stay on her feet. "Tonight," she croaked.

And tomorrow, she would pretend everything was the same.

CHAPTER FOURTEEN

Gil was angry.

Thea didn't know what she'd done to stoke those coals, but she couldn't deny the anger that visibly smoldered within him. Maybe it hadn't been her. Maybe something had happened in the brief time they'd been separated. Or maybe she truly had taken too long, frittered away valuable time, robbed him of something that couldn't be replaced.

The realization that she knew so little about his mission had never been so stark. She didn't know what timeline he ran on, didn't know how easily it could be jeopardized. So when they reached the room at the inn, she put her head down and sat on the floor with the trousers she'd started and not yet finished.

Even with the two lanterns and several candles he'd scrounged from somewhere, she found it difficult to see. Her tiny stitches disappeared into the dark brown fabric she'd selected. She tried to keep them steady anyway. Even if her stitches were shaky, they'd be strong, and if a few went wayward, it wouldn't harm the integrity of the clothing she made. But she wondered what it would do to the magic.

Focusing on the needle was difficult. She should have been refreshed after a bit of fun in the village, reassured after seeing there would be niches for her work to fill and ensure she'd have a good life after they reached Danesse and she had a chance to settle. Yet her thoughts kept drifting back to the steel she'd seen in Gil's eyes and the way she'd seen through the illusion the cloak draped over him. It shouldn't have been so transparent. She'd have to check the seams on his cloak next, ensure nothing had come loose. Even a damaged garment would retain its magic, but breaking threads did make it weaker.

His shadow passed over her as he paced the room. She tried not to flinch. He paced like a trapped predator, back and forth across the room. Each step was silent, solidifying the mental image. She'd seen pelts from great cats found farther south, where dense jungles demanded stealthy hunters. That he was dressed in black solidified it more.

When she finished one long seam, she put down her work. "May I see your cloak?"

Gil paused mid-stride. He said nothing, but she saw the question in the way he looked at her.

"I'd like to check something. To be sure the illusions work well together." It wasn't entirely untrue. They were supposed to build upon each other, but they had to be similar enough that his appearance wouldn't change when a single piece was removed. His cloak, his shirt, the trousers on her lap, they'd all build the same image.

His hand drifted to the clasp and the cloak slid from his shoulders a moment later. The false image she'd crafted fell away like dust as he held out the cloak for her to take.

She accepted it without comment. His demeanor did not welcome conversation. Her brother had been the same way. Whenever Ashvin grew angry or frustrated, he grew solemn, and an unwelcoming shadow followed his every step. It was one of few things about him she didn't miss.

The green cloth was easier to see by lantern light and it didn't take long to check all the seams. Everything was intact, as perfect as when the project left her hands. It had to be something else, then. Some other reason for reality to bleed through the illusion. Admittedly, she knew little about that sort of magic. Forbidden as it was, the power used to weave glamours into garments still held plenty of secrets.

Satisfied by the durability of her work and unsatisfied by lack of answers, she focused on tracing the seams with her fingers and replicating the image she'd created.

Above her, Gil still paced.

It was easier to look at him now. For some reason, she found his true face less threatening; perhaps because it was easier to picture how he'd look when he smiled. Thea glanced his way as he crossed in front of the lanterns yet again. The silence had grown troubling. His voice would be a comfort. "How far is it to Danesse?"

He paused near the door. "Ranor is small. If we encounter no issues, we'll be there in two days."

"That bodes well for easy trade. The roadways are clear and simple, then?" She tried to smile, but still took the sense he was angry. Maybe if she redirected his thoughts from whatever made him pace like that, he'd relax.

"Simple, and there's little to see in Ranor. Nothing but fields for the sheep and orchards full of pear trees between here and the capital." He lingered where he was, though he regarded the door with suspicion. It seemed unlikely that anyone might eavesdrop on two simple travelers, but anything was possible.

Thea made a soft humming sound. "Are your boots sheepskin, then? They look thicker than that."

"Cowhide. The eastern portions of the country are flatter, better suited to letting cattle range. Not in the numbers you'd see in Kentoria, of course. The Ranorsh favor sheep and goats, which are easier to keep on the hills."

"And pears. An odd assortment of things to keep." Goats and sheep meant quality wool would be easy to come by, though.

"Agriculture is one of the things I know little about. But I do know pears favor cool and wet climates. You'll have to try the perry. It's one of their finer exports, and one of few that are welcomed in Kentoria. A good quality drink." He laced his hands together behind his back as he spoke, lending him a businesslike air.

It was better than the pacing. Thea let herself relax. "Is that so? You don't strike me as a drinker."

"I am not, save when social situations demand it. Substances that dull the senses are unwelcome in my profession."

"I would imagine so."

After that, Gil had nothing to say, but he eventually slipped past her to settle on the edge of the bed. She was glad to see him sit, though she wouldn't say it. Without him crossing between her and the light, it was a little easier to see, and without him looming, it was easier to concentrate on her work.

The silence that followed was more companionable. Thea looked over her shoulder once to see him sitting with his elbows on his knees and his mouth resting against his clasped hands, his eyes closed. Thinking, or maybe meditating. As long as he rested, she liked it. That they were once again in a room that sported one bed had not escaped her notice, but she didn't doubt he'd take the floor as soon as she finished her work.

Inch by inch, she worked her way down the long seams for his legs. She put power there, magic to lend endurance and keep him sure-footed. The reinforced knees promised strength and stability. She added loops to hold the straps for his dagger sheaths secure, and deep pockets, just because. Every step of the way, she layered in illusions. It proved a challenge; the illusions on the cloak were sewn into curves, but pants provided only two. Instead, she worked elements of her existing design into any place they would fit. The long seams gave rise to the ordinary looks she'd created; the pockets were meant to store secrets. The front closure, too, though she smirked as she pushed magic into the stitches there. The memory of his laugh when they'd discussed that before warmed her heart.

Last of all, she hemmed the cuffs. They folded twice, sturdy and neat, and the near-invisible stitches she used to fasten them in place let her work in more elements of what should be left unseen.

When the last stitch was in place and the thread knotted and cut, Thea sat back and closed her eyes. She didn't know what time it was, but it had to be late. Her neck and shoulders ached in ways they hadn't in ages and she lifted a hand to rub one of the stiffest spots. There was still the shirt to go.

Strong fingers slid across her shoulder, displacing her hand. She started to question, but Gil pressed into the aching muscle and yielded a groan instead. He shifted to sit behind her, his powerful hands working into each tender pressure point in her back.

"You've done well," he said.

The simple praise sent a small thrum of delight through her, but she couldn't revel in it now. "Shirts are fast. It shouldn't take long. I'll make something simple, so the fit won't matter as much."

"How many hours?"

The question betrayed an urgency he hadn't expressed before. Something had changed. News he'd heard while checking in? Or had the festival's presence driven home just how far behind they were?

"I don't know. A few. I can finish by morning." Or, she thought she could. She didn't know how far off morning was.

His face turned toward the shuttered window as he considered. Did he know the time? His expression told her nothing. "I don't think we will have time on the road." The statement was soft, apologetic.

She understood. "Or the light."

"Or the light," he agreed. "But I'll need buttons up the front."

And buttonholes took time. Maybe she could speed up the process by using loops instead. "What for?"

"Peeling off a tunic overhead after sustaining an injury is remarkably inconvenient, and uncomfortable, as well. My shirts always button." He touched his chest, drawing her attention to their presence.

Thea was surprised she'd never noticed. Button-front shirts were not popular in Kentoria and had not been for some time. But then, his boots were Ranorsh, and she'd asked questions about those. Maybe she'd seen the style and unconsciously decided it wasn't important. "Buttons," she said with a nod. "I'll need to fit you for it when it's partway done."

"Whatever you need."

What she needed was rest and a good night's sleep, but she wasn't about to tell him that. She pulled a piece of dark fabric from the sewing basket to check its size. She'd packed more than necessary, unsure what else would be needed. The first piece was too small. She chose another, this one a soft cream. Ordinary, befitting the disguise she was meant to make. The dark colors he wore were flattering, but they stood out. "I wish I had a good gray," she said as she spread the cloth on the floor and took her scissors, chalk, and measuring tape from the basket. "It would suit your eyes."

"No one will see my eyes when I'm wearing it," he said.

Thea pursed her lips. "That's true. Stand, let me take measurements for this."

He rose and spread his arms.

"You've had things custom made before," She said as she fitted the tape across his shoulders.

"What makes you think that?"

"Just an observation. You know how to move." She worked out the shape of the pattern blocks in her head as she noted each number.

"I have had practice." He turned appropriately for her to measure the length of his spine and the width of his sleeve. "I don't know that I've ever worn anything that wasn't made for me."

Thea motioned for him to rotate in place so she could draw the tape around his chest. "The king outfitted you well."

"Kentoria did. The king wanted little to do with me, aside from choosing for me to exist."

"And then you killed him." She raised a brow as if to ask him to elaborate.

He offered a tight smile in return. "Not that king."

Of course. Gil told her he'd been trained young. That meant Garren Rothalan had to have occupied the throne when he received his first assignments and the equipment to go with them. "The old king, then." It was strange; no one had called him that when he still ruled. It was only after his death that his age became relevant. None of his sons had been given the opportunity to age.

None that she'd known.

The few secrets Gil shared about his mission floated through her mind, mingling with the numbers she needed to remember. She tried to chase them away, but they wouldn't go. Somewhere out there, a king remained. What would change when Gil found him? How did he know where to look? Maybe that was part of what distressed him. If a meeting with his contact had been delayed, and that meeting had been arranged before she was in the picture, maybe it meant they risked losing vital information. If that was the case, she'd just have to sew faster.

"He was a capable ruler, if not a kind man. But his eldest, Calem... Calem would have been a great king." Gil's eyes grew wistful as he spoke and Thea looked at him in surprise.

"You knew him?" she asked.

"I knew all of them. But Calem was my friend."

Thea's hands grew still. There was such weight in his words that her own heart sank. "I'm sorry. The plague took my mother, too."

His brows knit and he closed his eyes. "It was not the plague."

This time, her pause was not from sympathy. Everyone had mourned that tragedy. Garren Rothalan's eldest son had ruled no more than five months before illness swept Kentoria. The magic-fueled apothecaries couldn't work fast enough; many had been lost. The newly-crowned Calem Rothalan had been one of them. She couldn't help her frown. "What?"

"Poison." When he looked at her again, layers of loss and anger shone beneath the shadows in his eyes.

Thea's pulse sped. "Word from the palace said—"

"Aleron thought it best if the truth wasn't known," Gil said. "The plague was a time of fear for Kentoria. They did not need more. He was not ready to take his brother's throne, and the losses of the plague offered time for his grief. Time to prepare himself for the role he didn't expect he'd take. He sent me to find whoever killed Calem. I found nothing." Frustration edged his voice.

"Aleron ruled almost a year." She made herself focus on taking remaining measurements, then knelt to mark them on the fabric. She'd only brought a light colored chalk and it hardly showed against the pale cloth. "Did you look for all that time?"

"I've never stopped looking."

Thea didn't know what to say. She opted for simple repetition. "I'm sorry."

Half of her was tempted to ask about the others. She still didn't know who lived, but she wasn't sure she should push. Gil offered information on his own terms, and she'd only just coaxed him from his dour mood.

The longer she considered, the less important the question seemed. She'd seen Gaius killed and he'd confirmed the death of Calem, so only two options remained. Aleron had been a gentle ruler, hesitant in his choices but sure once he made them. Lucan, the king before Gaius, had been impulsive by comparison, but most had agreed he tried to make decisions with Kentoria's best interest at heart. Thea was less charitable. Lucan's orders had led to her brother's demise.

Still, while Thea hoped Aleron was the king Gil sought, anyone would be better than Gaius. After his brothers, Gaius had been a monster, a single-minded fury that cared nothing for his people and focused all his strength on the development of guard and military forces. With how powerful Kentoria already was, it had left everyone wondering whether he feared attack, or if he planned one of his own.

A new thought crawled through the back of her head and she bit her lip. Maybe he had reason to fear. "Did he know you were coming?"

Gil cocked his head to the side. "What?"

"King Gaius. Did he know?" Perhaps that was why he'd bolstered the guard.

"If he didn't, he was a fool." He nudged her scissors closer with his boot. "But I've distracted you enough. Continue. By your leave, I'll rest while I am able."

"Suit yourself," she murmured. She wasn't ready to give up conversation, but she'd get no more out of him now. Still, a new sort of hope flickered inside her as she cut the fabric and settled to sew. By Gil's estimate, there were still two days of travel left. She would have her answers by then. If Aleron still lived, the kinder of the kings and the king she had first petitioned for help, perhaps she could someday go home.

CHAPTER FIFTEEN

ALARM BELLS CLANGED through the village streets. Thea jerked awake at the same time Gil rolled off the bed. He landed beside her with a quiet thump, daggers already in his hands.

Panic clawed at her throat. She'd fallen asleep with her back against the side of the bed and his shirt lay unfinished on her lap.

"Pack everything," Gil said as he swept his cloak from the floor beside her and stalked to the door. "We're leaving. Now."

"But I'm not finished yet!" She gripped the shirt with both hands and raised it, as if it might change his mind.

"Later. Pack. Meet me downstairs." He slid into the hallway and shut the door. Voices rose with questions and she caught the deepest tones of his response, but couldn't make out the words. Elsewhere, perhaps in the main room below, someone shouted.

Thea swallowed hard. She didn't know what might stir a quiet village to panic and she wasn't sure she wanted to. Biting back fear and frustration, she crammed her sewing into its basket and took her bags. Gil's still waited on the bed. Was she supposed to bring those, too? She chewed the inside of her lip a moment before she picked them up, as well. Only after they bumped against her back did she recall what one of them contained. Her stomach lurched.

More voices rose in the room below, too muffled to make out, but their distress was unmistakable. She pushed into the hallway, expecting to find other people fleeing. Instead, a handful of village folk scurried past on their way into the rooms. More than one cast her a worried look, but she pushed on.

Gil stood empty-handed at the foot of the stairs, conversing with a man in armor made of metal plates sewn to leather. "They won't stop me, and neither will you. You can stay and hide or you can help. It makes no difference in how many I'll cut down."

"They'll dig you no grave here," the man replied.

"There won't be a need." Gil glanced back as he heard Thea approach. He nodded his appreciation when he saw the bags. "Come. We have a head start."

"Ahead of what?" she asked.

"Your funeral," the armored man said.

Gil took her arm and tugged her toward the door. "Raiders from the mountains. Attracted by the festivities last night, no doubt."

Thea pulled back. "Then we should stay and help."

"*We* have somewhere to be," he growled through clenched teeth. He opened the door and held it wide with a foot so he could pull her through. No matter how firmly she put down her feet, she wouldn't have been able to resist. He was too strong.

Her protests were verbal, instead. "But we could help!"

"No."

"You've been teaching me to fight."

"I said no," he snapped.

Thea caught the edge of the doorway as he tried to drag her outside. She anchored her feet against the frame and hauled back until she tore her arm free of his grasp. Had she not been clutching the doorway with all her might, she might have fallen.

He turned to stare at her in surprise.

She leveled her eyes with his and rubbed her arm. His fingers left a red mark behind, betraying how urgent he found the situation. "We have to do something."

For a long moment, he held her gaze. Then, inexplicably, he cracked a smile. "Leave the bags."

She hadn't thought he would change his mind. One after another, she slid them off her shoulder, depositing all their belongings and the basket of sewing supplies just inside the door.

Gil looked past her to the innkeeper who had grown ashen. "Barricade the door. This won't take long." With a flick of his wrists, daggers appeared in his hands.

Thea followed him into the street. With his token left behind, she knew he was sincere. She drew her knife and oriented herself to the sound of voices. Men she'd seen about the village the night before clustered near the smoldering remains of the night's fire. They wore armor, though sparsely, and the weapons they carried were not befitting of any sort of guard. Simple villagers, then; those who had risen to the call to protect their homes.

Gil approached them, though he was already pointing a dagger toward the southern foothills. "There are fourteen on the slope. That will be the main attacking force. Others will come from the sides."

A man at the head of the group turned to squint toward the hills. "Fourteen?"

Thea couldn't count them, either, though she saw the muddled shapes of people descending toward the village. "How can you see them?"

"Moreover, who are you?" the man asked. He hefted an axe in his hands that was better suited to cutting through wood than men. It was an obvious threat, but Gil ignored it.

"Travelers who arrived yesterday." He nodded Thea's way. "We encountered a number of brigands in the mountains and she wishes for us to help."

The man scoffed. "Ranorsh women don't fight."

Gil smirked. "Which is why I married a Kentorian. There." He pointed west and the whole group followed the gesture. "Thea, assist with them."

She drew her dagger. "What about you?"

"I shall disable the others. What these men do with them afterward is none of our concern. And then," he paused and raised his eyebrows, "we will depart for Danesse?"

"Yes," she promised.

"Very well." He flowed toward the oncoming raiders with his green cloak fluttering at his back.

"Blasted fool," the armored man grumbled. "Your husband's off to get himself killed."

Thea suspected he would be all right. "You're welcome to assist him," she suggested as she brushed the pad of her thumb across her knife's edge. It rasped across her skin, sharper than her best scissors had ever been.

He grunted. "We're safer in numbers, and you're safer inside. Your knife is pretty, miss, but we can't spare anyone to protect you."

Part of her wished she could say she didn't need protection, but she wasn't sure. That was why Gil had left her with the villagers, wasn't it? So there were more people around to aid her while she fought? She tried to appear confident as she pointed out motion to the east. "I'll be no trouble, but they might."

The armored man swore. Another group advanced from that direction and Thea added them to her mental tally. Fourteen for Gil. Seven from the east, eight from the west. To the north, where the sheep roamed, the fields were clear.

"So many," someone else whispered. "Have Kentoria's guards gone slack? Letting so many through?"

"We've never needed Kentoria to protect us," the armored man growled. "We don't need them now. Go hole up with your family if that's what you want. Those of us with spines will chase them off!"

A shout went up from the eastern group of bandits, a

discordant show of bravado that struck Thea as forced. It didn't mask the sound of clashing weapons or the panicked cries that came from the south. She gripped her dagger and dared not look, but she knew what those sounds meant.

That Gil struck first had already given them the upper hand.

"Let's go!" the armored man roared as he thrust his axe toward the sky. A few energized shouts rose in answer.

When they went east, Thea went with them. She didn't understand their movement or reasoning, but she supposed combat strategies came from experience. It was their village, one they'd defended their whole lives, though the doubt and distress she'd heard in the one man's voice at the numbers made her wonder how great their chances were. The group she moved alongside was a dozen or so men, plus herself; they outnumbered the smaller bandit groups, but only as long as they met them individually.

The armored man led the rush and lunged into the raiding party with a bellow. His axe smashed into the enemy leader and Thea flinched. She'd never seen real violence before the throne room. She was unprepared for it now.

The village men positioned themselves around her. Whether it was deliberate or by instinct, she didn't know, but she slid forward to take on a raider by herself with a silent vow that she wouldn't weigh them down.

Her presence was a boon. The raiding party gaped at sight of her, her illusion-dark hair flowing like a banner in the wind as she dove forward and stabbed for a man's gut. The blade glanced off his armor, but the strike knocked the wind out of him and he stumbled. A villager finished the job.

A new worry streaked through her as the first raider collapsed. Gil's lessons had focused solely on how to kill. What if she didn't want to?

"So," the village band's leader roared over the clash, "Kentorian women do fight!"

The exclamation bolstered her and she responded by diving

in to slash her dagger across a bandit's thigh. The man howled as he went down. There, she'd disabled one. She didn't have to kill anyone. She didn't have to be like Gil.

And yet he did not kill, either.

Each strike that landed without doing more than causing injury gave her a new appreciation for everything he'd done. The guards in the palace and the ferry, the brigands in the mountains —he'd managed to fend them off without landing a single fatal blow. All it would take was one slip, one strike with imperfect timing. She pulled many too soon, leaving her opponents without any injury at all, but the village men were right there to defend her after every mistake. She was smaller, faster, but also without armor and at higher risk. She darted out to strike like a snake, then retreated behind the wall of their weapons and stronger bodies. They worked out a rhythm before the last man went down.

Before he did, the second wave hit.

The group from the west came at their backs as Thea landed her last strike and someone else drove the bandit to the ground. They turned too late for a perfect defense and the village men scattered like a fan, leaving Thea exposed.

She dove forward, toward the nearest raider, and slashed at his thigh. It was the fastest way she'd found to disable them, a strike they weren't expecting. But this man wore more armor, and her blade bounced off and stole her balance.

As she reeled, a club came for her head.

A hand snapped out to catch it a moment before the green cloak swirled past her cheek. Gil wrenched the club from the bandit's hand and surged forward with his knife. He struck hard and fast, and more times than necessary. The raider collapsed, screaming, and Gil started to follow.

"Don't!" Thea cried. She caught his arm before he could stab again.

He froze.

"Don't forget," she breathed.

He slid back and let the village men descend on the man to do what they would.

Step by step, Thea reeled him backwards. His muscles were coiled tight beneath her hands, powerful and tense, yet he yielded to her touch as if hers were a grip like iron. His breath came hard and heavy, but he did not strike her as winded. He was too steady, too controlled, poised like an angry beast ready to fight.

Ah. She softened her touch and stroked his arm as she removed him from the fight, stepping backwards over groaning bandits left struggling on the ground. It was anger that boiled through him, present in every fiber of his being. A rage he could hardly contain. She'd seen that stance in him before, though she hadn't recognized it then. She'd been too distracted, too frightened, focused on nothing but the nightmare unfolding before her as he slaughtered the king.

As the last raider went down, some of the tension slipped from him and he turned to search her face. "Are you hurt?"

Thea shook her head. "The men on the slope?"

"Disabled." Not killed. He glanced toward the villagers to be sure they'd heard. A handful of them split off in that direction.

The determination in their step gave her pause. "Will they kill them?"

"It is their right to do so. The people of this outpost may defend themselves how they please." He tilted his head toward the inn they'd come from, then started off that way. "You need only focus on what we're doing, and right now, we are going to Danesse."

"What? Right now?" Thea stumbled over somebody's arm as she followed. The man groaned. "Sorry," she muttered.

"That was the agreement, was it not?"

"Well, yes." She just hadn't expected it so soon. She started to return her dagger to its sheath, then paused in the middle of the road. It was dirty.

Gil walked only a few paces farther before he stopped. "We

will go upstairs. Clean our things and ourselves. Then we will continue out of the city."

It was all so anticlimactic that she didn't know what to say. She turned her dagger point down and bowed her head as she followed him to the inn's front door.

It did not budge when he tried to push it open.

"You did tell them to barricade," Thea murmured.

"Indeed." He knocked instead and cleared his throat. "Your men live and your raiders are dealt with."

A rustle and scrape on the other side made them both lean closer to the door. "Identify yourself. Who's out there, and how do we know?"

Gil blinked. Had he not considered that? "The traveler in green," he replied, fingering the edge of the cloak. It bore several dark spatters Thea knew were not mud. "I believe I will need a change of clothing. I trust nobody moved the bags my wife left beside the door?"

A low murmur of discussion followed, then a few grunts and thumps as whatever blocked the way was moved. The innkeeper opened the door a crack and peered out at them, his face less ashen but his hair more disheveled. "By the One," he muttered as he looked them up and down.

Thea tried to smile. "Water and a washbasin would be much appreciated."

"No doubt," the man mused. "Come inside. I'll send it up to your room."

Gil offered his arm as the door opened and Thea took it with a subdued smile. Just inside the doorway, their bags and the sewing basket still sat.

They scooped up everything and someone—the innkeeper's wife, Thea assumed—shuffled up the stairs ahead of them to deliver a basin and towels. "Warm water will be right up," the woman said as she left it all on the tiny table near their room's door.

"Cold water too, please," Thea said. "It's better for washing out stains."

"Of course, Miss." The woman bobbed her head and disappeared into the hall.

Gil deposited their bags on the bed, then inspected his clothing. The black of his shirt and pants hid much, but with how spattered his cloak was, Thea had no doubt the rest of him was covered in blood.

"I don't suppose that shirt is close to being done?" he asked.

"It is. I need to try it on you and mark where the buttons should go, but I should be able to finish fast. If you let me." She found herself grateful only her hands were sullied. The only other garment she had was the dress Gil had helped her cut in two.

"Good." He started to remove his cloak, then thought better of it and stopped. He removed his boots first, something that could come off without revealing his true face.

Thea waited by the basin until the innkeeper's wife returned with two earthenware pitchers. One steamed pleasantly and she took both with a murmured thank-you. She started with the warm water as the woman excused herself and closed the door. A sliver of soap waited in the bottom of the basin. Thea moved it before she poured the warm water into the bowl.

While she scrubbed her hands and arms, the soft rustle of fabric reached her ears and a warm blush colored her cheeks. She would not look while Gil was changing. She wouldn't even think about him. She picked every bit of dirt from underneath and around her nails, then rinsed and dried her hands. "All yours," she announced when it had grown sufficiently quiet.

"Good. Mark this, please, and see if you can finish it while I wash my things." Gil wore the finished trousers and half-finished shirt, she saw when she turned. He held the front closed, but the illusion was already effective. The dirty cloak lay on the floor and his appearance remained as it had been; that of an exceptionally ordinary man.

She made herself smile as she crossed to the sewing basket to take her glass-headed sewing pins. They'd be more visible against the fabric than the pale chalk had been. The faint markings had made her nervous, but the shirt fit well. It hung loose to his hips, granting plenty of space for him to tuck it in beneath his belt. The sleeves were loose, too, but fitted at the cuffs, and the collar folded in a fashion similar to the coat collars she'd seen about the village. It was a good style, a quality blend between what was popular in Samara and what she'd observed of Ranor. Something new, with plenty of opportunity to be successful. The idea of designing a new trend was appealing.

"I'll be quick," she said as she straightened the meeting of the two halves of the shirt's front. She pinned the layers together first, then marked placement for buttons at regular intervals. Long hours of practice had given her an accurate eye, but she'd still double-check with her measuring tape before she attached anything. "Just the loops to make and buttons to sew on. Here, there will be buttons on the cuffs, too."

Gil raised his arm obligingly so she could mark where they needed to go.

She adjusted the placement of them on the first sleeve several times before she was satisfied. "While you're stuck here, I must ask something."

"I doubt that's true, but you're welcome to take advantage of the delay," he replied playfully.

She gave his arm a gentle swat before she moved to the other sleeve. "You had no interest in helping the village defense. Why did you change your mind?"

He hesitated.

"I know you probably don't care if these people live or die," she added. "And I know you've probably seen this before. They seemed to have practice and the bells mean they're used to this sort of thing, but you were ready to leave. Then you stayed. Not only stayed, but you smiled about it."

His arm turned, ever so slightly, giving her better access to the unfinished cuff. "There are two reasons. One is that I feel partly to blame. I've been through Post—this village—many times in my life. You're right in that they deal with this on a somewhat regular basis, but the majority of the rangers who ferret brigands out of the hills are Kentorian. I fear these sort of attacks may grow more common in the coming weeks."

"Why?" She slid in the last pin to mark button placement, but did not let go of his sleeve.

"Because Kentoria's forces will be occupied. Looking for us. Me." He offered a rueful smile.

"Oh." She hadn't considered that, but it made sense. "And the other reason?"

His smile changed, softening at the edges as thoughtfulness touched his eyes. "Because I ordered you to leave, and you told me no."

Thea's brow furrowed and she raised her gaze to his.

"You resisted with everything in you," he said. "You didn't crumble or back down. I... enjoyed that."

In her moment of stubbornness, the fact she was defying him never crossed her mind. She searched his eyes, struggling to find an explanation for her behavior before she realized he expected none. Her attention slid to the pins and she cleared her throat. "I'll have this done within an hour." She removed the few pins that held the front closed, leaving those that marked button placement, and pushed the unfinished shirt back over his shoulders.

For a moment, she regretted her decision. Silvery scars peppered his bare skin, pale against his warm complexion. She halted with his shirt halfway down his arms, studying the marks. There were too many to count. None of it was surprising. He was an assassin; risk came with every job he took. A jagged mark just above his heart caught her eye and she swallowed back the wave of sadness it brought. "Oh, Gil." She raised her head.

His eyes locked with hers and his breath hitched. Fire burned in his eyes with an intensity she'd never seen, a blaze that threatened to burn through her illusions and swallow her whole.

She didn't dare move, trapped in his gaze, unable—unwilling—to tear herself away.

"You make it difficult," he whispered, "for me to be a better person." Then he drew back, peeled the shirt from his arms on his own and pushed it into her hands.

Tension left her in a rush and she sucked in a breath.

He moved past her to wash his arms, shaking his head.

Thea didn't know what to say. She rearranged the shirt in her hands and made herself sit. The sewing basket was right there, still open, waiting for her to finish her work, but her fingers were sluggish and clumsy as she gathered what she needed to finish the job.

Gil scrubbed his hands and then ran his fingers through his hair. The illusion rippled around them, the strands shimmering between brown and the dark ashen blond that was their natural shade. "I am not deserving of such attention."

All of a sudden, she couldn't see the thread between her fingers. Distraction blurred everything and she blinked hard to clear her mind and eyes. "I don't think you get to decide that."

"I am being honest, Thea. Whatever you think of me now, I have not always been... this." He leaned against the table for a moment before he gave his head another shake and scooped his discarded clothing from the floor.

"I don't know what you mean," she said, though she thought she did.

"Then I will be blunt, and you may rue me for it. There has been no shortage of women in my life, and I have not always been as discerning as I now try to be. When a man is offered anything, you'll find very few refuse it."

She had known. And she wasn't surprised. He was eloquent, charming, a gentleman in ways that surprised her. Recollection of the way he'd stood before her during the festival's dance, his mouth so tantalizingly close, sprang to her thoughts with such force it made her blush. What sort of woman would refuse? Light knew she wouldn't have. She squeezed her eyes closed. "If you think to spare my virtue, then you're too late. The last man who thought to become my husband was not so considerate as you."

Gil turned, but said nothing.

The thread was still twisted around her forefinger and thumb. She made herself roll it into a knot and licked her lips. If blunt honesty was how he preferred to communicate, so be it. "My father sought a marriage for me as a means to save his business. A powerful nobleman's second son, a marriage for wealth and security. They offered a high bride price and my father ordered me to secure it by any means necessary. I was not to anger or refuse my betrothed in any way."

His brows drew low, a deep furrow between them. "You should bear no such burden."

She snorted. "But I did, and I did it poorly. My betrothed and his family made sure my father knew as much when they canceled our union a mere week before the wedding."

"You should command better than a transactional marriage."

"Is that not what this is?" She motioned between them. "A transaction? A means for us to get where we need to go, a trade of stability for an illusion?" Her fingers curled in the unfinished shirt in her lap.

Gil's expression grew pinched.

She didn't know why she'd asked. It was a sham, all of it. Nothing more than her first arranged marriage had been.

Yet even as she scolded herself for the confusing emotions that gripped her chest like a vise, the thread between her fingers grew blurry again, this time with tears. She fought them back as she attached button after button, chasing magic down her fingertips and into each stitch so she could be done. Closures, for silence. For hiding. For security. Secrets.

He finished scrubbing stains from his things and hung them across the table to dry as the last closure was finished.

Thea blinked hard as she cut the last thread and thrust the shirt toward him at arm's length. "Here. My end of the bargain is complete."

Gil regarded it in silence, then crossed the room to draw the shirt from her fingertips. "Thea."

She refused to look at him, refused to let him see her weakness and emotion as hot tears spilled from her eyes.

He didn't let her hide. Slowly, he sank to kneel before her. His warm hands cradled her face, his thumbs wiping each tear from her cheeks.

Her breath caught in her chest and she choked back a sob. Gil pressed a thumb to her lips as if to still it as the fingers of his other hand tangled in her hair. He drew her closer, until she could no longer bear to look at the ordinary illusion she'd forged. She closed her eyes, envisioning him as he really was—his handsome face, his smoke-gray eyes, the hints of red in his beard that caught the morning sun—and when his lips finally claimed hers, she surrendered so readily that everything else fell away.

Relief and elation exploded in her chest, a whirlwind of fluttering feelings she'd fought down for so long. So desperately, she'd wanted this; the heat of his hands against her skin, the tender brush of his mouth on hers, the taste of his lips as he took what she'd so fiercely wished for him to want.

But fear, dismay, and heartbreak surged right along with her joy. He was a killer, a monster, a man who should have terrified her to her core. Yet when he finally broke away, she couldn't help the rush of butterflies as he rested his brow against hers.

"You are worth far more than any bride price," he whispered. "And you deserve far better than me."

Slowly, he released her, and when he stood, the shields she so often saw him use to bury emotion were back. "Pack your things."

Her heart sank, but she nodded as he drew on his new shirt. Her mental image of him as he was warred with her eyes, but the illusion won, stronger and better than anything she'd ever designed. He was a plain man, as unremarkable as his name, and it was too late for anything to change.

Gil had his mission, and they had their deal.

It didn't matter how they felt.

Their marriage was still a lie.

CHAPTER SIXTEEN

HE DID NOT KISS her again.

More than once, Thea caught Gil looking at her. Sometimes the glance was wistful, other times so solemn that she feared what he might be thinking. Each time, she reminded herself it didn't matter. They were so near to Danesse, to her new life. They'd part ways soon, and she did not expect she'd see him again.

Instead of blunting her feelings, that thought process made things worse. When they stopped for the night to camp at the edge of the road, Thea rested her head against his shoulder and Gil did not stop her.

As they neared the Ranorsh capital, they saw more travelers on the road. The lack of bold colors in the wardrobes of passersby reassured her the plan to offer things she dyed herself was wise. She'd have a future here, but the longer she thought about it, the more she realized it still felt hollow.

She no longer saw herself happy alone.

"I've realized what's wrong with me," Thea announced as they passed another farm settlement. They'd spoken less often after leaving the inn and the look Gil gave her now was something between expectation and surprise. She chanced a smile, though the way it curved her lips felt insincere. "I've developed Sartherian Madness."

His brows lifted. "Is that so?"

"Think about it. You're a dangerous man who's appeared in my life without warning. When we met, I was sure you meant to kill me, but now that we've been stuck together for some time, I..." She trailed off without finishing. She what? She certainly didn't idolize him the way Sartherians idolized the king who tore their country asunder. She didn't complete her thought, but he still chuckled and replied.

"There are two problems with that," he said. "Firstly, we aren't in Sarther. You've never even been there. I am relatively sure it only counts as Sartherian Madness if it happens there. Kentoria likely has its own name for it. Secondly, the Hostage King of Sarther spent months conditioning his subjects by forcing them to endure deliberate suffering from which he could rescue them. Had he tried to move from the cause of the problem to the solution in a span of weeks, I don't think anyone would have fallen for it as readily. And thirdly, which I just thought of, I absolve myself of any responsibility for your madness because I never intended to cause you difficulty, nor did I intend to..." Like her, he trailed off, and his face fell.

Thea gazed at him hopefully, willing him to finish the thought she couldn't.

He did, but not in the way she hoped. He sighed and stared off into the distance, where the city of Danesse rose from the heart of the river valley. Their downhill trek made things easy, and his pace remained steady, but she took the distinct sense he wished he could slow down.

"It will be difficult to part ways with you," Gil said after a time. "I did not anticipate that I would so greatly enjoy your company."

"Nor I, you." A lump rose in her throat as she admitted it.

"But Rilion surely waits," he added. "He is more tangled up

in this than is fair to him, and I cannot let him down. I only pray he has not tried to continue without me."

Thea nodded. An informant's role was dangerous. The one Gil worked with risked much by entangling himself in Kentorian affairs. "His name is familiar to me. I swear I've heard it before."

"You should have. It's the most popular name for Ranorsh males there is. Rilion was one of their legendary heroes, near mythological in status."

"That would explain it." She lowered her basket and let it sway. It was lighter now, holding just the extra fabric and her supplies, as well as the skirt and bodice of the dress she'd sacrificed earlier in their travels. She'd find a way to mend that once they settled. A change of clothes sounded heavenly after the journey they'd been on. A blessing that it wasn't summer. With the autumn bite in the air, she did not sweat.

Now and then, they passed people who nodded their way. The friendliness was a curiosity. Danesse was a large city; not as large as Samara, but worthy of its title as capital. Yet the people they encountered greeted them as if they were familiar faces, neighbors in a cozy village like the one they'd left behind.

Gil caught her turning her head as another handful of travelers departing the city greeted them along their way. "Ranor's hospitality is my favorite thing about the country. Why I've always enjoyed my visits, despite their troubled history with Kentoria. I believe you'll like living here."

"Maybe." A region known for being warm and welcoming was one where her business would likely thrive, once she established roots in the community. But it was strange to think of living somewhere she knew so little of the culture. She didn't even know what legend the name Rilion was from. "I just can't help but worry. I shouldn't be afraid of being somewhere alone, but everything here is unfamiliar, and once you go, I'll... have no one." She winced as the words left her mouth. She sounded pathetic.

He pondered that for a time, opening his mouth to speak and

then closing it again. A moment passed before he tried again. "Under normal circumstances, contact would not be wise, but if I am able to return to Kentoria after my task is complete, if there are any messages you would have me deliver... A friend, maybe, or family—"

"I have no family," she said, sparing his breath. "Or, none immediate, anyway. My parents are gone, as is my brother. There is my cousin, Elia, but after the mess I've left behind for her, I would be surprised if she wished to speak to me ever again." She'd thought of poor Elia and the work she'd left behind several times, but she could do nothing but hope all had turned out well.

Gil nodded in both acknowledgment and understanding. "I am sorry." For which part, he didn't specify. He didn't have to. Her life had grown so pitiable that he could have chosen any part of it and offered an apology and it would have fit.

"You don't have to be." She forced a smile. "But you said *if* you return to Kentoria. Do you not mean to return with the king?"

"Intentions are nice to have, but rarely practical. There are risks to everything. I'm sure you understand." The clipped way he related his answer told her the subject was unwelcome. She let it rest, and they passed into Danesse just after sunset.

At the edge of the city, they visited a tiny office where their passports and marriage license were examined and stamped for a dozenth time.

"It won't be the last," Gil murmured wryly as they returned to the streets.

The wide avenues here were lined with colorful glass lamps, and although these were more permanent than those in the small outpost village, yet they remained largely unlit. Thea could not imagine it was practical to fill and light lanterns every night, but she had expected a celebration of the pear harvest would be underway here, too. There were no striped awnings to be seen, no stalls offering preserves or pear butter. She scanned storefronts and shops with tall glass windows, but they boasted ordinary wares. She'd have to dig deeper into the city's offerings if she wished to try the perry as Gil suggested.

"Now to find Rilion," he muttered beside her.

Thea doubted she could assist. "Do you know where he lives?"

"If he is home, there is no way we can reach him without notice. But I may know a way to request a meeting." He must have decided that was the best course of action, for he veered down a side road without warning.

"I thought you said we were going to stay with him," she said. "Does that not involve going to his home?"

"Well, yes, but you'll have to trust me when I say it's best to wait for him to lead the way. It's better for everyone if we are not seen entering or leaving."

Thea frowned. "Do the disguises not help?"

"In this particular situation, the disguises may make things worse. But we will see what he says when we meet." His smile was tense and wholly unreassuring.

She followed close at his back. Now and then, she considered reaching for his hand, but rationality chased the notion out of her head. How long did they have? A few more days, maybe. No more than that. She couldn't deny that something had changed between them, but his intentions were clear. He would continue his journey, and she would be left behind.

The knowledge stung, and she scolded herself for letting it hurt. This had been the plan and the intention from the beginning. This was what she'd agreed to, what they'd both worked toward. It shouldn't have rankled now.

Eventually, they came to a shop that appeared no different than any other. A cobbler, from the sign. Thea craned her neck to look at it before they went inside. The shop was well-lit but quiet, the day's work already over. A man tidied tools at the counter, while a boy swept.

"Not taking any more orders today," the man said.

Gil motioned for her to stop. "Wait here."

She remained by the door, but watched as he crossed the room. He spoke to the cobbler in a voice so low, she made out nothing, but the man's face revealed much. His eyebrows shot up his forehead, then drew down and scrunched together. His frown deepened, then he nodded and turned to the counter. From somewhere beneath it, he produced a scrap of paper and a grease pencil. Gil took both and borrowed the countertop to write.

"Come here, lad," the cobbler called to his son. "Need you to run an errand for me. I'll finish sweeping up."

The boy abandoned the broom and joined them at the counter as Gil finished his note and folded it shut. He provided a few murmured instructions, again too soft for Thea to hear, then passed the note to the boy and stood straight. The child trotted off through the door and disappeared into the streets.

Gil turned to face the cobbler. "Thank you. If it's no trouble, we shall wait here."

"No trouble at all, milord," the cobbler replied. He resumed cleanup, but cast Thea several curious glances.

Gil put away the pencil, back where the cobbler had gotten it from. He lingered at the counter as if he didn't know what to do with himself. That stance was familiar. She saw the urge to pace and the way he fought it down. So often, he'd come across as confident. Sure of himself and everything he did. Now, with the way he ran his fingers through his hair and concentrated on his steady breath, she noticed the cracks in his facade.

He *didn't* know what to do. Whether he should pace or be still, whether he should rejoin her or stay where he was. She solved that part for him, crossing the room to lean her hip against the counter and wait. "A boy as a messenger, hmm?"

"Children are unthreatening and easily trusted. He will get much farther in delivering that message than you or I." He propped his hands against the counter as he watched the cobbler take the broom and continue cleaning.

Thea watched, too. There was something charming about the simple tedium of keeping a shop. The rasp of the broom was soothing, pleasant, and she let it fill the air while they waited.

Outside, night deepened, and just when Thea began to wonder what they were waiting for, the boy returned.

"They're coming," the child announced before his father chased him into the back room.

The cobbler paused in the doorway and started to speak twice over before he shook his head and said simply, "I'll lock up after you're gone."

Gil nodded. "You have my thanks. We won't be long."

"Won't we?" Thea asked softly. The words had scarcely left her lips before a chorus of booted footsteps and the rattle of heavy armor flooded the street outside. A group of armored guards passed the window with lanterns in hand and a moment later, the door slammed open and she clapped a hand to her mouth.

All of a sudden, the familiarity of Gil's informant's name made sense.

It was not a mere informant named after a legend that stood panting in the doorway.

It was Rilion, Third Prince of Ranor.

CHAPTER SEVENTEEN

"I AM LATE," Gil announced.

The prince looked as if he might choke. "By the One, you're alive!" He crossed the room in a rush and greeted Gil by clasping his arms. Relief made his shoulders go slack, but a moment later, his lip twisted. "What's happened to your face?"

"I've been forced to admit that between the two of us, you are more handsome."

Now it was Thea's turn to choke. The statement was thick with the sarcasm of some long-running joke, but it fit with what she had heard. Prince Rilion's looks were the whole reason she knew who he was. He was dark-eyed, dark-haired, and bore such strikingly attractive features that half the women in Kentoria fantasized about somehow finding themselves his royal match. Elia had gone through a phase of it; she was of distant relation to some royal on her mother's side, and in her teenage years, she'd thought it possible. Thea kept her hand clamped firmly over her mouth to hide her smile. What her cousin wouldn't give to be in this random Ranorsh cobbler's shop now.

"I always knew you'd come around to it someday." Rilion exhaled hard and raked his hands through the hair at his temples. "Light, how could you do this to me? Getting to that outpost was no small feat, and then when you didn't arrive—"

Gil held up a hand to forestall him. "I don't fault you for leaving. I only feared you'd try to take things into your own hands. We have need of shelter, somewhere to hide while I evaluate the situation and prepare for the next step. Are you able to host us?"

"We?" Rilion repeated. His eyes darted to Thea.

She didn't know whether to bow or merely greet him, given the informal way he spoke with Gil. In the end, she gave an awkward curtsy and bowed her head.

"A Threadmancer," Gil said. "I will tell you everything, but you know we have little time."

Rilion straightened as if the title impressed him. "That explains your face. I can give you someplace to stay, but my father must not know. You'll be restricted to one of the guest houses. One of my personal guards will escort you there, and I will join you after I've supplied a sufficient excuse for why I am not at dinner." His mouth twisted with a caricature of a smile.

Gil snorted. "Be hasty, then."

The prince stepped away, but not before sharing a rude gesture.

Gil waved a hand and moved to Thea's side. Rilion gave orders to his men with just a flick of his fingers. One remained while the others fell in beside him on their way back to the palace.

"Now you see why trying to reach him at home was a poor idea," Gil said dryly. He fished the last of his Ranorsh currency from his pocket and left it on the counter before he nodded to the one guard who remained.

Thea could have laughed at the absurdity of it all. "And you didn't think to warn me?"

"The fewer people who know what we're up to, the better."

The guard led them from the cobbler's shop and Gil closed the door securely as they left. His statement had not been posed threateningly, but it left her unsettled, so Thea remained silent as they followed the guard through the city's streets.

A few curious people stopped to watch them pass, but no one lingered long. Thea worried their guard escort would draw unwanted attention, but the one leading them was not the only guard wandering the city. After she spotted two others speaking with people on the street and giving directions, she relaxed. Bothering members of the guard with something as menial as navigation was unthinkable in Kentoria; it gave the armored men here a softer image.

Eventually, they reached what she could only describe as a manor. The guest house sat in a yard ringed by a stone wall that wasn't too tall to climb, though the gardens on the other side were pristine enough to indicate no one tried. The guard opened the wooden gate and ushered them through. The house itself was built of stone inside a frame of towering logs and boasted two and a half floors. The windows were dark, but a lamp of golden glass burned by the front doors. That it had two doors reminded Thea of the red granite palace in Samara. She'd only seen it twice; both times had ended with executions. A shudder ran down her spine unbidden.

The guard preceded them, but instead of opening the doors, he knocked.

A long, awkward silence dragged past before a maid answered.

"The prince's guests," the guard offered as explanation.

The maid smiled and opened a door wide. "An honor to host you, milord. Milady. Have you taken your meal?"

Gil stepped forward first. He walked with his hand on the hilt of a dagger. His cloak almost hid it. "No. His Highness intends to join us, but we are uncertain when. It would be rude to enjoy his hospitality without him."

"Of course, milord." The maid gave a tiny curtsy. "Will your escort be joining us?"

"I will await His Highness while the guests settle," the guard replied.

Thea climbed the two steps to the door and found herself wishing she wore a skirt. The simple outfit she'd made for travel was hardly appropriate for dining with a prince. Rilion hadn't seemed to notice their state of dress, though. Perhaps appearances meant little in matters of assassins and kings.

The manor's furnishings were well-suited to entertaining noble guests. Rich tapestries and plush rugs decorated the space and antlers of various shapes crowned the walls. The furniture was all dark wood, the upholstery a deep gold. Thea couldn't recall the last time she'd been anywhere that had upholstery. Her own family had given up such luxuries when her mother passed.

Gil scarcely looked around. "If I know Rilion, he'll be late. Prepare a room for us."

"Two rooms," Thea corrected.

He glanced at her, startled, but wiped his face clean of expression an instant later. "Of course."

"Two rooms," the maid repeated pleasantly. "Shall I draw a bath?"

Thea's heart leaped. "You have the facilities for that?" After weeks of travel, she couldn't imagine anything better.

"Well, the house is too small for each guest's quarters to have their own bath, but we have a nice central space for private ablutions."

"I believe she would enjoy the comfort," Gil said. "Show us where we may take our rest first, if you please. Then draw the lady her bath."

The maid nodded and beckoned them with a hand. "This way, milord. Milady." She slid through the house with a flowing grace.

Thea was all too happy to follow, her dusty travel clothing forgotten.

They trailed up the stairs, where the maid pointed them to separate rooms. She gave Thea long enough to deposit her bags and the sewing basket in her assigned quarters, then led the way to the private bath. A wide, square wooden basin sat in the center of the bath chamber. Beyond it, a merry fire crackled in a wide stone hearth. A black cauldron steamed above it.

"Do you always have bath water at the ready?" Thea asked.

"Oh, yes. We never know when the royal family will need to host guests. There's always someone here, and the house is always ready to welcome visitors." The maid smiled so her eyes crinkled. They were the same rich brown as Prince Rilion's; the same brown she'd unknowingly given Gil. It was no wonder that man at the inn in Heartroot had believed Gil was Ranorsh.

"Well, I appreciate the foresight." Thea slid her fingers through her hair and studied the shelves against the walls. Several held jars of oils and soaps. Others held herbs and flower petals. She picked one up and turned it to examine its contents through the glass. "Am I allowed to use these?"

The maid busied herself with scooping water from the cauldron into the bath. "Of course, milady. Shall I help wash your hair?"

Thea almost said yes. At the last moment, she remembered the illusions. Once her clothing came off, her hair would be red, and her trickery would be revealed. Rilion knew she was a Threadmancer, knew she'd created an illusion for Gil, but the fewer people who knew about her power, the better. "No, thank you. I can manage on my own. After being on the road for so long, I'd appreciate the time to soak and relax in private."

"Of course, milady." The maid curtsied and finished transferring the heated water, then readied a towel. She said nothing else.

After the maid departed, Thea checked the latch on the door. The lock was so flimsy she doubted it would keep anyone out. Her housemate was polite enough she had little concern about him walking in; she couldn't picture him so much as trying. But the maid concerned her, so she locked it before undressing, all the same.

The reddish tones in her auburn hair had grown unfamiliar. She ran her fingers through her tresses as she regarded the water. It was not as hot as she might have preferred, but she had gone years without the luxury of a whole bathtub. Weeks without the luxury of soap had been bad enough. She contemplated that for a time, then selected several jars and bottles from the shelves. She had to make herself presentable for their company. Smelling pleasant was a good start. Yet as she sank into the water and opened each container to breathe its aroma, she found it wasn't Prince Rilion who crowded her thoughts.

What sort of fragrance might Gil like? She thought something with spicy notes. Or maybe he'd prefer if she were as feminine as possible. Something sweet and floral, then. One of the bottles contained an oil scented with honeysuckle. She smelled it twice, then nodded. That would do. She'd perfume her hair with it when she'd washed, and then...

Her brow furrowed. Then what? They'd speak with Rilion, he'd make the necessary arrangements for Thea to stay in Danesse, and Gil would leave. In a few months' time, he'd send documents rendering whatever persona he'd chosen in his passport deceased, and she would be alone.

That word hit her thoughts hard. Alone. Not free. Danesse no longer offered freedom, and she was no longer sure what freedom was. The ability to do as she pleased? She was losing that, too. Freedom wasn't just choice any longer, she realized as she sank shoulder-deep into the wooden tub. Freedom was the way her heart fluttered when he'd kissed her, when his fingers tangled in her hair, when her soul was set alight by the soft sweetness of his words. She wouldn't taste that—or him—again.

When Thea had washed, she reconsidered the honeysuckle oil. It was a foolish idea, the whims of a love-struck and naive girl. Yet they were still to meet Prince Rilion, and she still needed his help. Allowing herself some feminine charm could be beneficial.

As she dried her hair and begrudgingly donned her grubby

travel clothes, she wondered if there had been any point. Perfume wouldn't hide the dirt.

Her assigned guest room had been arranged to welcome her back. A tray of dried fruits with a pitcher of some sort of cider waited on the dark wood table, just in case she'd grown hungry. A variety of dresses lay on the bed, giving her pause.

"There ought to be something there to fit you," the maid said as she bustled in with an armful of wood. A little fire burned in a narrow fireplace in the corner of the room, chasing the chill out of the air, and she left the wood beside it so the flames could be fed through the evening. "His Highness said milord and milady would look a good bit different after freshening up, so don't worry. The prince keeps interesting company. We're all used to it by now."

Thea couldn't help her thoughtful frown. "Is Prince Rilion here already?"

"Just arrived. Settling a horse for milord in the stable out back. He'll be in to join the two of you before long. Shall I help with your hair?"

"Please." She couldn't fathom why Rilion would betray their illusions so readily, but she wouldn't pretend to understand the machinations of royals or assassins.

The maid closed the door while Thea selected a dress. The green one drew her attention, but the color made her hesitate. It was similar to a shade she could accomplish with cocklebur, but who knew what had been used? The fabric she'd used for Gil's cloak had been one she dyed herself, a mixture of crushed flowers and copperas.

"You've heard the stories too, have you?" the maid asked. "Don't worry. Ranor has mountains aplenty, but we're sparse on mining facilities. Our mountains are good for rock and not much else."

Reassured, she shed her dusty clothing, grateful to have it back off her newly clean skin. "You believe the rumors about dyes making people ill, then?"

"Oh, it was all the gossip about Danesse. The king's always refused to import textiles, saying it would be bad for the wool market here. He's been looking to push exports instead, since Ranor's artisans can prove our dyes are safe." The maid took the dress from the bed and helped Thea into it. It buttoned up the back, an unfamiliar style and one obviously meant for noblewomen. She would have never been able to get into the dress on her own.

"Is there demand for brighter dyes in Danesse?" Those she had experience with were made primarily with plant-based components, though she'd tried her hand at a few blends using earth-based pigments.

"That, I couldn't say. Working for the royal family, I already see the best there is to be had. There's no shortage of bright colors in royal wardrobes, but I'm sure you know that." After the last button was secured, the maid crossed to a small vanity where a polished silver mirror hung against the wall. She fetched a brush and ran her finger over the coarse boar bristles before she pulled back the vanity's stool. "Come, sit. Don't want to keep His Highness waiting."

Thea doubted they'd wait for her. Rilion's business with Gil had been delayed enough already.

The maid worked the tangles from her hair with a deft hand, then produced a bowl of pins from a drawer. She wove strands above Thea's ears into braids and pinned them together at the back of her head, covering the meeting point with carefully positioned curls. "There. That's suitable for dinner with a prince. Come, milady, I'll show you to the dining hall. Cook will be ready for me to serve things by now."

"Thank you." At the height of her father's success, Thea's family had hired servants. Now, that seemed such a distant memory that she couldn't recall how she was meant to reply. She checked her reflection once, then made herself follow the maid. Her bare face was far too plain. A hint of something on her cheeks or lips would not have been amiss, but there was nothing more to do.

Thea smoothed her hands down the front of the dress and steeled her resolve. She would meet with the prince and speak of her needs, and with fortune, the night would bring peace.

CHAPTER EIGHTEEN

Voices carried through the house. Thea recognized Gil's, muted as it was. His voice was strong, the cadence of his speech comfortable. It always was. By comparison, Rilion sounded soft and uncertain, but that could have been because of the matters they discussed. Both men fell silent when she appeared in the doorway with the maid. Her dress made her self-conscious, though she knew the cut was flattering. The high-collared neck turned down like the coats in the outpost village, exposing a panel of gold silk that matched the trim on the sleeves. A band of gold ran around the waist, too, accentuating the shape of her hips.

Gil had changed clothing, too. The soft gray of his shirt made his eyes stand out, and if his hair was darker, it was only because it was still wet. She didn't know how he'd found time to wash, but he was good at making her wonder. He offered her a slight smile.

"Yes," Rilion said, indicating she'd interrupted their conversation. "Shall I retrieve it? I think you'll find it humorous."

Thea raised a brow, but Gil's smile widened. "Please do," he said.

The prince shook his head and waved a hand before he excused himself from the dining hall. That he hadn't greeted her left Thea uncomfortable, but the way Gil inspected her from head to foot chased away her worries. He liked what he saw. She recognized it in his eyes.

"I have just finished explaining why you are here," Gil said when his attention returned to her face. "He is displeased with my chivalry, but there's nothing to be done or undone now. We shall discuss your residency over dinner."

"And your mission?"

His smile faded. "After that. In private."

Of course. She tried to smile back, but faltered. There was no point in trying to hide her disappointment. Somewhere along the line, she'd begun to assume he would eventually tell her everything. Now, standing in a guest house belonging to the Ranorsh royal family and waiting for the prince to return, she had no choice but to admit she still knew nothing of value. She'd been given a vague sense of what his mission entailed, knew he'd taken it upon himself to pursue it, but nothing beyond that. How foolish it had been to think she had earned knowledge.

"Look, see?" Prince Rilion said as he returned. "You can't deny it's funny." He unfurled a piece of paper. A poster, Thea realized. A *wanted* poster.

Gil burst into laughter, a sound so deep and merry, it warmed her heart and spiraled her into dismay at the same time, for her face was the one emblazoned on the decree.

"So you see," Rilion continued with a wry smile, "my confusion was well-founded."

One more laugh, then Gil wiped his eye. "Ah, Light's mercy. He thought I'd been bested," he explained.

"How in all the One's glory did they decide *she* was the assassin?" Rilion laughed too, though he turned the poster to examine it more closely now. He didn't go so far as to hold it up beside her, but it was obvious he compared the illustration to Thea's face.

Her cheeks burned. It made sense. This was why she'd run. But why was it only her? "He's not mentioned at all?"

"Not a word." The prince's demeanor softened some as he tossed the poster onto the table. "They delivered it by hand, demanding my father turn her over if she appeared. At first, I thought it a ridiculous mistake, but when I went to Post..."

A quiver of uncertainty ran down Thea's spine. She'd expected to be a wanted woman in Kentoria. That whoever had taken control of the country might be able to seize her from within Ranor's borders had never crossed her mind. She'd thought she'd reached safety. Now, she wasn't so sure.

"The image does her no justice." Gil drew back a chair and motioned for her to sit. The maid had vanished, but a rattle on the other side of a small door at the far end of the room explained where she'd gone.

Thea crept forward to take the offered place. Rilion positioned himself at the head of the table, and Gil put himself between the two of them. She only sat when both men had.

"I agree." Rilion flicked the end of the poster and it rolled itself up again. "Now, introduce us, will you?"

"Of course. This is Thea, my Threadmancer, whose illusions kept anyone from noticing my resemblance to my wanted poster." Gil's voice was thick with sarcasm. "According to her passport, her name is Theadora Emroth. Thea, this is Rilion, Third Prince of Ranor. But I suspect you already knew that." He lifted his eyebrows as if to goad a reaction from her.

"Named after the hero," she replied sarcastically, too.

"Ugh. Don't remind me." Rilion made a show of rolling his eyes. "They should have given that name to my eldest brother. As it stands, I think they're expecting entirely too much from me."

"But you are helping me," Gil said. "That may be seen as heroic in time."

Thea laced her hands together in her lap. "If I may, Your Highness, why *are* you helping him?"

Rilion rubbed his mouth. "Because I'm a fool. But truthfully, because we are friends."

"I thought assassins didn't have friends," she intoned.

Gil shrugged. "To be fair, I've never actually agreed with your assessment that I am one."

She narrowed her eyes at his pedantry.

"I don't think that's an argument you're going to win," Rilion said. "Everyone who has ever sat at my father's table knows what you do. You've just never been caught at it, and all that means is that you're very good." He reached for his cup, then paused with a frown when he saw it was still empty.

"I am good at many things. There are just only so many places I can be at once, and that is why I am here now." Gil leaned across the table to grab a dark bottle. Its cork had already been removed and stuck back in place, so it would be easy to pour when the time came. He pried it back out of the bottle and filled the prince's cup.

"You're not supposed to do that," Rilion said.

"I'm not supposed to do many things. It's never stopped me before." Gil smirked, but grew serious as he filled Thea's cup. He left his own empty. "But we've spent enough time on idle chatter. I am in need of a favor."

"Another, you mean," the prince grumbled.

The maid returned with a platter on either hand. She laid them both in the center of the table and busied herself with carving meat and filling plates.

Thea leaned forward to address her. "Could you bring a pitcher of water, please?" She tilted her head toward Gil's empty cup.

The maid nodded and bustled back to the kitchen, where the cook still rattled dishes.

"Yes, another." Gil did not look Thea's way, but his hand brushed against her thigh beneath the table. She froze. He'd never dared touch her before—not like that. Her chest tightened and her heartbeat thumped in her ears.

Rilion made a show of leaning back in his chair. "As if I've not done enough for you already. What is it this time?"

"I promised Thea the opportunity to start over. An apology, if you will, for accidentally upending her life." Gil's mouth tightened. "She will need to be granted residency under her new name. I have promised to pay for a building to help her establish a new business here. A Threadmancer's services will be useful to your people."

The prince made a face. "You know my father doesn't allow women to lease or purchase property. Backwards and rotten old man. The only way she can hold a building is if she inherited it."

"Or if my husband buys it," Thea said.

"You are married?" Rilion asked as he reached for his cup.

She nodded toward Gil. "We are, yes."

The prince choked on his drink.

"Forged documents," Gil said, so quickly he came across flustered. Perhaps he was. "In order to take her past the waypoints in the mountains more easily."

Rilion gave him an incredulous frown.

Gil straightened as the maid returned and filled his cup with water. "Those documents should allow us to settle things. The building will be purchased in my name—my assumed name— and passed to her upon my supposed death."

"Dying again, are we?" Rilion asked dryly.

For a moment, Gil appeared aggrieved. "Will you aid me with this or not?"

Thea spared a glance toward the rolled-up poster, then averted her eyes. Half of her wanted to see all that had been written. Did the people of Kentoria really think she'd defeated Gil? It made little sense. The guards had seen them fleeing together. The country was sure to be in turmoil, though, and she knew how easy it was for information to become tangled.

"Fine," Rilion sighed, exasperated. He took his fork as the maid finished serving each of them and excused herself from the room. "Explain what you need, and I'll make it happen. You've run out of favors, but this..." He trailed off, studying Thea with a speculative eye. He nodded. "I will do this."

Relief washed over her, a greater comfort than the warm bath she'd just climbed from or the soft bed that still waited upstairs. Thea sank in her chair and pressed a hand to her chest. "Thank you, sincerely. I never imagined I'd be forced so far from home. Until we reached Danesse, I wasn't sure there was any hope left."

"It hardly seems fair to punish you for being caught in his scheming." Rilion pointed at Gil with the end of his fork. "Regardless of your reason for being here, I see value in welcoming more artisan mages into the city. You may know this already, but it's not uncommon for those with the talent to leave Ranor once they become proficient in their craft. I fear our economy is not as robust as others. Many seek greener pastures."

"I doubt there are many places better for a Threadmancer," Thea said. "I saw the number of sheep your country possesses, and the quality of their wool, as well. Kentoria favors larger livestock. Cattle and such. There's not much of a market for wool spun from cattle, if that's something that can be made at all."

The prince chuckled and gave an understanding nod. He was not charmed or flattered, but he was receptive to her needs, and that was all that mattered.

They discussed her plans for a shop at length. They spoke of design and where she could source supplies, her intention to provide woolen fabric dyed in new colors not commonly available, the types of magic she considered her own specialties, and what would be forbidden. She wasn't surprised to learn illusions were outlawed in Ranor, but Rilion said nothing about the illusions she'd made for herself, or those Gil would surely continue to wear.

Eventually, though, as she knew it would, conversation lulled, and there was no way to avoid what was left to come.

"Well," Gil said at last. He'd been silent through much of her conversation with the prince, letting her take the lead, allowing her the space and authority to explain her needs and how she planned to make herself useful. "Now that we've established what you can do for Thea, I suppose we must discuss what you've done for me."

Rilian had been cheerful for much of their chatter. Now his mouth drew down and he grew solemn. "Yes."

Gil raised a hand in signal for him to wait, though it was unnecessary. The prince leaned back in his chair and gazed at Thea, his dark eyes once more shaded with supposition. "The manor's maid will see you upstairs," Gil said. "I shall see you in the morning."

"Of course." She met his gaze, her expression as guarded as his. Thoughts of his hand on her thigh stirred butterflies in her chest. Instead of enjoying them, she envisioned herself crushing each of them beneath a boot. The time for that was past. She offered the prince a curtsy and excused herself from the dining hall. The maid met her at the doorway and waved for her to follow. Together, they climbed the stairs to her room.

"I'll bring breakfast to your room in the morning, milady, no need to get yourself out of bed," the woman said as she opened the door. "Have you any requests?"

"None for breakfast," Thea muttered. The unwanted clothing had been removed from her bed, but she spied her illusion-imbued garments folded alongside them. "I do have one request, and I admit it may be odd."

"Oh, that makes me curious," the maid laughed.

Thea mustered a smile. "This clothing is beautiful, but I admit I prefer my own. Everything I brought with me is filthy after travel, and the dress I brought is in need of repair. Could you show me where the washing is done? I'd like to help wash my things so they can dry overnight and I can deal with them tomorrow." The maid's eyebrows rose, so she added, "I don't doubt your skill with domestics, but I'd feel better if I could be the one to wash my damaged dress. Just to be certain of what I'll need to repair it."

"You're right, milady," the woman said slowly. "A very odd request. But..." Her eyes flicked toward the curtained windows, considering.

"I don't think it'll take long, not with the two of us." Thea didn't know if cajoling would help, but the maid's expression softened.

Eventually, the maid nodded. "All right. Let's get your things, I'll take you out back and we'll scrub it up all fresh before it gets too late."

Thea released her breath in a whoosh. "Thank you. I can't say how much I appreciate it." She hurried to retrieve her cut skirt and bodice while the maid collected the trousers, tunic, and undergarments she'd abandoned earlier. They exited the room together, but the maid turned a different way than before.

"I'll take you out the back way, so we don't disturb milord and His Highness," she said. "Knowing how men are, they'll be up half the night talking stratagems and whatnot."

The notion of the two men arguing over plans and possibilities made Thea snort. "I don't know if Gil's that talkative."

The maid cast her a curious look. "Is that so?"

Something about the woman's tone was off. Thea didn't know what or how, but it left her unsettled. "Perhaps with the prince, he would be. They do seem to be good friends." Despite Gil's assertion that he had none. He'd refuted her suggestion he might, as he'd refuted her insistence he was an assassin. Before, she'd thought he was just being difficult. Now, she couldn't help wondering how much of what he'd said had been subtle misdirection.

Misdirection she'd clearly fallen for.

"Here we are," the maid announced as she opened a door and chilly nighttime air flowed in. It was cold enough to make Thea shudder, but once they started scrubbing, the cool air would be a comfort and a relief.

Just outside the back of the house, there was a stone-walled well and a small cobblestone-paved workspace. A washtub sat upside down beside the well, and the well's bucket sat on the ground beside it. The maid lit a lantern, turned over the tub, and dropped the bucket down the well. It hit the water with a smack a second or two later.

"The washing bat's over there, leaned up against the wall," the maid said.

Thea retrieved it as the other woman filled the tub with enough water to suit their needs. They dropped the clothing into the tub and took turns pummeling the dirt loose, though Thea took more care with the dress. That, she scrubbed between her hands, working the fabric against itself. She hadn't touched the skirt again since she'd climbed from the river with Gil's help, a part of their travels that now seemed long ago.

"Goodness, look at the dust," the maid exclaimed. Even in the dark of night, the cloudy swirls of dirt that filled the water were obvious.

"Now you see why I wanted to wash things," Thea said with a laugh. "We hardly stopped. Just long enough for me to sew travel clothes. My dress wasn't well-suited to the task." She fingered the tattered edge of the skirt, wistful.

"Well, if you're half as good a seamstress as it sounds like you are, you'll have it fixed up in no time." The maid nodded to herself, then pointed to a rope line. "Here, let's rinse and string them up. I'll check in the morning and if they're dry, I'll bring them up with your breakfast."

Thea wrung as much water from the garments as she could. "Thank you. I appreciate your help."

"Always happy to help, milady. Sometimes folks hardly know how much they need it, but it's always nice when one sees the truth of things." A bit of a spark lit the woman's eyes.

"I haven't asked your name yet," Thea said.

"Oh, begging your pardon, milady. I'm Inaley, though most visitors just call me Ina. You're welcome to use either, of course.

Are you ready to head back to your quarters? I'd be happy to take you, milady."

"Thea, if you please." She'd like that better; she was no one here, closer to the maid's social station than that of the men inside. Or, that of the prince, at least. Surely Gil's position as the crown's assassin had given him some sort of rank, but Thea grudgingly admitted she didn't know that, either.

"Of course." Ina grinned at her, then tilted her head toward the door. "Let me stop by the kitchen to get some coals from Cook's fire. We'll warm your bed right up."

Warm blankets sounded heavenly. "Thank you." Thea savored the idea as she finished spreading the wet clothing across the lines. She didn't want to dry her hands on her dress, so she shook them and rubbed her chilled hands together until they were no longer dripping.

Minutes dragged by and Ina did not return. Had she gone ahead to the room? Thea hadn't realized she was meant to follow. She crept back through the doorway by which the maid had led her out, but the hall was dark, and she heard nothing. No rattle from the cook in the kitchen, and no whispering footsteps from the maid.

Thea retraced her steps through the hallways and up the stairs. The lights in her room were lit, though Ina wasn't there. Farther down, light spilled from another door, open little more than a crack. Voices spilled along with it. Wary, Thea paced closer.

"I've done everything you asked, but I won't do this." That was Rilion; there was heat in his voice that hadn't been there before.

Gil's followed, but it was low, dangerous, again the voice of the assassin who had spirited her out of Samara and into the wilderness. "Then everything you've done has been fruitless. I will not be deterred. Not now, not when I am so close. I will continue to Angroth, with or without you."

Angroth. The country lay to the north, just beyond the

northern ridge of mountains that framed Ranor. Was that where Gil's destination lay?

"You've *been* to Angroth," Rilion snapped. "You've been to Lyrangroth, to Vahar, to Helmsor, to Havrek. When does it end, Gaius?"

The name hit her like a thousand pound weight. Thea's stomach lurched and her stomach constricted.

No.

"It ends when he's dead," Gil said. "Or when I am."

No.

"Then you'll die alone."

Shadows breaking across the light warned her of movement, but her feet were leaden and she could not make herself move.

The door opened wide and Rilion stepped into the hall. He scarcely glanced her way as he stormed past. Gil followed, drawing a breath to continue the argument, thunderheads unlike anything Thea had ever seen brewing in his eyes.

Until they fell on her.

He froze.

Thea stared. "Gaius," she said. The name she'd so hated was no less bitter on her tongue as she looked upon him, her heart twisting in her chest.

She hoped he would correct her. Pause and explain whatever she'd misunderstood.

Instead, the storms in his eyes grew cool as winter wind, and a hard shield of neutrality shut his anger away. "Yes," he replied, though his lip curled with disdain.

Her hand went to her chest, as if to catch the pieces as they shattered, but his words reduced her to dust.

"I am your king."

CHAPTER NINETEEN

G<small>AIUS</small>.

The merciless king Kentoria hated. The warmonger whose armies made allies squirm. The man she thought she'd watched die.

Thea swallowed hard, but it went down like broken glass. "I —I saw—"

"What you walked in on was exceptionally complicated. You would not have believed me if I explained." His voice stayed low and steady, but she read the danger in his stance. Was that it, then? If she ran, he'd kill her?

She backed up a step, shaking her head.

"You may think of me what you wish. What I must do does not change."

"You said you sought the king." Not that he was the king. By the Light, had the very pretense by which they traveled been a lie, all this time?

"I did not," he replied. He was patient. Calm. This wasn't how he was supposed to be. Gaius was known for being angry, violent. Why couldn't he be the version of himself she hated? Why must he still be so steadfast? He considered his words carefully before he went on. "I said a king yet lived, and that I would see him where he belongs."

Thea struggled to remember. Was that all he'd said? How had she not seen through that? "The king in Samara, the man you killed—"

"As I said," he interrupted, "the situation is complicated. I am willing to explain."

But she didn't know if she wanted to hear it, and that was a problem. She backed farther down the hall. He didn't pursue her. Did she want him to? To refuse to let her go, to sweep her into his arms? The memory of his lips on hers and his fingers in her hair twisted like a knife in her chest.

"You kissed me," she spat.

"Yes." His shoulders relaxed, if slightly. "And I would again, if you would have me."

Even as everything inside her splintered, the softness in those words lit a spark within her chest. She shut her eyes and tried to stamp it out. He'd betrayed her. Lied to her. Deceived her. How dare her emotions betray her, too? "Who are you?" she asked at last. Perhaps that question should have been where she started, the moment he'd walked out that door.

Again, he considered his answer before he spoke. "I am Gaius Gilgarion Rothalan, fourth son of Garren Rothalan and rightful king of Kentoria."

She flinched at the middle name. *If you mean to lie about your identity, do it by bending the truth,* he'd said. Had he introduced himself as Gilgarion, rather than just Gil, she would have known. "And you are an assassin?"

"Yes." The answer came simply this time. No dancing around the subject. "I am—was—my father's blade."

"His own child," she breathed. How could a father expose his own flesh and blood to such cruelty?

"Yes."

Thea no longer knew what to say. She stared at him for some

time, her face as guarded as his, lest he see the way she crumbled inside.

All the times she'd looked at him and warred with feelings. All the moments at the end, when she'd wondered if she could convince him to stay—or at least come back when his mission was complete. She'd been a fool.

"Were you going to tell me?" she asked at last.

Gil—Gaius—hesitated. "I wished to." Yet that wasn't an answer, not truly.

"You kissed me." She'd already said that, but her mind circled back to it without cease.

"Yes." He'd said that before, too, but this time, his voice softened. Worry creased his brow, the most expression she'd seen from him since he'd stepped from that room.

She tore her eyes away and stared at the carpeted floor beneath her feet. A thousand questions warred for the right to leave her tongue. In the end, none of them did.

For a time, the hall was quiet. Rilion had gone; Ina had never resurfaced.

Just when she thought she could bear the silence no more, he spoke.

"For years, I have pieced together bits of information, locating the man who had my father and brothers killed. His last attempt was reckless, and now I know where he is. I depart for Angroth in the morning. Regardless of what happens to me, Rilion will see that you are given a home and a chance to start over."

Thea couldn't find her voice. All she did was nod.

"Had I the power, I would wipe clean your slate and let you return home to Kentoria, but I cannot promise that. This situation—I spent years building it, knowing my family's killer would eventually come for me. The staging is precarious. I cannot reveal myself now, and I cannot guarantee I will live long enough to do so in the future."

Absolving himself of responsibility. Asking her to

understand, without telling her anything of substance. She should have been angry. Instead, she was only hurt. "You would go alone?"

"I have reached the end of Rilion's goodwill, as I have exhausted the goodwill of others I once considered allies. My fight has cost others a great sum. He will not accompany me." He spread his hands, resigned.

And he would not stay to explain. The need to understand pricked like a thousand needles, but Thea could not make herself ask.

Somehow, her silence told him everything. The corners of his eyes grew pinched. "I cannot ask you to go with me. I cannot guarantee your safety outside Danesse. You saw the raiders in the outpost village. I have no doubt they were meant to look for me."

Knowing who he was, that did not come as a surprise. "And what if you didn't ask?" By the Light, what was she suggesting? She hardly recognized the words coming out of her own head. He'd crushed her. Hurt her. Misled her the whole way. Going with him was out of the question. She was supposed to stay here, to start over, to forge a new life. Life was all she had *left*.

Yet after coming so far, it seemed a minuscule thing to risk. She had reached her destination, but there was nothing for her here. No home. No friends. Only a hope those things might eventually be—that she might still have the will to seek them after watching her heart walk away.

The realization hit her like a slap in the face.

"Take me," she whispered. "Take me with you."

"Thea—"

"Don't leave me here. Don't leave me behind. Not after everything we've been through." Tears hung on her eyelashes and she fought to hold them back. She didn't want to cry. Not now, of all times, when she wanted to be strong. So many times, she'd given up her fight. She would not crumble now.

He stepped closer. The movement was halting at first, as if he was uncertain it was what she wanted. His second step was more confident, but his words were not. "I thought you wanted this. To be here, to start over—"

"I want you," she blurted.

Gil's shoulders slumped. "I cannot promise that. I cannot promise I'll survive what I must do. How can I give you what I do not know I will possess?"

She couldn't stop the tears. They grew thicker, blurring her vision. After all they'd done, how far they'd gone, why was she still so weak? "Then give me what happens before then. The you here, now—"

He swept in before she could finish and dropped a kiss upon her mouth.

Thea molded herself against him as his arms curled around her body, sliding her hand through the short hair on the back of his head. This was what she wanted. Where she belonged.

His arms were home.

"I dared not hope," he whispered.

Neither had she. She scrubbed tears from her eyes with the heel of her palm and rested her forehead against his. He was too tall; he had to bend forward just so she could reach him, yet he bowed when she pulled him down as if he would have gone anywhere she desired. "I want this to be real."

"I am the king," he replied. "When we return, I can make it so."

Her assassin. Her husband. Her king. Reality swirled so fast, it left her dizzy. "By the Light, Gaius," she breathed. "Who did you kill?" It hadn't been the king. *He* was the king. But he was not the king she'd known, not the man she'd recognized. He'd severed that man's head, right in front of her.

He grew solemn. "Someone I believed I could trust. I was mistaken."

"A decoy?" Nothing else made sense.

He nodded. "Selected to sit in my place, to execute my orders while I was left free to continue my search. So far as most of

Kentoria knows, he was Gaius Rothalan. But there are members of the guard who know the truth, and the members of my council knew, as well."

"They'll rule in your stead?" She'd been so eager to escape Kentoria, she'd hardly considered how the country might manage without a king.

"As well as they are able, until my return. Or until Rilion notifies them of my death. I have left orders, and I pray my substitute was the only traitor in their midst."

Thea shook her head as she tried to grasp it all. Light's mercy, but her head was spinning. "How did you know? How did you find him?" And how much damage had been done to her homeland before he'd been caught?

"My sources led me back to Kentoria, where I discovered he had not executed all of my orders. Instead of working to strike an alliance with Ranor, he prepared for a coup, bolstering the Kentorian armies with men loyal to his cause. Whatever it may be." He muttered the last beneath his breath. A hint of steel had returned to his eyes and posture, but his arms around her were still gentle. "His confession came with his dying breath, and now I know. The man I seek hides in Angroth. To kill him may be to incite a war, but I am ready."

She exhaled hard. "I don't understand. Why hunt him further? Why not wait for him to come to you?"

"Because by now, he is sure to have heard Kentoria's king is dead, or he will hear soon. He will assume that means the coup was successful. So I carry his assassin's head to his doorstep. He will soon learn he's killed the wrong king."

Thea shuddered. She'd tried so hard not to think of what he'd carried, and hadn't been able to fathom why he'd kept it in his bag.

"I know you find it distasteful," he said, as if reading her thoughts. Maybe he'd just read the shiver that ran down her spine. "If it means anything, I did not enjoy the process. But a message will be sent, and even if he slips away, I want—need—something to show I do not fear him."

She made herself nod. She wouldn't pretend to understand. "What must I do? How can I aid you?" The last thing she wanted was to beg he give her his final days, then become a burden that weighed him down.

"You will learn to fight. It's not far to the heart of Angroth, maybe a third the distance from Samara to here, but it will have to be enough."

She thought she could do that. Even now, she carried the dagger he'd let her borrow. The way it rubbed her bare leg was uncomfortable, and having it hidden beneath the skirt of her dress was inconvenient, but leaving it in her assigned room had felt wrong. "I'll prepare to continue travel. The maid and I washed my illusory clothing. It's drying now."

"Good. Since your face is the one on that poster, you'll need to remain unrecognizable." He frowned as if he found that thought unpleasant. Perhaps he did; he twisted his fingers in her reddish curls and breathed deep.

Ah. So he did like the honeysuckle, after all. Thea's face warmed. She'd wanted him to find her appealing. Now, standing with his arms draped around her and his eyes half-lidded as he inhaled the fragrance of her hair, she was embarrassed. Would she have done such a thing if she'd known who he was sooner?

He opened his eyes and stepped back. "Provisions," he muttered as he snapped his fingers. "I'll need to let him know."

"Rilion?" she guessed.

"Yes." He gave a wry sort of smile and turned for the stairs. He didn't tell her to stay, so she trailed along behind him.

What would the prince say about her canceled plans? Would he say anything? He'd said little about Gil's quest, or of Gil... Gaius... himself. Again, her cheeks felt warm. No wonder Rilion had choked when she'd identified herself as Gil's wife.

They found Rilion in the stable, though why Gil thought to look there, Thea didn't know. He stood, rubbing the forehead of a horse. The animal crunched on some treat, but already rooted at the prince's coat pockets, looking for more.

"That's enough for you," Rilion muttered as he stepped back, guarding his pocket while the other horse present came and leaned over the stall door.

Gil said nothing, just stood in the stable's doorway.

The prince slipped something to the second horse, then sighed. "She's going with you."

"Your assistance in settling her here may yet be needed," Gil replied.

Rilion bowed his head. "We'll hope it doesn't come to that." He stroked the second horse's neck, then made a sound of frustration. "I didn't bring enough horses."

Thea peered past Gil's shoulder, examining the nearby tack first, then the animals. "But there are two."

"Yes," Rilion said flatly.

She blinked. "Does that mean..."

Beside her, Gil gave one of his rare, but genuine grins. "It would seem so."

Reluctantly, the prince nodded.

The party was now three.

CHAPTER TWENTY

AT THE CRACK OF DAWN, Ina arrived at Thea's door, bearing a tray of porridge, sliced fruit, and steaming tea.

Thea ate while the maid laid her clean travel garments across the foot of the bed. The two halves of her dress were there, too, but she'd already decided to leave those behind. Speed was necessary for the coming trip. Anything she could do to lessen Gil's burden would help.

Her thoughts rolled around that man like waves tumbled about the rocks at the shore. Reconciling that he was Gaius, the king, with her knowledge of Gil the assassin and his charming ways seemed an insurmountable task. But it had only been one night, and merging the two identities in her head would take time.

"You knew, didn't you?" she asked as she sipped her tea.

Ina lifted her head. "Knew what, milady?"

"Who he was. Gaius."

The maid offered a coy smile. "Oh, we get so many guests. I couldn't possibly keep them all straight, milady. Even if I have been working for the royal family since I was thirteen."

Thea snorted and cradled her tea close. "You're as bad as he is, bending the truth like that." She should have been mad at him for it, too. In the heat of the moment, realizing all he'd hidden, she'd been angry. But the feeling had been fast to fade, and she wasn't sure if it was because his reasons made sense, or because he'd kissed the sense right out of her.

Ina chuckled softly to herself and finished tidying the room. All that was left for Thea to do was get dressed and take the things she couldn't leave behind. Anything she left would be set aside for later, just in case they stopped by Danesse on a return journey, which made it easier to decide.

Of course, that assumed there would *be* a return journey. Every time she thought of the risks, she grew convinced that accompanying him would slow him down and increase the likelihood of Gil coming to harm. Yet he'd been pleased when she asked to go with him; relieved, even. He'd said he could not ask her to go, but he'd been fast to grant permission when she asked.

Risky or otherwise, he wanted her there, and that would have to be good enough.

By the time Thea dressed and descended the stairs, the men were outside. Rilion had gotten a third horse from somewhere, and all three were saddled and ready for the trip. Each horse bore a bedroll on the back of the saddle and bags of provisions to either side. Thea had left most of her things in her room, packed into the sewing basket so they would be easy to store until she came back. If she came back. In a strange way, that offered comfort. If she didn't survive, it wasn't as if she'd miss the books she'd brought along and hadn't gotten to read.

"Have you any riding experience?" Gil asked as she approached. It would be hard to think of him as anything but Gil today; he wore his illusory clothes, giving him the face she'd crafted to go with the name. That face would likely always be Gil in her head, no matter what she knew of his identity.

"I'm afraid not." Thea liked the idea of horses, but her family had always resided in Samara. There was no room for anyone within the city to keep them. The king had his own pastures just beyond the city's walls, space for the animals to graze. Not the king, she corrected herself. Him. Gil. Gaius. Except he was the king. By the Light, she was going to have a headache in no time.

Rilion hummed thoughtfully under his breath. "We'll give her the bay. She's more sweet-tempered than the others."

Thea did not know what bay meant, and she looked between the horses in hopes one would be identified.

Gil stepped toward the pretty brown mare with the black mane, tail, and legs. "Bring your bags. I'll show you how to fasten them."

She only carried one bag now. She slid it from her shoulder and held it in her hands as she approached. "Do they have names?"

"That one's Molasses." Rilion busied himself with preparing his own horse, a dappled gray gelding with sleepy eyes. "This is Nib, and the red one is, ah, Socks."

Thea observed the white markings at the reddish horse's hooves. "Yes, I see."

"People who name horses tend not to be creative," Gil said.

"No worse than what people name cats. Or dogs." Thea's family had never owned dogs. Just the old gray cat, whose flat face made him appear perpetually grumpy. He'd been sweet. "My mother's cat was named Toddles, but we mostly called him Tod, for short."

"Toddles?" Rilion repeated with a small laugh.

"His legs were shorter than the rest of his litter. He wobbled when he walked." She grinned, an expression the prince returned. He seemed warmer this morning, despite his claims the night before that he wouldn't accompany them on the journey.

Gil's fingers were deft when he tied her bag to the saddle, his speed too hard for her to follow. He undid the knots and showed her again. "People aren't often much better with names. We're both examples of that, aren't we?" He raised his brows at Rilion, who gave a snort.

Thea tried tying the bag on her own. It held. "Because Rilion is a common name?"

"As is Gilgarion," the prince said. "There are some scholars who speculate they're the same person, you know."

"And others who say they are rivals." A competitive spark lit Gil's face.

Rilion rolled his eyes. "Two interpretations of the same story is a far more likely explanation, and you know it. Just like you know the One whom the Ranorsh revere and the Kentorian deity of Light are likely the same. They're just offshoots of the same faith."

Gil raised a finger in warning. "I am not having that argument again."

Their back-and-forth was charming. Thea giggled to herself. "Again? Do the two of you talk at all outside of debating?"

"As a matter of fact, the similarities between the legendary hero Rilion and the hero Gilgarion were the reason we first spoke," Rilion said.

"Don't think I didn't notice you referred to only Rilion as legendary," Gil said.

"I don't know that I've heard of either one. Beyond the names being common, that is." Although Thea couldn't recall any other Gilgarions, and it was only Gil's middle name, not his first.

Rilion brightened. "Is that so? I happen to have recently read a new perspective on the likely origins of the heroic legend. If you'd like, perhaps I could—"

"Save it for the road," Gil said, slapping his friend's shoulder.

That was certainly what they were; friends. Seeing the playful camaraderie between the two of them warmed Thea's heart.

In a strange way, it brought her comfort, too. They'd dealt so little with other people along their journey. Seeing Gil banter good-naturedly with someone other than herself reassured her that was simply the way he was, not only a front he'd put on while they traveled. The way a man behaved around his friends was telling, sometimes.

Gil boosted Thea to the saddle and helped her settle, then climbed onto his own mount. Rilion did, too, and once he was settled on the gray horse's back, he drew up the hood of his cloak.

"Just a moment, now!" Ina called from the kitchen's back door. The maid hurried across the cobbles with a bundle in her arms. "If you're going north, the lot of you can't go like that. Not with cloaks alone." She spread her arms to present three coats in the Ranorsh style.

Thea beamed. "I was just wondering if I should have made a cloak for myself. Thank you, Ina." She leaned down to accept the gift from the maid, who moved from horse to horse to distribute the coats.

Gil ran his hand across the red collar of his.

"Your favorite," Thea remarked.

He cracked a smile.

"Thank you," Rilion said sheepishly as he draped the coat across the front of his saddle. That was a good place for it, too; it would keep his legs warm while the weather was pleasant enough that wearing it would have been uncomfortable. Thea spread hers across her legs, too.

"Yes, thank you." Gil reined his horse toward the gate. "Now we should go. We've tarried long enough."

Ina waved them off without so much as a word of farewell before she retreated into the kitchen.

Once she was gone, Gil's face grew stony. "Is she trustworthy?"

"Few are," Rilion answered simply.

They rode from Danesse in silence. Gil led, but they rode in a casual formation so the two men in cloaks wouldn't draw attention. Thea had no doubt Rilion was not supposed to be joining them. Whether or not he'd befriended Gaius, and Gaius was now king of Kentoria, everyone knew the cordiality between Ranor and Kentoria was strained. It made their friendship all that much stranger.

"How *did* the two of you become friends?" Thea asked once they were clear of the city. The sky overhead was clear blue, but pale with the hint of coming winter. Before long, there would be snow on the ground.

"Our fathers once tried to strike an alliance," Gil said. "Others had tried before, but while Ranor is not outright antagonistic, it's safe to say there's no love between our two countries."

"King Garren brought the princes in hopes one would strike it off with my sister," Rilion added. "With the exception of Calem, that was. Calem was already betrothed to the princess of Nylmeres at that point."

Gil nodded. "Calem stayed behind to oversee things in Kentoria while we were away. Being the youngest, it was unlikely the Ranorsh princess would care to see me at all. I tried to convince my father to leave me behind. He refused."

"To be honest, my younger sister fancied him a good deal," Rilion said. "But she was nine, and my father was not looking for an early betrothal. She is still coddled as the baby of the family. On the other end of things, my elder sister is seven years my senior, and I believe we are the same age." He motioned between Gil and himself.

"I am eleven months older than you," Gil corrected.

"The same age," Rilion repeated soberly.

Thea grinned to encourage them to go on.

Gil fixed his eyes on the horizon as they worked their way north. "The princess was content to entertain Aleron and Lucan, but she didn't care to entertain a child as well. I was twelve at the time, I believe, and I had recently acquired new... skills... in my training."

The emphasis he put on that word made her lean forward in the saddle. "Do I dare ask what sort of skills those were?"

"He picked every lock in the palace he could find," Rilion said.

A logical skill for an assassin, and one she could see a boy using irresponsibly, too.

"Specifically, I picked the lock to a library." Gil smirked at the memory. "The king's private library, filled with all manner of political secrets. The last place I should have been, and yet, I wasn't alone."

Rilion scratched the bridge of his nose. "I, ah, wasn't supposed to be there, either. When the door opened, I thought I was about to lose my head."

Thea's amusement drained. She knew little about the sort of training Gil had endured, but she'd seen him fight. She could guess.

"He attacked me first," Gil said, confirming her fear it had ended with violence.

"I thought he was a spy." Rilion chuckled at the memory. "I'd been in the library all morning and hadn't seen our guests arrive."

"So you fought," Thea said slowly. It pained her to think of the outcome, but it couldn't have been that bad. Both of them rode alongside her. "Who won?"

The prince grinned at her. "Both of us, I'd say."

"We stopped as soon as we realized we'd be better allies than rivals," Gil said. "We stole fourteen books from his father's library and hid in the attic to read them."

Thea couldn't help but laugh. "And let me guess, you've been friends ever since."

"Well, sort of. He doesn't enjoy books anymore." Rilion sniffed. "I suppose I have to forgive him for that."

"I still appreciate literary pursuits, although I admit I've come to find historical documents and regional legends less than engaging."

Rilion gave a shrug. "He does not share my ebullience for research."

"Few probably do," Thea said. "I appreciate your passion for it, though. It's quite evident." It was something she understood, too; not because she shared the same field of interest, but because her family had often rolled their eyes at her enthusiasm over textiles and fashion.

"Passion is often admirable," Gil said in a murmur, "but I suspect now is not the time or place. Look. There may be trouble."

Both Thea and Rilion shifted in their saddles to look farther north, where the hard-packed dirt road wound into the mountains.

Somewhere ahead, still a few miles off, smoke rose from the hills.

CHAPTER TWENTY-ONE

SEVERAL MILES TO THE NORTH, they found the burned-out remnants of a small village. Little more than a farmstead, Thea thought, though the number of buildings and their shapes made it obvious there had been several houses.

"What happened here?" Rilion asked no one in particular as he slid from his horse and dropped its reins. It shifted in place, but did not wander.

Thea was not sure she could dismount on her own. Before she could try, Gil appeared at her side. She slid down into his arms, grateful for the assistance.

He released her as soon as her feet were on the ground. "The buildings are too far apart for the fire to be accidental."

"So it's arson, but..." Rilion trailed off. He scanned the smoldering remnants of buildings for a time, then trudged toward the ruins. He found a farmer's hoe along the way, miraculously unburned, and used it to scrape through the ashes and glowing coals. "That doesn't seem right."

"What doesn't?" It looked like the site of any other fire to Thea. There was little left of the houses, only fallen stone and charred wood.

Gil stalked toward the ashes. "No remains."

"Not even animals." Rilion tossed the hoe into a pile of ashes. Gray motes swirled into the sky. "How old do you think it is?"

"Hours. It burned some time this morning, I'd think." Gil turned to search the nearby hills, but if he saw anything, he did not say. "We would have passed them on the road from Danesse."

"Unless they didn't go that way." The prince glanced to the north.

Thea tried to follow his line of sight, but a flutter of something caught her attention. She walked that way, instead.

At the corner of a mostly-fallen shed, a scrap of deep red fabric fluttered. She cocked her head. "That's a Kentorian weave."

Rilion headed her way. "We're rather far north for Kentorian riffraff, aren't we?"

"Consider who you're traveling with," Gil said.

The prince snorted. "Fair enough."

Thea reached for the fabric. The moment her fingers brushed it, a jolt of *something* lanced up her fingers. She jerked her hand back with a yelp.

Gil tensed. "What is it?"

"Magic." She shook her hand. It still prickled. "I don't know what sort. It could be from someone with a talent for weaving, or another Threadmancer."

Rilion perked at the statement and reached past her to take it. "You can feel that?"

"Because I'm a Threadmancer, too. I can feel some things. Sometimes. A good Threadmancer can hide the magic, so it won't stand out to anyone but an artificer, but..."

"Let me see." The cloth stuck fast where it was snagged. Rilion pulled until it tore loose, then flexed the fabric between his hands. A puzzled frown worked its way over his face as he brushed his thumbs across its surface. "There's... hmm. I'm not sure what to make of that."

Thea's brow furrowed. "You sense something?"

"I have a bit of a talent for it," the prince admitted. "I've not had the training of a full artificer, of course, but it's a good skill for anyone with historical interests to have."

Gil crossed his arms. "And do you plan to tell us what you feel, or are you just going to stand there and fondle that like it's a lover's handkerchief?"

Flustered, Rilion pushed the bit of cloth into Thea's hands. "It's resistance magic. The fabric is made so it can... hmm, how to explain it? It repels flame."

"Then you'd explain it by saying it repels flame." Gil reached out and for a moment, Thea thought he meant to take it from her hands. He drew his fingertips across its surface. She already knew he couldn't feel it, but perhaps he'd notice something they hadn't. "You said this is Kentorian cloth?"

She nodded. "I'm positive of it."

His fingers tensed against the scrap. "Is there any way you could tell who made this, or when?"

Thea wished she could. "That's beyond my ability. If there were fewer Threadmancers in Kentoria, then maybe I'd know something about their power signatures, but there are at least a dozen." Just one fewer, now that she was gone.

Gil exhaled softly, but she heard his frustration.

"So we have an arsonist swathed in enchanted clothing from Kentoria, a bordering country Ranor doesn't quite get along with." Rilion scrubbed a hand through his dark hair. "Yet there are no corpses, no bones. Not even those of animals. Any ideas what that could mean?"

Thea looked to Gil as if to ask his thoughts. His eyes narrowed with thought and instead of replying, he stalked toward the northern side of the village. At first, she thought he studied the nearby hills nestled at the foot of the mountain. It wasn't until she went to join him that she saw he was examining the ground. She hung back, staying out of the way.

"When they departed, it was in an organized group, but they went fast." Whatever marks told him that, she couldn't see them.

"Farmers should be settling for winter, not abandoning everything and venturing into the mountains."

Unless they hadn't a choice. Thea stuffed the scrap of fabric into her pocket and then nibbled on her thumbnail. "Where does this road lead?"

"Angroth," Rilion said. "Not much between here and there."

Gil grunted softly and turned to go back to his horse. "Then perhaps we'll see them on the road and find answers along the way."

A sliver of doubt twisted Rilion's expression, but he said nothing and returned to his mount.

The road yielded no further clues before nightfall. Thea did not understand how as many people as the farmhold must have housed could disappear from the road so swiftly, especially with animals in tow, but the men offered no suggestions.

There were no established campsites like there had been along the road between Kentoria and Ranor, so they stopped only when they were too weary to go any farther. At least, Thea and Rilion were weary; Gil roved up and down the road while they set up camp, searching for signs or indications they may have missed. He still maintained the group had gone north along the same trail they followed, but the road was narrow and unkempt, and it was a marvel Gil saw any tracks at all.

Eventually, he returned. Thea had already spread her bedroll, and she sat cross-legged on the cushion and gnawed dry rations while Rilion started a fire. It was too cold to go without it, but seeing the flames spring to life in the night made her think of the ashes of the settlement they'd left behind. She couldn't imagine a group of travelers stopping without a camp, but there had been no signs they had even stopped for rest. She chewed absently while she watched the fire. The paper-wrapped bars in the supply bags tasted all right, a blend of grains and nuts held together with fruit paste, but the cold weather made them hard. Maybe next time, she'd wait for the fire and warm one up, first.

"Find anything interesting?" Rilion asked as Gil removed a bar of his own from his bags.

He didn't remove his bedroll from his horse yet, just sat on the ground near the campfire. "Have the number of raids and robberies near the borders increased of late?"

Rilion blinked slowly, as if he didn't understand the point of the question. "They've increased in recent days, but I wouldn't say there was any noticeable change in the past few weeks. Come to think of it, the increase started months ago."

Gil gave a slight frown. "In the spring?"

"Yes. Why? Does that relate to something?"

Thea understood. "Your coronation." She paused to wipe a crumb from her lip. "Or, the other you's coronation. Your decoy."

"Lucan's death." Gil nodded. "What of the neighboring countries? Have you heard anything from them?"

"No. Or, not that I'm aware." Rilion stared at their provisions as if unable to decide whether he wanted any. "It's possible my father has kept such discussions to himself, but as far as I know, nothing has been out of the ordinary. Angroth and Lyrangroth have reported nothing out of the ordinary, but ordinary for them is to simply not report things. They're very insular that way."

"And Vahar?" Gil asked.

"Nothing. But their southern edge has the benefit of not being up against the mountains, where it's easy for ruffians to hide. There was..." The prince's eyes narrowed as he turned his gaze to the fire. "There was something from Nylmeres. Just something in passing that our quarriers picked up from their miners. Something about having to lock up tools in the mines. Theft had been bad. But theirs is such a sliver of border up against ours. Most of their range is shared with—"

"With Kentoria," Thea finished. She thought of the scrap of fabric in her pocket. Red was an unlucky color, but it also reflected the nature of fire, making it an ideal choice for such a garment. "Are most of Ranor's raiders Kentorian?"

Rilion nodded. "We are on good terms with Vahar, and as I said, Angroth and Lyrangroth tend to keep to themselves."

Thea looked to Gil for confirmation she understood what he wanted to know.

He licked sticky remnants of his nut-and-fruit bar from his teeth. "It is safe to say however my opponent infiltrated my kingdom and swayed my decoy to his side, he has used that weak point to try and destabilize Kentoria's alliances, as well."

"But we aren't your allies," Rilion said.

"Ranor isn't, but you are. And neither your brothers nor your father hate me. I am arrogant enough to believe they would be willing to negotiate a formal treaty with me, regardless of the difficulties they had with my father."

Thea suspected he was right. She'd found him charming from the very beginning. As a king, that charisma would serve him well. But alliances had nothing to do with the puzzle piece that still sat in her pocket. "So whoever arranged the deaths of your father and brother is pushing the worst Kentoria has to offer to cause trouble. That doesn't explain why the people they attack would go north, into the mountains, instead of toward Danesse. That smoke was visible from just a few miles outside the city. Shelter wasn't far off."

"It does not, but I have my suspicions." Gil slapped his thighs and rose to his feet, abruptly changing the subject. "Rilion, fetch your weapon. It's been too long since we sparred."

"What, now?" Rilion asked, though the question was pointless. Gil had already drawn his daggers.

Thea stood instead. "I'll fight." They hadn't practiced for days, and while it wasn't so much time that she thought she'd lose what little skill she'd gained, there was a sense of urgency she couldn't shake—something that warned her of the need for a blade.

"Very well." Gil beckoned her to the empty space that hardly justified the title of road.

She stepped over tall grasses to join him, dagger in her hand.

She'd hardly set her footing before he came at her.

Though he'd drawn two, Gil fought with only one blade, the other held behind his back. Every strike was calculated, measured, designed to make her think. Real combatants wouldn't fight that way, he'd warned her during their first match. They'd strike hard and fast, aiming to debilitate.

The first five swipes and stabs, she dodged or parried. The sixth slipped past her reach and his dagger came in for her ribs.

At the last second, he twisted his hand and jabbed her side with his index finger.

Dead.

He'd recited the word often enough in the early rounds of their lessons that he no longer had to. She drew back to readjust her stance.

He didn't give her time. The next round of blows came faster, but she was primed for them; he didn't make contact until the tenth attempt.

"Good." He gave a firm nod and stepped back to let her breathe.

She relished those few seconds of respite and the sound of his approval, too. No matter how many times they sparred, he always offered reassurance when she'd done something right. Most people she fought, he'd told her, wouldn't be experienced soldiers. They'd be rough-around-the-edges sorts who'd grown up brawling without training. Practice made them effective, but it would do the same for her.

This time, she sprang first.

He wasn't surprised. He deflected her blade and spun to tap her back.

"Am I allowed to make suggestions?" Rilion called.

"For Thea, or me?" Gil gave her three seconds to recover,

then came at her again. He moved like water, ebbing and flowing, always in motion.

Thea knocked his blade aside and darted into the gap. Her knife drove toward his chest and something jabbed her side. His other hand, dagger turned so she wouldn't be cut.

"Watch both hands," he murmured. "I am not the only person who can fight with both at once."

Rilion cleared his throat as he approached. They stepped apart, pausing their practice. "You're mirroring some of his movements. You're a good bit shorter than he is, so you don't have the same strength behind some of these lunges or swings, and they won't land on him the same way." He grasped the back of her dagger hand and repositioned her arm. "Focus on going in low and you'll pass under his arms more often. His height is a weakness for him. His stomach is right at stabbing height."

She studied the way he stood her, then extended her arm to full length. The tip of her dagger was level with the hollow where Gil's rib cage would split. A little higher and bone would halt a strike. Lower, and almost anything would be fatal.

Rilion nodded his approval. "You'll have more strength going in like that, with the full force of a stab. You're standing too upright, trying to match his height, and that takes strength from your arm."

Thea lunged forward in an experimental attack. It didn't land, but she came closer.

From the way Gil looked at her, he approved, too. "I have difficulty seeing her as a knife fighter. She'd be better with a sword. She's graceful."

It was the first compliment of the sort he'd given her. Thea felt her cheeks warm and was grateful the flickering campfire hid the color.

"I could teach her," Rilion suggested. "I have more experience with a regular sword than you do."

Gil held his hands to the side, daggers balanced on his palms, and shrugged. "I'm certain you could, but you're overlooking one problem. We haven't brought any swords."

His hands closed on his daggers again and he swept forward, but not toward Thea. This time, he went for the prince.

Rilion stifled a shout and leaped backwards. His knife was out by the time his feet hit the ground. "That's unfair!"

"Have you ever known me to be fair?" Gil drove him back toward the fire, but after a few steps, Rilion found his rhythm and held his own. The prince snarled something under his breath, not quite words, but agitated enough that the sentiment was clear.

They were well-matched; Rilion wasn't as nimble or practiced, but it grew clear he was familiar with the way Gil moved, and he anticipated almost every blow. Thea considered letting them fight on their own. But fighting in a group was something they hadn't had an opportunity to practice, and she wasn't going to let it pass. How many more practice sessions would they have before they hit trouble?

She leaped forward to engage Gil from the side.

He hadn't expected her to join. Surprise flashed on his face and vanished a moment later, replaced by concentration. Her stab did not reach him, nor did Rilion's. The three of them shifted, rotating toward the fire and then around it, a flurry of stabs and slices, swings and jabs.

Fighting alongside Rilion gave her confidence, but Thea couldn't deny that Gil was *good*. His footing never faltered and his defense never failed, even as they both hammered against it. At the same time, he forced them sideways and spun them toward the fire. It limited their movements and forced them to split their attention between the campfire and their target. With how well Rilion had matched him on his own, the message was clear. Skill alone would not overcome strategy.

She bounded forward and kicked the campfire. A shower of embers burst around the toe of her boot and a flaming log flipped end over end to crash into Gil's legs.

He hissed and leaped back. His black boots spared him the burn, but the movement left him open.

Thea surged forward, curling her hand.

Her finger jabbed between the ridges of muscle in his stomach.

"Dead," she announced.

Gil raised his hands in acknowledgment of her success.

Rilion pumped a fist in victory.

"A good effort, and an unexpected action." Gil flashed her a grin. "But next time, you'll have to do it alone."

She smiled back.

"Ah, come on. That's all the more reward you give her?" Rilion jammed his knife into place and went after the burning log. It had rolled a short distance and he used a stray stick to herd it back to the campfire.

"Certainly not," Gil said as he slid his daggers into their sheaths and stepped forward. "I have something much better to offer." There was a sparkle in his eyes, dull beneath the illusion, but something not even magic could hide. Approval. Pride. And just a hint of anticipation.

Her heart fluttered in response. She'd done well, met his expectations, and for the first time, she felt she might have something beyond sewing to offer.

She tilted her head back and welcomed her victory kiss.

CHAPTER TWENTY-TWO

SHE DID NOT BEST him the next time, or the next time, or the time after that, either. They trained each morning and again at night, sometimes with sparring matches during the day. Occasionally, Rilion joined in, and other times he fought Gil by himself.

"You're fighting harder than before," Thea remarked one evening after he'd jabbed her in the ribs and stomach fourteen times. Some of those had been hard enough to leave bruises. She refused to complain. It was another message, something she needed to learn from if she wanted to survive. Gil meant her no harm. Anyone else would kill her.

"That is the general point of training. As your skill advances, you are matched against more competent opponents." He took a long drought from his water skin, then reclined so he was propped on his elbows.

"That means you were holding back more than I thought." She didn't know why she'd expected otherwise. There was no one else to train her; of course he'd temper his skill.

The smile he offered was tight, hardly a smile at all. "There is no one of lower skill here to teach you. Rilion is competent, though not my match. If you'd prefer, you may train with him."

"Thank you for volunteering me," Rilion put in sarcastically.

Maybe she should. Thea considered it as she finger-combed through her hair. It hadn't taken long for it to become gritty again. She longed for the bath in Danesse. She'd never experienced anything like it and probably wouldn't again.

Why wouldn't you? a small part of her objected. Tiny as that inner voice was, it was enough to make her pause and pursue the thought.

If they made it through this ordeal alive, they'd eventually return to Kentoria. How many times had Gaius kissed her? No matter how she clung to the false identity he'd presented, he *was* the king, and returning to Kentoria would end with him on the throne. What would she be then? She dared not imagine herself as a queen, regardless of her heritage. Her family had been noble enough that her pedigree had the potential to overshadow their downfall, yet gentle kisses and tender moments hardly warranted any fantasy of marriage. But oh, Light, she wanted it.

She'd entertained the idea of being his wife before. His real wife, not a position falsely assumed to make travel and business easier. A wife bound to him before the Light, honored with vows, cherished the way she'd always imagined she could be—

No.

Thea squeezed her eyes closed. She couldn't risk setting her heart on that, no matter how badly she might wish for it. Even if he wanted that—wanted *her*—they were not yet through the mountains between Ranor and Angroth, and the worst was yet to come. She couldn't think of it now, not even to dream. He'd been clear in explaining the risk. The chance she could lose him was hard enough. If she allowed herself to know—or even *believe* —he meant to wed her in the end, the fear of losing him would leave her paralyzed.

Actually losing him might kill her.

She steered her thoughts in other directions as he and Rilion spoke. They studied the stars and planned their course, and she still was not sure where they were going or why, beyond that they believed the person Gil sought was there.

"Not that far north," Rilion was saying. He pointed vaguely toward the east, making her wonder what she'd missed.

"But north of Passgate." Gaius—he was kingly when she looked at him, stroking his chin in thought like that—stared into the sky as if it could hold answers. "We're at least two weeks away from that settlement, and that's assuming it hasn't yet snowed in the mountains."

Thea wasn't confident making that assumption. The air had grown bitter at night. More than once, she'd caught the scent of snow on the wind, though she had yet to see so much as a flurry. It seemed impossible for the ground to still be bare farther to the north. "Where is Passgate?" she asked.

Both men blinked at her. Her lacking knowledge of geography wasn't a problem as long as they had Gaius to lead them, but a general sense of where they were and where they were going would be wise to have, if... No, no ifs. She'd already decided she wouldn't think of that.

"Angroth is shaped something like a teardrop," Rilion said, curving the fingers of his left hand into an approximation of the country. "Passgate would be about here, halfway up the western side." He touched his right index finger to the general location.

It told her less than she'd hoped. "And where are we now?"

He slid his finger down to the very bottom of the curve, nestling the edge of his nail against the fleshy web between his forefinger and thumb. "Ah, about here."

"Angroth is near the length of Kentoria, from the northernmost mountains to our southern coast. The horses will make us faster going across the valley, but we'll slow again in the hills." Despite the subtle crease of frustration between his brows, Gaius was calm. How had she ever looked past that unshakable nature and thought him anything other than what he was?

Rilion scratched the back of his neck and sighed. "We still don't know where exactly the place is, though. Intelligence offered by the sources I can reach will only get us so far. Aside from knowing he's in Angroth—"

Gaius raised a hand. "Knowing that is enough."

If anything, the extra distance would give her more time to train. More time to practice, make herself useful, and more time by his side. That was why she'd come, Thea reminded herself. Two weeks in close proximity, traveling the mountains and valleys with him only an arm's reach away.

Solemn, she burrowed into her bedroll and gazed at the stars. Maybe she'd sleep better if she kept him that way in the future. An arm's reach away, close enough to touch when the night's sounds frightened her awake.

Tomorrow, she'd lay her bedroll close.

"Well now," Rilion said. "What have we here?"

Thea craned her neck to see, but he'd already reined his horse to a stop and dismounted. Whatever it was, he knelt to inspect it.

Gaius dismounted, too. The closer they got to their destination, the more solidly that name cemented itself in her mind. Even with the unseemly face she'd given him.

He crouched beside Rilion and touched the ground with fingertips reddened by the cold. They'd spotted a few stray snowflakes early that morning, but they'd all roundly denied it. No one wanted to consider the impact of snow. Now, whatever it was they saw made snow a greater threat.

"How many?" Gaius asked so softly, the wind almost carried away the words. "What do you think?"

Rilion pursed his lips.

Unable to restrain her curiosity, Thea slid from her mare and inched forward to have a look.

Tracks. Clear ones, more defined than what even those left near the burned settlement had been.

"It's got to be dozens. Look how thickly they're layered." Rilion spread a hand and waved at the marks as a whole. "And they've been by recently, too."

"But we still haven't seen anyone," Thea said. "How can they move so swiftly in numbers so large?"

"Simple. There has to be something we're missing." The prince shrugged, then stood straight. His gaze tracked to the north, then the west.

Gaius did the same, though the turn of his head was barely perceptible. "They've not headed toward Passgate."

Thea wasn't sure of the directions or distances, but she, too, saw how the trail meandered west. "Is there something wrong with that?"

"Angroth isn't known for its large number of settlements." He dusted his hands together as he stood. It meant something to him; she saw it in the distant look that filled his eyes.

She paced closer and squinted at the horizon, unable to determine what he was looking at. "What are you thinking?"

Rilion had already returned to his horse. He stopped with his hands on the saddle and listened instead of mounting again.

A long moment dragged by before Gaius finally drew breath and spoke. "We shouldn't go north."

"Where, then?" Thea asked.

"West. The same direction our missing farmers went."

"Back into the mountains?" They'd only just escaped the slopes of those between Angroth and Ranor. The valley ahead had been wide and welcoming. Now they gazed across rolling foothills that promised hard travel and slow going. Slower, once the snow fell.

"If that is where they take us." He turned and waved for her to get back on her horse. She'd gotten better at mounting and dismounting on her own, and she was able to climb back into the saddle without much difficulty.

Rilion mounted, too, then leaned forward in the saddle as if it would help him see farther. "It's a recent path. Cut by the feet of many travelers. There are no cities that way, not that I know of. Mines, maybe, but they wouldn't attract such a large group of travelers."

Especially not when those travelers were Ranorsh. What could have sent them across mountains and into a neighboring country? Thea had rubbed the scrap of red fabric daily, hoping it would provide answers. It still hadn't.

"Then we should see what has attracted them." Gaius pointed to a narrow line that threaded through the grasses and scrub adorning the foothills. "Their trail is there. We will follow it as far as we can."

So they did.

The trail wound on, seemingly forever, and it only grew wider as they followed it. Eventually, another trail intersected with it, and its width was doubled again. By the first evening, the three of them could ride abreast with room to spare, and ruts from wagon wheels had joined the countless marks from sturdy boots and animal hooves.

"Wagons bearing what, I wonder?" Rilion mused to himself when they stopped for rest. He sat facing the west, but there was little to see. The trail disappeared into the night, and Gaius forbade a fire.

"Too close," he'd said, without explanation.

Thea dreaded what danger that meant and hoped spreading her bedroll right beside his would help stave off the worry when she slept, but it didn't. She woke often and rolled ceaselessly in her bedroll. Only when a strong, warm hand reached out to smooth back her hair and caress her face did she find respite from the uneasy dreams, and she woke tired the next morning.

They resumed travel at the break of dawn. Gaius scouted ahead on foot while Rilion led his horse. That he felt there was a need for scouting put Thea on edge. She couldn't tell if Rilion felt the same; the prince had a steady quality about him, much like what she'd seen of Gil during their travels, though he lacked the same measure of passion and energy. Or maybe his passion simply rested elsewhere. When he'd spoken of his studies, he'd had a spark in him, too. She dared not think herself the sort of person who might befriend a prince, but when everything was over, she hoped she would have the chance to know him better.

Their horses walked, letting Gaius outpace them easily, but they caught up with him near noon. From the moment he came into view, he walked toward them. How far ahead he'd gone, there was no telling.

"I've found your settlement," he announced when they were close enough to hear him speak his normal volume. Given the natural strength of his voice, they paced forward a bit farther before the horses stopped of their own accord. Their reaction amused Thea. Even the horses found him commanding.

"All the way out here?" Rilion sounded only half surprised. He scanned the hills, but there was nothing to be seen, and the ground had grown rockier, making the trail harder to follow.

Gaius nodded. "I recommend we turn the horses loose and continue on foot."

The prince snorted at the suggestion. "I am not turning the horses loose. These are good horses, and well trained. Do you have any idea how much a good Ranorsh steed costs?"

"A pittance compared to what's in your father's coffers, I'm sure."

Thea patted her dusty mare's neck. "I like Molasses. I'd prefer not to leave her. Is there somewhere safe we could leave them, instead?"

"Tying them somewhere would practically guarantee they'd be stolen, or else eaten by predators found in the hills." Gaius frowned to make his inconvenience clear, but he reached for the reins of his red gelding. They would keep the horses. "We will ride single file."

He took the lead and Rilion took the rear. The placement made sense; Gaius knew where they were going and Rilion was a stronger fighter than she, but it felt like being sheltered and she wasn't sure she liked that. She was under no illusions about her skill, but she hoped to make herself useful somehow. As of yet, she'd provided nothing Rilion couldn't.

Well, almost nothing. She supposed he could, in theory, provide the kisses, but somehow she didn't think Gaius would appreciate them. The tiniest hint of a smirk curved her lips and she raised a hand to wipe it away, disguising the motion by pretending to pull a stray hair from the corner of her mouth.

The path curved around a hill ahead. Instead of cresting it, Gaius turned his horse toward a rocky stretch that sloped upward, higher into the mountains.

They rode for what felt like hours before Gaius dismounted and flashed a hand signal telling them to do the same. The silence was telling. Thea climbed down from the saddle with caution and gave Rilion a curious look, but the prince only shrugged. She twisted the reins in her hand and continued on.

At last, a peak came into view.

"Leave the horses," Gaius whispered as he beckoned them forward. "They can't go far."

Reluctantly, Thea let Molasses go and crept to the peak to see what required them to make themselves so small.

A half-built fortress bursting with workers nestled in the steep valley below.

CHAPTER TWENTY-THREE

THE SOUNDS of construction rang against the mountains, faint from distance, but present. The echoes of hammers and pickaxes made Thea's eye twitch.

"How in the name of the One did they get all these people here?" Rilion asked in a murmur.

"What name is that?" Gaius crouched and inched as far forward as he dared, studying the lay of the buildings. Thea did, too, though she didn't know what she was looking at. The fortress looked strange compared to the surrounding mountains. Flat, square. Shapes common in Kentoria's architecture. Ranor's buildings had been taller and more angular. She didn't know what to expect from Angroth.

"I'm not saying it," Rilion replied, irritated. "You know it's forbidden to speak it."

"But writing it doesn't count, somehow?"

"His word can be written because it's knowledge the One has given to us. If the name is part of that, then—why are we discussing this now?" The prince made a sour face and returned his attention to the scene below.

Thea was already counting. "I don't know how to categorize the people down there. There are so many people working construction, but there are soldiers, too. Hundreds." It was hard to make out more than the minuscule shapes of people, but many carried large poleaxes or halberds that made them easy to spot. "Where did they all come from?"

From the way Gaius scanned the fortress from end to end, he was counting, too. "Settlements like the one we passed."

There were children, too. Thea didn't see them often, but now and then, a tiny person ran from one side of an open space to another. She shifted her attention outward, to the slopes. If there were fences, she couldn't see, and the pale bodies of livestock would have blended into the snow-dusted mountainside if not for their shadows. "What could convince people to come so far? Is there a shortage of work in Ranor?"

"No," Rilion said, "but if you offer enough money, just about anyone will move. Why here, though?"

"The southwestern region of Angroth is the best place someone who wants to go unnoticed could choose to settle. It's not as if there's anything down here. Not here, and not in Lyrangroth on the other side of the range." Gaius glanced west, toward the higher peaks. Looking for trails through the mountains? Thea saw none, but she'd already learned he was better at finding anything out of the ordinary.

"They aren't all Ranorsh people, though. We would have noticed this sort of exodus." Rilion studied the mountains, too, then turned to make sure the horses hadn't left.

Thea worried her lower lip between her teeth. "I can't be sure, but I think at least half of them are Kentorian."

Both men looked at her in surprise.

"Their clothing," she explained before they could ask. "It's too far for me to see clearly, but the shapes—the outline of their silhouettes is consistent with Kentorian fashion."

Gaius squinted at the workers near the top of the fortress. They were working on some sort of wall, transporting stones and mortaring them in place. "How would so many Kentorians get this far into Angroth's mountains without being noticed?"

That was a question for Rilion; as a prince, even a Third Prince, he should know.

All Rilion offered was a shrug. "I certainly haven't seen that many migrants."

For a time, they were all quiet.

Thea stifled a sigh. "So what does all this tell us?"

Again, Rilion looked sour. "My information may have been somewhat incorrect. This is how the outpost was described to me, but they definitely indicated it was north of Passgate."

"Maybe it was," Gaius said. "Maybe they moved."

The prince waved a hand at the construction. "Considering how many people have moved without notice, I'm willing to consider the possibility."

"So this is it?" Thea asked. "This is where we're supposed to be?"

"Maybe." Gaius didn't sound convinced.

"You know there's only one way to find out." Again, Rilion looked toward the horses. He made a small sound of exasperation and hurried that way. The gray dapple, Nib, was headed down the slope.

Thea thought he might return to finish that conversation, but instead, he climbed onto his wandering horse. She glanced to Gaius. His eyes were intense, focused. Did he envision his target there, hiding in that fortress? Leading it? Her nerves prickled with anxiety. "How do we find out? Sneak in?" she whispered.

"No," he said, a wry twist to his mouth. "We walk in the front door."

The descent back the way they'd come ate up the rest of the day.

"They'll close the gates at nightfall, I'm sure," Rilion said as the sun dipped below the ridge of mountains to the west. "Do we make camp again, or press on?"

"We'll venture as far as we can. Even with the fastest horses the world has to offer, we wouldn't make it to their settlement tonight." Gaius sounded frustrated.

Thea sympathized. It was hard to be sure what they were doing was even the correct choice. They'd turned to follow that trail on a whim. The fortress being there was promising for their cause, but if they reached its walls and discovered it wasn't the destination they were after, they'd be several days behind. Would that much time affect the likelihood of finding whoever pulled the strings of power in Kentoria? She hoped not, but Gaius had already spent years searching without finding what he sought. Delays now were not promising.

The sky remained bright for some time after the sun dipped out of sight. When the first hint of gold appeared, they halted for the night and set up their meager camp.

Rilion scrounged enough sticks from the nearby hills for a fire. Gaius did not object when he cleared a patch of dirt and piled them to light. Instead, he paced restless circles around the campsite.

After his third lap, Thea left her things behind and touched a hand to the dagger on her thigh. "We should practice."

He slowed, then shook his head and continued his circuit. "If you are not ready by now, nothing I do tonight will change that."

It was fair, and probably true. She knew she'd gained skill, though that hadn't been hard, since she'd known nothing when they began. Now she could hold her own in one-on-one combat, though the few times Rilion and Gaius had teamed up against her, she'd struggled. She thought that reasonable. Gaius could track and manage a seemingly endless number of opponents at once, but not everyone was him. No matter how much training she'd had, she was still a seamstress, a Threadmancer, a noblewoman whose hands had scarcely touched a weapon before this ordeal.

When he did not stop pacing, she finished spreading her bedroll. "Come sit with me?"

Gaius slowed again. This time, he considered the request. No objections came to mind, Thea supposed, for he strode over to sit at her side.

Satisfied, she leaned her head against his shoulder.

Rilion watched as he worked to start the fire. He'd witnessed affection between them enough since they'd left Danesse; nothing improper, only kisses and embraces that rarely lingered. There was speculation in the way he studied them, though, and Thea didn't think she'd seen that before.

She shut her eyes so she wouldn't have to ponder it. "You're worried. About tomorrow? That we won't find what you're looking for?"

"That we won't find him," Gaius said, "Or perhaps that we will."

He sat stiff, his shoulder still as stone beneath her head. She inched closer. "After all this time, you've still never told me who exactly it is we're looking for."

"I don't know, and therein lies part of the problem."

"Oh." That would be a problem.

"I've always told myself I would know when I see him, but perhaps that isn't true. I may know him. Or it may take time for me to be sure." Gaius rubbed the back of his neck. "If I am to be truthful, I never saw him. But I have seen what he has done to my family, and he will answer for it."

Thea rubbed his arm. "I'm sorry."

"After all these years, we still don't even know why." Rilion held out his hands before the tiny fire as the flames took hold.

"Rilion has been aiding me since my father's death," Gaius said. "For a long time, he has been the only one to help. Calem cared, as did Aleron. Lucan..."

"Lucan cared," Rilion said. "In his own way."

Gaius stared at the ground and Thea rubbed his arm again. She didn't know how to comfort him; not in this. She'd known people who suffered loss, had suffered loss of her own, but this was different. His whole family. The stability of the kingdom he was supposed to rule. All gone.

Eventually, he drew a breath to speak again. "Calem could have been a threat to many countries in this part of the world. He was well-liked. It made sense for an assassin to target him, but I never found any trace, no signs anyone had breached our defenses. It was worse than chasing a ghost. At least ghosts have sightings."

Thea nodded. That was, she assumed, part of why everyone believed it was the plague. The king had died so swiftly during the plague, an illness that took its toll within a matter of days. The palace had been closed against disease, and only a madman would have passed through the city at that time. The revelation it had been poison still shook her.

"For all that I mourned Calem as a friend, as well as a brother, Aleron was harder. You know what they said. An accident. Ill luck on the hunt." He snorted softly. "It was in the shelter of his own quarters. I was the one who found him. I'd just come back from searching. I was to offer a report. Had I arrived only a few hours earlier, I could have been there. I could have stopped the assassin. I know I could."

"You don't," Rilion put in. "You have no way to know that. You could have been asleep in your chambers and it would have happened, all the same."

Gaius frowned so deep, Thea thought the furrows in his brow might never smooth out. "Or I could have been there. I was Aleron's blade. As I was Calem's, as I was my father's. I failed them all."

"You've done all you could." Thea hugged his arm. It would have been too difficult to get her arms around him from the side. "But what about Lucan? All these deaths are so different, I don't know if..." If she had the right story? By now, she expected not, and she shouldn't have asked.

But he didn't seem to mind, and he laid a hand atop one of hers. "Lucan was... difficult. He was already paranoid after Calem's death. After Aleron, it became unbearable. He began sequestering himself in his quarters, refusing to see anyone, even... no, especially me. He feared me. He accused me of having killed Aleron, at one point. I swore my loyalty to him a thousand times. I swore it on the Light, I swore it on our blood, I swore it on anything he asked. But it was never enough, and in the end, he..."

Her hands tightened on his arm.

He swallowed and closed his eyes. "He could bear his fear no longer. In the end, that was what killed him. And to an extent, it was my fault."

"You've been saying that for months," Rilion said. "It's still not true."

Thea cast him a frown, then looked to Gaius. The lines of the face she'd given her didn't match the shadows cast by the fire, not quite. It gave him an unsettling look. "Why do you think that? Just because he was afraid of you?"

"Because I gave him reason to be afraid. He gave me orders I didn't agree with. My role was to be the king's blade, a weapon with which he could strike. I wasn't supposed to refuse. But his paranoia went too far. I tried to reason with him, to convince him the people he wanted me to kill had done no wrong. That harming people who were supposed to be on our side would destabilize Kentoria and its alliances. But he insisted, and I felt I had no choice. I was sworn to him a thousand times over."

Her heart twisted. She knew the cost of Lucan's paranoia all too well. "You can't blame yourself for his actions. We all know he was..." Mad? She couldn't bring herself to say it, even if she was sure the word fit. Even if it was a milder word by far than the curses that first sprang to mind. By the Light, would it ever get easier to think of her brother? She cleared her throat lightly and continued without fitting any word to the former king at all. "He arrested many innocent people throughout Samara. Executed people who didn't deserve it. No one was safe, but that wasn't your fault."

For a time, Gaius said nothing. When his eyes reopened, they bore a deep sorrow, darker and heavier than the illusion she'd spun over their color. "I tried to make my peace with what he wanted me to do. Tell myself it was for the best. That I'd sworn to serve him and I would do so until the end. I couldn't. By the time I refused to lift a blade in his name again, I'd already shed far too much innocent blood."

Thea ran her hand up and down his bicep. She didn't know what to say. What would comfort him? She had nothing to offer but the story of her own loss to the same king's illness, and that was hardly a story that would make anyone feel better. Yet there was little else to say, except the simple words that left her mouth. "I understand."

And she did, at least on the surface. It made perfect sense that Lucan would fear him. That a man with the power to strike a king dead would refuse to obey was terrifying. She saw how it could drive him to the brink. And she understood the quandary Gaius had been left with, though she lacked the fortitude to think of the things he must have done. He'd been forged into a weapon; all he knew was how to cut.

To rise and refuse to cut anymore must have been far harder than anything else he'd done.

Rilion scratched the back of his head and sighed, long and deep. "To an extent, Lucan probably had reason to fear. I had hoped Aleron's death was the end of it, that Gaius wouldn't be a target. We can all see that wasn't the case. I don't mean to excuse Lucan's paranoia, but an assassin came for Gaius, too. We still don't even know why."

Thea's eyes snapped to his face. "You don't?"

Gaius nodded, resigned. "We've never turned up even so much as a clue. For all that I've searched since Calem's death, I've found nothing. No motives. No demands. Only more uncertainty. My father was old when he passed. He settled late in life. We all expected it, and Calem was ready to take the throne. For a long time, I believed his death was by natural causes. Now, I am no longer sure. It's only an assumption, but I have reason to suspect he was poisoned as well. All with no traces left behind, just as it was with Calem."

"But we're close," Rilion said. "I have a good feeling about this lead. We're going to find answers soon."

"Perhaps." Gaius took Thea's hand in his and pulled it to his mouth so he could kiss her knuckles. "But I have been sullen long enough. A king should not be given to sulking or self-pity, and I have indulged in both enough tonight. We should rest while we are able. Tomorrow, we'll find answers."

Answers, or yet another mystery.

CHAPTER TWENTY-FOUR

By MID-MORNING, they rode toward the massive gate on the east end of the fortress. The steep valley around them housed more animals than Thea first realized, along with shepherds and goatherds. The people in the fields paid them no mind.

The gate was closed. A handful of guards stood outside, their faces painted with varying levels of boredom, though mild interest shaded their eyes as the three of them grew near.

"Haven't had many folk come a-horseback," one guard called. His accent was definitely Kentorian. "Who're you?"

"We heard there was work here," Gaius replied. It wasn't what the guard asked, but the man didn't seem to mind.

"For the right people, yes," the guard said. "What can you do?"

Gaius gestured to Thea first. "My wife is a seamstress. My brother is a scribe. I... well, I can do whatever may need strong hands. I have experience with a blade, or I can aid construction."

"A scribe?" The guard's brows rose and he glanced to Rilion. "Are you good with numbers, too?"

The prince nodded. "Oh, yes. Is there a job to fill? Inventory, maybe?"

"Managing His Majesty's accounts. We've a few scribes who

are good with numbers, but not as many as we need. Here. Prove it, read this, and I'll let you in." The guard rooted in his pocket for a moment, then produced a piece of folded paper.

Rilion dismounted and trudged forward to take it. He blinked. "This is a recipe for acerglyn."

The guard laughed. "Oh, you read fast. Double the numbers on those measurements, there."

"Double is entirely too much alcohol," Rilion muttered. "Ten gallons of water, one gallon of maple syrup, four and a half teaspoons of brewer's yeast, one and a half cups of maple sugar—"

"All right, all right." The guard snatched the paper back before he could finish. "Maybe that was too easy. Hey, woman. You're Kentorian, right? Do you know how to make syrup?" He waved the recipe at her.

Thea blushed. "I never worked in—"

"I know how," Gaius interrupted. "I don't know how good the sap runs are this far north, but can teach anyone who's willing to learn."

"Ah, good! It's been far too long since we had a proper drink." The guard grinned, an expression shared by several of the others. One of them turned to knock on the gate and whisper a password to someone on the other side.

The gate came open and one of the men pointed inside. "You'll go up the slope to the first shack on the right. You'll check in there and let the clerk inside know what sort of jobs you can do. Approval for you to stay will have to come from His Majesty, but the clerk there will take you to him."

"Thank you," Gaius said. He dismounted, then helped Thea from her horse. She no longer needed the assistance, but he'd scarcely touched her since they'd left Danesse. She relished the strength of his hands against her waist and the warmth of his body as he let her slip close enough to steal a hug. He squeezed her arms, but then let go and led the way toward the shack. The gate ground closed behind them.

"I didn't know you knew how to make syrup," Thea said.

"I don't."

She faltered. "You don't?"

"It's not as if we'll be here long enough for them to figure that out," he murmured.

Rilion stifled a sigh.

She lowered her voice. "Are we going into the shack, then?"

Gaius nodded. "We'll check in. Receive our assignment and instructions to meet whoever they think is their king. Once we do that, we should be free to wander and ask questions."

Thea wasn't sure asking questions was wise. Remaining as unmemorable as possible would be to their advantage. But this was his quest, his goal, and she would let him take the lead.

"I have some concerns about all this," Rilion said.

"As do I. The situation is not ideal, but we should explore it as fully as we are able. It may be revealed that this is the wrong place entirely, in which case we will move on and head for Passgate." Gaius stopped outside the shack and looked for somewhere to tie the horses. There were no hitching posts or fences nearby.

"I can hold them," Thea offered. "You still have our documents, right? If you can't check in for both of us, you start, and I'll wait here."

"Very well." He passed her the reins.

Rilion did the same. "What documents does she mean?"

"Our marriage license. And our passports. I hope you've prepared a name."

The prince blanched. "A name?"

"When I travel, I am Gil."

"If we're supposed to be brothers, then I'm Ril."

Gaius snorted. "No one would believe that."

"I guarantee there are parents out there who would absolutely name their children Gil and Ril. I am your younger brother, and I am grateful that for the moment, you look the part." Rilion opened the door and motioned for Gaius to go first.

Gil, Thea told herself, setting his other name in mind. She'd only just gotten used to his real name. Now she'd have to watch herself to be sure she didn't slip. By the Light, what was she going to call him after they were through with all this?

The men slipped inside. Thea shuffled her feet and took a moment to stroke her horse's nose. Molasses gave her a friendly nudge, then searched her hand for treats.

"Nothing for you," she said, spreading her hand to show it was empty. The other two horses remained still. Holding three was a terrible idea, she realized belatedly. If one tried to go anywhere, she'd lose all of them. For now, they seemed content to stand and rest. With luck, they'd be given a decent stable while the three of them were there.

Or maybe that would be no luck at all. How they planned to get back out of the fortress, nobody had discussed. If the horses were stabled somewhere out of the way, it would be an added layer of challenge to their escape. If they *could* escape, she thought grimly as a man with a halberd strolled by. Most of the apparent guards bore little to no armor, but there was a fierceness in their eyes as they roved the courtyard that told her they'd be no easy fight.

Maybe there wouldn't be a fight. Maybe this king wasn't the enemy Gil was after, no matter what Rilion's information said. She didn't even know what that information was.

"Hello," she offered to another passerby. Most of the people who meandered past on their way to complete duty or business were more interested in the horses than in her, but a few returned her smile with small, nervous ones of their own.

Eventually, the door beside her cracked open and Rilion slipped out. "I'm finished," he said. "He needs you in there for your part."

Thea passed him the reins and shuffled toward the door.

The inside of the shack was dark and cool. She blinked hard as the shadowy shapes inside resolved into people. Gil leaned against a counter, while a woman scarcely tall enough to see over it inspected their passports.

"Here she is," he said. There was a fondness in those words. The genuine quality of it warmed her heart.

The woman rose on tip-toe to look at her. "A seamstress, you said? Can you weave?"

Thea blinked. "With the right tools, yes."

"Spin wool?"

She hesitated.

Gil gave his head the slightest tilt, encouraging her to answer.

"I'm out of practice," she said, opting not to bend the truth. "But again, with the right tools. And perhaps a bit of time to refresh my memory."

"Hmm." The woman sniffed. "No children?"

A furious blush heated Thea's cheeks. "We're newlyweds."

"But we pray," Gil added.

Her blush grew so bright, she suspected one could light a candle by touching it to her face.

The woman sniffed again. She had no stamp, but she produced a quill and a bottle of reddish-brown ink and penned something in both passports. "Light willing, then. I believe His Majesty will have you, but the final say is his. Your appointment will be one hour before the dinner bell." She slapped the passports down on the counter and pushed them forward.

"Thank you," Thea said with a frown. "But if the bell hasn't been rung, how will we know what time it is?"

The woman stared at her as if she didn't know what to say.

Gil swept the passports into his bag. "We'll just wait. Is there assigned seating for audience seekers?"

"The antechamber of the King's Hall. You will be asked for your appointment time. Tell them, and the steward will call for you when it's your turn."

"Thank you." He took Thea by the shoulders and steered her

toward the door. "Oh, one last question. We came by horseback. Is there a stable where we may let our animals rest?"

"We haven't many horses," the woman admitted. "So we haven't any facilities. Ask about the fort proper and you'll find someone to see to them, I'm sure."

Gil nodded and urged Thea out the door.

She shrugged out of his grasp. Guiding her hadn't been a condescending action, but protective. Part of her relished it, but they didn't know what waited ahead. She had to convince him to focus elsewhere, to move onward without worrying about her. She welcomed his touch, but she would not become a distraction.

"Where do we go from here?" Rilion asked as Thea reclaimed her horse.

"We're supposed to ask around for somewhere to stable the horses. The clerk inside didn't know where they could be put." Thea patted Molasses on the shoulder.

"I will walk around and inquire after somewhere they may be kept," Gil said. "I will return shortly."

Rilion snorted softly. "Try to temper your aristocratic tongue while you're at it."

Gil said nothing and paced off across the rocky courtyard.

Thea gazed after him as he stopped to talk to person after person and explain what they were after. They couldn't just stand outside the clerk's office forever, so she drew her mare into a slow, easy walk. Rilion followed with the two horses he led. It wasn't as if they'd be hard to find. They were the only people with a team of horses.

"So," she said after a time. "Should I call you Ril now?"

"People don't refer to each other by name very often," he said dismissively.

"That wasn't what I asked."

"I am aware of that. You may call me what you wish. I don't think my name is any hazard, even here. It's rather common."

"So I've heard." She turned her head. Gil was walking with

someone now, headed toward what she assumed was a storage building of some sort. Surely they weren't to tie up the horses there.

Rilion volunteered no further information. It was just as well; they'd have to be mindful what they spoke of now.

They completed a circuit of the main courtyard before Gil returned with two young men trailing at his heels.

"They will tend the horses for us," he announced. "Their father came to work as a farrier, but there are no horses, so he works as a general blacksmith instead."

The story was irrelevant, but the conversation made a good cover. She laid a hand to her horse's nose. Molasses tried to nibble her fingers. She pulled them away. "Oh, good. She could use a good brushing, it's been such a long ride."

"We'll take good care of them, ma'am, don't worry," one of the youths said in a clear Kentorian accent. By the Light, her estimate of half the camp being Kentorian was coming up modest.

The other young man pointed to the west end of the courtyard. "There's the King's Hall, up there. Can't miss it. Whenever you're done, you can come out to the field just beyond the east gate. We'll have them out there grazing, and we'll show you a safe place to tie them up at night and picket them during the day."

"Thank you both," Rilion said as he passed them the reins.

Gil offered a few more instructions, then turned to lead the way toward the so-called King's Hall.

Thea turned her head to watch the two young men depart with their steeds in tow.

So the horses would be just beyond the walls. That would either make them easy to get to during an escape, or it would doom them by forcing them to find a way past those walls to recover their mounts. Thea prayed for the former, then scolded herself. She should pray for something safer than a need for escape. The discovery they were in the wrong place, maybe. Or that they'd walk through the doors into the King's Hall and discover the man Gil sought for his revenge was already dead.

At that moment, the full weight of what they were doing finally hit her and she slowed to a stop.

She understood the nature of his quest and had disconnected that act from the charming and gentlemanly companion he'd been. She stared at his back as he walked with his chin up and his back straight, kingly and merciless, just the way she'd always heard. There was no denying his identity now. Just as there was no denying what the outcome of this would be.

Sooner or later, they'd find the man Gil was after, and that man would die.

As he climbed the steps to the King's Hall, she had a fleeting vision of him flinging the doors wide and commanding attention from the moment he stepped through. Instead, he opened only one door, then motioned for her to precede him. Her hand itched for her dagger's hilt, so she curled her fingers into her palm and squeezed her fist tight. There was little risk yet. No one knew who they were or why they'd come, and they were supposed to have an audience with the king. A flashback to the *first* audience she'd had with a king put a grim smile on her lips.

"I've never seen such a frightening look of amusement," Rilion said as he slipped in after her.

"Just remembering the first time I met Gil." She was tempted to turn and bat her eyes at him as he followed the two of them into the antechamber, but they were not alone, so she kept it to herself.

Gil wore a smirk of his own. Perhaps he'd made the same connection. "This meeting may go the same way."

Rilion muttered something under his breath and trudged farther into the room. There were no chairs or benches, only the smooth stone floor. A handful of people leaned against the walls or sat on the floor, waiting their turn to be seen. The prince picked a place against the wall and settled with a sigh, never looking back to see if they intended to join him.

Come to think of it, Thea didn't know if they'd be seen together or separately. They should have discussed that possibility on the way over.

"If their king is efficient, it won't be long," Gil said as he leaned against the wall and crossed his arms over his chest.

"And if he's not, at least we'll be well-rested." Rilion smirked and leaned back with his hands folded behind his head.

A pair of doors at the end of the antechamber opened and a man in red-trimmed green livery stepped through. He pointed at each of the people waiting and made a face. "Ten only? The count is worse every day. All of you, come along. You'll be seen now, since there are so few of you."

Thea hadn't even decided where to settle. She shrugged and waited for Gil to take the lead.

The steward gave them an unimpressed once-over before he led them through the doors.

The hall on the other side was impressive. High pillars supported an arched ceiling, and a fine red carpet ran the length of the floor to a high, white stone dais. The throne was there, but its back was turned toward them, flanked by two guards. On the other side of the throne, people stood, facing the doorway to speak to the fortress's king. Curious.

The steward stopped them just inside the doors and sorted them into two rows. "You may not look upon His Majesty unless he calls for you. Your business may be stated from behind him, but you shall still bow." He straightened a man's collar, then moved on to push down the hood of Gil's cloak.

Gil caught his arm and opened his mouth to either protest or doom them all, when one of the doors to the throne room slammed open.

"Your Majesty!" A scout in travel-worn clothing hurried forward, past the objections of the steward, to drop to one knee before the dais and the back of the throne. "I bring news from Kentoria. You've done it. The false king is dead!"

"Dead?" The word was touched with surprise and delight.

Well, there was their answer. Thea glanced to Gil for direction, or perhaps just acknowledgment, but the look on his face was stricken.

"By the One's mercy," Rilion whispered.

Thea's eyes darted to the throne as a man stood and turned, and when she saw him, she understood.

Before them stood the true king of Kentoria.

CHAPTER TWENTY-FIVE

"LUCAN." The name scarcely escaped Gil's throat, a tangled pair of syllables that betrayed the gnarl of emotions behind his pinched eyes.

Had she not seen him before, his face burned into her memory by the hatred he'd inspired, Thea wouldn't have believed it.

The supposedly-dead king ignored them. Instead, he strode down the steps toward his scout and barked a laugh of delight. "They've done it? They've actually succeeded?"

"Word has come with those who now flee Kentoria to avoid its collapse," the scout said. "The false king Gaius was slain before the usurped throne. Your kingdom awaits you."

"Long live King Lucan," one of the armored guards shouted.

"Long live King Lucan!" repeated every other person in the room, aside from Thea, Rilion, and Gil. Their silence earned them a long, suspicious glare from the steward.

It didn't matter.

Gil was already moving.

"Wait." Thea tried to catch his arm, but he slipped from her grasp and stormed toward the throne—toward his brother— with his eyes ablaze and one hand jammed into his bag.

Rilion spat an oath.

"A false king," he snarled as he tore the preserved head from his bag and held it aloft by its hair. "Here is your false king!"

A wave of shrieks rose from the peasants before the throne as he flung the head at Lucan's feet. The man recoiled at the same time his guards sprang forward.

A guard banged in through the doors behind them and Rilion was on him in an instant, blade flashing as he landed a swift series of blows and tore the halberd from the guard's hands. He rammed its pole through the handles on the doors, barring the way.

Someone sprang for Thea and she jerked her dagger from its sheath before she saw who it was. The steward. He was unarmed and his eyes grew wide as her blade swiped across the front of his uniform.

"Who are you?" Lucan spat at last. His arms curled to his chest, half in repulsion, half in fear. "What have you done?"

"What have *I* done?" Gil pressed a hand to his breastbone, then whirled to meet the two guards that rushed him. He should have been at a disadvantage, bearing knives against their polearms. Instead, he flung two of his smallest knives. Both thudded into the joint at the shoulder of the guards' armor, cutting deep, disabling their arms. Both men shouted as their weapons dropped.

Gil strode forward. "I saw you. I mourned you. I *wept* for you. And all this time..." His voice cracked.

This was not how this was supposed to go.

Thea drove the steward back with a series of jabs. The man relented and fell to the ground, sheltering his head with his arms.

The peasants still screamed. All of them ran, though there was nowhere to go. How was there nowhere to go? Thea scanned the room in disbelief. The fortress's throne room had been constructed with only one entrance? She glanced back, to where Rilion stood with his back against the doors and a foot on his downed guard's shoulder to keep him face-down on the floor.

Lucan looked from the injured guards to Gil, his lip peeled back in a snarl, even as he shuffled backwards. "Who are you?"

Gil tore the cloak from his shoulders and cast it to the floor. The illusion masking him slid away like shimmering grains of sand.

Lucan's eyes widened.

Thea's did, too. That shouldn't have happened. She'd layered magic into every piece of his clothing, just to be sure—her eyes slid down. By the Light, where was the clothing she'd made? He wore something different, something Ranorsh.

Understanding struck her like a slap and she spun to glare at Rilion.

The prince blinked at her, as if unsure what she wanted. *He* wore Gil's clothing. The illusion had no effect on his appearance; it hadn't been tailored for him. Light! When had they traded clothes? She hadn't noticed at all!

"You," Lucan snarled at last. "I should have known. I should have known that was too easy."

Gil stepped past the false king's head. He pointed at it as he passed. "You did this. You turned him against me. You tried to kill me."

"Yes," his brother sneered.

"Why?"

"You've not come to me to pose as a fool," Lucan snapped. His shoulders hunched and he inched backwards. "You know why. You've always known. Or at least suspected."

Gil's brow furrowed.

Lucan's mouth twisted, first with surprise, then with disgust. "Or perhaps I've given you too much credit." He halted his retreat.

The doors shuddered. Angry cries rose outside them. "Now's a good time to hurry!" Rilion shouted.

Thea looked between Gil and Rilion, torn between helping brace the doors and offering Gil support.

The injured guards took up their weapons. Gil had already passed them; they were to his back. She gritted her teeth and ran.

She intercepted the first guard as he lunged. Her dagger was barely enough to throw the attack off course, but the spearhead of the halberd surged past Gil's side instead of through him.

He seized the pole as it sailed past and shoved hard, spilling the guard to the floor and wrenching the halberd from his hands.

Lucan gave a harsh, bitter laugh. "You see? You *see?* This is why, Gaius. This is exactly why! Because you were taught this. You were given this gift. You knew that oversight, that slight, and you were pleased. You all were pleased."

"I don't know what you're talking about."

Lucan scoffed. "Don't pretend you never noticed. Don't pretend you didn't see what our father left behind. An heir, a spare, a blade to bear. What was left for *me?*"

"You're as mad as you were before you died," Gil snarled.

Dark fury lit in Lucan's eyes.

At the doors, the guard under Rilion's foot grabbed him by the leg and pulled him off balance. He went down hard.

Thea spun to help him but the guard was already on his feet, tearing the halberd's pole from the doors. The doors burst open and a wave of guards poured in.

Smug satisfaction replaced Lucan's fury and he paced backwards to put more distance between himself and his brother. "It was them or me," he said. "Father made his choice, and I made mine."

"I was sworn to protect you!" Gil protested.

"Then you failed." Lucan gestured toward him. "Seize him! Kill him! Finish what others could not!"

Rilion clawed his way up the doors. He couldn't hold them back against the guards alone, nor could he risk letting the surge of enemies pin him against the wall. He retreated to join Thea at Gil's back.

The first time a guard swung at her, Thea reevaluated her understanding of combat. All of them carried spears or halberds. They held an advantage when she was a short distance away, but their reach was long and their swings left them vulnerable. She gained the upper hand when she darted in beneath the poles to stab at the breaks between pieces of armor or, as more of the newcomers sported, gaps where they wore no armor at all.

Flaws in their defenses. An awkward force, hastily assembled, without proper equipment. As long as they kept her at the end of their polearms, their lack of armor was no trouble. The moment she made it past the sharp end, it was their undoing. She was no fighter, but even she bested several guards before Rilion made it to her side.

"Don't let them get to Gil!" she cried.

"Really? I thought he might want to invite them to tea," Rilion growled behind clenched teeth. He was faster, better trained and better prepared than she. Before long, he downed two guards—disabling, wounding, never killing—and seized one's halberd. He twirled it before transferring it to his off hand. "What I wouldn't give for a sword right now."

"Maybe you should have packed one." She chanced a look over her shoulder.

Gil climbed the dais. Lucan still inched backwards.

The wave of guards had slowed. Thea looked to the doors and almost laughed. The common folk who had been in the throne room choked the doorway, struggling to pass the guards who tried to push their way in, clogging the path so neither group could get by.

"Brace yourself," Rilion warned her.

She tried, but her eyes drifted back to the scene behind them. She wanted to be there. Be by Gil's side, be his support.

The prince followed her gaze and groaned, though he shifted to stand before her and held his knife and stolen polearm ready. "Fine. I'll buy you as much time as I can."

Gratitude washed over her. "I'll be back." Then she turned and ran, taking the dais steps two at a time.

"I would have gladly lived every day in your shadow." Gil raised his voice; Lucan had retreated farther and now cowered behind one of the grand pillars.

"Only until you knew!" The king clawed at the pillar as if he wished to climb it, or perhaps burrow into the stone.

Gil stopped. Uncertainty and dismay warred on his face. Neither emerged victorious; instead, the familiar mask of steel resolve slipped into place, cold and hard.

Thea's heart sank.

No one had slipped past their defenses.

No one had escaped without a trace.

The betrayal had come from within.

Slowly, Gil's hands went to his daggers. "I would have followed you to the ends of the earth."

Fear stole the color from Lucan's face. "And so you have." One hand dipped beneath his robes.

"Thea!" Rilion shouted.

She spun just in time to dodge the spear aimed for her head. She darted close and struck.

Metal rang behind the pillars. "You refused me!" Lucan snarled as he met Gil's daggers with a blade of his own. "Turned against me in my hour of need. I gave you an honor, having you execute the traitors in our midst, but you turned against me and joined their uprising. I tested you and you failed!"

"There was no uprising," Gil snapped. Their blades clashed again. "There were no traitors. Only innocents you sent to the axe."

Innocents.

Thea's heart skipped a beat. Her second stab went wide and glanced off the guard's armor. The dagger bounced back hard and she lost her grip.

The guard lunged forward and seized her arms.

Memories—nightmares—swirled through her head. Her brother's face. The headsman's axe.

Execute the traitors.

"Rilion!" Gil's shout snapped her back.

She twisted in the guard's grasp and tried to stomp his foot, but he wore sturdy boots and her heel made poor contact. Her eyes darted toward Rilion, fearful for what she might see, but he was running toward her. He was not the one who needed help.

"Take her," Gil ordered. Lucan was down before him, gasping for breath, hands up, pleading.

Thea's throat tightened. "No—"

"I do not wish for you to see." He didn't so much as look her way.

Again, thoughts of her brother surged. *Don't look, Thea.*

Tears flooded her eyes.

Don't look.

Rilion seized her arm and ran for the door as the tangle of bodies there cleared and a new rush of guards began. She tried to resist, to linger and help Gil's fight, but Rilion's grip was too determined. They reached the door and the prince shoved her behind him as he spun his stolen halberd. He'd changed hands again; he fought with the polearm and struck with the dagger when he knocked weapons aside and lunged close.

Her hand went to her dagger's sheath out of reflex before she remembered the blade was gone. She needed a weapon. A blade. Anything.

Her breath caught as she remembered, and she tore her bag from her shoulder. She'd brought so little, the burden so light she'd all but forgotten.

She pulled out her scissors and launched herself forward.

A halberd swung for her side. She dropped to the ground and kicked off the floor to launch herself upward and drive the end of her scissors into the guard's stomach. The tip of the closed blades couldn't pierce his gambeson, but she hit hard and he doubled over as the air left his lungs.

Another guard came at her over his back and she slammed her scissors against the halberd's blade. The polearm shattered against Kentoria's finest steel. The guard stumbled, but another was fast to take his place. Thea snapped her scissors open as an axe descended on her, catching the pole and wrenching it sideways. Rilion went in under it, his quick stabs sending the guard to the ground.

They pushed through the swarm in the antechamber of the King's Hall. Suddenly, the way before them parted, the guards flowing to either side, rushing to aid their king.

Rilion planted a hand against her back. "Go, go!"

They sprinted forward together to burst into the daylight, already short of breath. Warning bells clanged across the fortress. The ranks of soldiers had already grown thin, and the courtyard teemed with panicked bystanders.

Rilion threw down his polearm and jammed his dagger into its sheath. They'd escape faster if they blended in.

Thea didn't know what to do with her scissors. She glanced at their blades before she rammed them into the dagger's sheath.

The main gate was open. People spilled from the fortress to the valley like a cascade of water, hundreds more people than she'd fathomed.

"There." Rilion pointed. On the slope, their horses trotted back and forth, avoiding the surge of unfamiliar faces.

Thea cut that way without guidance. Her legs burned and a stabbing pain shot through her side. She clamped a hand to it and pushed onward. As they grew near, Rilion gave a sharp, staccato whistle. A tone the horses knew, for they perked their ears and turned toward them. She no longer needed help mounting, so she ran to Molasses and dragged herself into the saddle. Her arms shook so they almost gave out.

"Where are those boys?" Rilion growled as he climbed onto Nib. "They're supposed to be watching you, blast them."

"Be grateful they aren't." Thea reined her horse toward the slope they'd climbed that morning, then paused.

The third horse tried to follow them. Rilion turned him around and gave his rump a slap to set him in the direction of the fortress gate. Then he urged Nib downhill. "It's the best we can do," he said between breaths.

She looked back toward the gate as Gil's horse trotted toward the flow of strangers. She watched—hoped—for something more.

Don't look.

Ashvin's last words whispered in her thoughts.

She squeezed her eyes shut and turned away.

CHAPTER TWENTY-SIX

THEY'D RIDDEN for over an hour when Rilion called a halt. They were back in the wilds, little more than a rutted trail telling them where to go. The hoofprints their horses left behind the day before still lingered, bold against the mingled tracks of farmers and animals they'd followed. Those farmers and animals were long outpaced, if they were coming this way at all. Would they abandon the fortress so readily? Thea thought they might stay put after it became clear they were in no danger, but then she second-guessed herself. They'd abandoned their lives in Kentoria, Ranor, and who knew where else, and they'd held those far longer.

Thea's sides ached when she clambered from the saddle. She held them both and stifled a groan.

"There's a brook over there. Cuts through the rocks." Rilion pointed toward a ridge not far off the path. So what was why they'd stopped here.

She led Molasses over the rocks so she could drink, though her muscles protested every move. The mare trudged along and her step gained more spirit when she noticed the water. Thea let go of the reins and sank to the ground, rubbing the muscles in her calves.

For a time, Rilion stood in the middle of the trail and gazed back the way they'd come. Then he sighed and led his horse to the water, too.

Thea smoothed back her hair and let her head hang.

Don't look.

The same words had echoed ceaselessly in her head as they fled the valley. She'd fought to keep her eyes trained on the trail ahead, to guide her horse behind Rilion's, to focus on the escape. Now she could breathe, and the voice of doubt reared in her mind a dozen times over, all at once.

She'd failed in the one thing she'd wanted to do. To ride at his side, to see things through to the end. She'd let herself be herded away, crumbled when the price was most dear. They'd abandoned him to die.

Yet didn't he deserve it? After all he'd done, all the lives he'd taken, the life he'd been *about* to take—

No, she told herself firmly. He didn't deserve that. No one deserved it.

They'd crossed rivers, mountains, had been challenged half a dozen times. He fought with care and precision, crippling, disabling, never killing. Even in the throne room, with Lucan on his knees.

He'd told her, early on, that he'd meant to kill only once more.

She'd never fathomed it might be his own brother.

A small, hiccuping sob tore free of her throat before she could catch it.

Rilion startled at the sound.

"I don't know what's happened," Thea choked. "I don't know how it came to this. Everything's fallen apart in the last hour."

The prince looked troubled. He studied her, then glanced away. For a time, the only sound was the rustle of the wind in the grasses and the sound of their horses as they moved along the brook and drank.

Eventually, Rilion sighed and returned his eyes to the

western horizon. "I warned him, once. Said this was a possibility. I was... too soon in sharing it, I think."

Thea lifted her head.

"There are poisons that mimic death," he said slowly. "I cautioned him that with the extent of Lucan's paranoia, and with Kentorian burial traditions, we couldn't be certain. In Ranor, bodies are burned and returned to the earth."

And in Kentoria, they were buried in hardwood caskets lined with dried leaves. She rubbed her brow. The dead kings were buried privately, somewhere on castle grounds. How hard would it have been to dig up Lucan's body so he could be revived with an antidote? Not hard, if your replacement was seldom home. Gil's determination to find his brothers' killer had provided a perfect window for escape.

If only things had spun in favor of Gil's escape this time.

She wiped her eyes with the back of her hand before more tears could form. "He told you to do this, didn't he? Ahead of time?"

Rilion's brows knit. "Do what?"

"Take me. Leave him there."

He hesitated.

Thea nodded and lowered her eyes to the water, watching as it trickled over the rocks. "I thought so."

"If I am being honest, I don't know why he let you come to begin with. To scare you off, maybe. He's never..." He exhaled. "He doesn't work with others anymore. Not often. Too many people have died because of things he's had to do."

Don't look.

Her eyes burned anew. She turned away. "That's what I'm afraid of." And what she desperately wished she'd had a moment to ask. Lucan's face, the wicked satisfaction it bore as he gave the order, was burned into her memory. But the king had only given the order. Execute the traitors. Another hand had swung the axe, and the executioner's mask the man wore had haunted her dreams every night.

Now her mind blurred that memory with the moment in the woodshed, when she'd seen Gil pull that mask from his face.

She tried to force it away. No matter what she'd seen, she did not know.

If he didn't make it out of that fortress, she never would.

"I needed to be here," Rilion said after a time. He gazed toward the west, a tense sort of hope betrayed in the set of his shoulders. He didn't owe her any explanation, but she sensed that he wanted her to ask.

"Is that why he brought you?" Or was he trying to frighten Rilion off, too?

He waved a hand at the valley around them. "Someone has to clean up all this. The people, that fortress. Someone will have to answer for it, and it's closest to the Ranorsh border. He wanted me to know what we needed to expect. A favor, in his own way."

"That favor could have gotten you killed."

"Well, yes. That tends to happen with him. That's why I don't know why he let you come." The smile he gave her this time was nervous, but resigned. "We have to keep moving."

No sign of Gil's escape, then. Thea dipped her hands in the frigid water and wiped her face clean, then rose. "How far?"

"As far as necessary. Back to Danesse. From there..." Rilion spread his hands with a helpless shrug. "We'll see."

She retrieved her horse and mounted without another word.

They rode on for another few hours before Rilion pointed out a small structure clinging to the side of the mountain. "We'll see if that's inhabited. Might make a good rest stop."

The sloping trail that led to the weather-worn shack was steep and rocky and they dismounted for the last portion of the climb.

Rilion passed Nib's reins to Thea before he knocked at the door. No answer came and with a little persuasion in the form of his boot near the latch, the door came open.

The inside of the shack had seen better days, but the presence of a bed with no mattress and a pantry with bare shelves revealed it had been empty for some time. He surveyed the interior, then stepped back to find somewhere to tie the horses. "There's an oven of some sort. See if there's any firewood left inside."

Thea did as she was told. Had they arrived after nightfall, it would have been too dark to make out the cobwebbed stack of wood in the corner behind the red brick oven. She pulled the logs one at a time to put them in place, mindful of spiders, though the cold made her fingers so clumsy she doubted any hiding pests would be more nimble. She'd just finished the stack when Rilion stepped inside.

"We'll stay here until morning," he said. "I have a few cuts and scrapes from that fight and I think we're far enough from the fortress for me to give them a proper inspection. There are rainwater barrels out back if you want to wash."

"I'll be all right. I can help tend your injuries, if you'd like." She didn't have a first aid kit, but she knew enough basic care that she thought she could get by. It was one of the things a lady of the house was expected to know, if only to tend the scraped knees of her future children.

"No, thank you. I'll be all right on my own." He gave her an awkward sort of smile, then glanced to the door. "Actually, I think I'll do it outside. Where the light is better. Here, there's flint and steel in my bag. See if you can get the fire going." He left his things on the table and then slipped outside with nothing but his water skin.

Thea took the hint. She retrieved what she needed from his bag and set to work getting the fire lit.

By the time he came back inside and closed the door, the fire crackled merrily, but it did nothing to lift the morose mood.

Gil *would* be back. She refused to believe otherwise. But neither of them spoke of the matter—or anything else—and when she finally spread her bedroll and gave herself over to sleep, the mask she'd always prayed to forget flooded her dreams again.

~

Low voices woke her in the middle of the night. The fire still burned, though dimly. A new log sat atop the pile, not yet touched by the feeble flames. Rilion's bedroll on the other side of the shack was empty.

Thea sat upright and listened close. A thump and scrape made her jump and she reached for the handle of her scissors, just in case. Leaving their horses outside made them easy to find.

The door bumped open and Rilion stumbled through with his arm around—

"Gaius," she gasped as she leaped from her bed.

He grunted a response as she slid forward and posted herself at his other side to help support him. A handful of cuts decorated the dark shirt he'd borrowed from Rilion, but the worst seemed to be an injury to his leg. From the way the fabric clung to his skin, she knew it was in desperate need of attention.

"Good thing we tied the horses out like that," Rilion said. There weren't any chairs, so he helped Gil settle on the floor by the fire instead.

"I'm just grateful you left one behind." A rueful smile tugged at the corners of Gil's mouth. "It was not my cleanest getaway."

"It's a miracle you got away at all." She tried to shift away, but he caught her and pulled her in to touch her forehead to his. His eyes closed. Her heart skipped a beat.

Don't look.

She drew back under the guise of inspecting his injury. "This needs to be washed."

"Laundry, at a time like this?"

"Spare me the jokes," she muttered. "This could become inflamed."

Rilion had already produced a small iron pan from his travel supplies and filled it from his water skin. "Won't give you much, but at least it'll be warm," he said as he tucked it into the brick oven beside the fire.

"Do you still have your cloak?" She leaned back to look. He didn't have his bags with him. Half his knives were missing, too. The sheath for his favorite, the one he kept on his right thigh, was gone. Shed when he'd sustained the injury to that leg, or cut loose during the same event?

"It's on the saddle," Gil said.

Rilion strode back to the door. "I'll get it."

Thea didn't know how to begin. She couldn't very well ask him to remove his pants. Instead, she scooted back and tugged the boot from his foot so she could begin at his ankle.

"What are you doing?" he asked in a murmur.

She didn't reply, just pulled her scissors from their sheath and cut her way up the leg of his pants, peeling the cloth back a bit at a time. It stuck unpleasantly.

"Thea?"

She couldn't make herself meet his gaze. Unspoken questions already threatened to choke her. She didn't need tears, too. New chips in her scissors made them catch and hang and she focused on cutting.

Rilion returned and shut the door against the cold. "A little worse for wear, isn't it?" He held the green cloak in one hand. The cloth was stained dark.

"It'll suffice. Bring it here." Thea held out her hand. She'd exposed the gash in his leg. "By the Light, this could have killed you."

"And would have, if it had been much deeper," Gil said.

She took his cloak when Rilion offered it, found an edge, and cut a piece from the fabric. Neither of the men said anything as she retrieved the pan from the oven and dipped the cloth in water.

Bit by bit, she cleaned what she could.

"It'll need to be sutured," Rilion said after the extent of the injury became clear. "Can you... you know..." He pantomimed threading a needle.

Thea snorted. "Of course I can." Not that she had, but sewing an injury shut couldn't be much harder than running a good seam.

"With magic?" the prince asked hopefully.

"Threadmancy doesn't work that way." She wasn't sure any magic did. "You can't insert power into something that lives."

Gil didn't so much as flinch as she wiped his skin clean. "You don't have to stitch magic into me. Just push it into the thread and let that do the work. That should be possible, shouldn't it?"

Thea doubted it. But the wound in his thigh was severe. If he wasn't seen by a proper medic, she doubted it was something he could survive. There had to be medics in Danesse, but to get there required crossing a mountain. Would he make it that long? "I can try," she said softly. Her heart cried that she *had* to. She couldn't let him fight all this way, only to fall ill with a festering wound after his quest was finally complete.

Rilion provided his water skin for the injury to be rinsed. While she tended that, he dug through her bag. She'd given herself a single, tiny sewing kit, little more than a pouch with a spool of thread and a few pins and needles. It took him time to find it and when he did, he wasn't impressed.

It would have to be enough.

"See if there's a little block in my bag, something wrapped with paper," Thea said as she chose a needle.

"This?" Rilion held it up between two fingers.

She took the wrapped beeswax from his hand and used it to liberally coat her thread. "This may be uncomfortable."

"More comfortable than being stabbed by a pikeman while mounting a horse, I'd assume," Gil said.

Despite his confidence, when she started, he flinched.

Rilion clapped a hand to his mouth and groaned in displeasure. "I'll go get more water." He snatched his water skin and excused himself from the shack before either of them could chide him for his weak stomach.

Then they were alone.

Thea made stitch after tiny stitch, all without speaking a word.

"You are angry with me," Gil said softly.

"I don't care if you killed Lucan." If she was honest with herself, she was glad. With his death, there was justice for Ashvin.

Just not all of it.

Gil did not reply. Expectation weighted his silence, yet he asked nothing. Of course not; he didn't need to. He already knew she was upset.

She couldn't make herself lift her head, couldn't look him in the eye. Even pushing the question to the tip of her tongue was enough to make her hands tremble.

His fingers brushed her cheek. "Thea, speak to me."

How could she ask? How could she live *without* asking? She shook her head and made herself focus. She was supposed to be pushing magic down the needle. She'd forgotten entirely.

"Healing," she murmured, blinking hard to clear her vision and gathering her strength. She willed power to gather in her chest, to push through her shoulder and down her arm. It prickled, white-hot, as it spilled into the needle between her fingers. "Health, wellness, whole—"

"Thea, please," Gil pleaded, curving his hand to cradle her face. His other hand rose to join it. His hands were warm, skin callused from all the years he'd spent gripping the hilts of blades. Or the handle of...

She tried to breathe and almost choked on the air, but once she found her voice, the words spilled free like pins strewn across the floor, sharp and small. "Lucan's headsman," she gasped. "Were you—Did you—" And then it was tears that choked her, instead.

Understanding dug a furrow in his brow and his thumbs moved to wipe the first tears from her skin. "Yes."

Everything within her shattered, a million razor-sharp shards of glass to cut her soul to pieces.

No denial. Not even hesitance. Just a simple answer, the brutal truth, the one thing she'd hoped from the beginning might be untrue.

Don't look.

Why did it matter? She couldn't see. The needle in her hand was so small it vanished as the first sob racked her shoulders.

Again, Gil's thumbs stroked her face, sweeping away the only part of her sorrow he held power over. "At the end, I was... the only one he trusted," he whispered, "and so I have done many things that shame me."

"My brother," her voice cracked. "He was all—all I had—" She couldn't finish. All speaking did was make her cry harder.

He shifted, drawing himself up to his good knee so he could lean forward and wrap his arms around her shoulders, cradle her head so her face was nestled against his neck. "I know my apologies can never be enough, but you have them. I never wanted this, and I am sorry. I am so sorry."

She wanted to sink into him and let herself be held. His arms should have offered comfort. Instead, they'd torn the last shred of happiness out of her life. She shook her head and pulled away.

He didn't try to stop her.

Thea wiped her own eyes and strode out the door into the cold night.

Rilion stood beside the horses. He put out a hand and said something, but she pushed past without stopping to see what he wanted.

She didn't know where she was going, but anywhere was better than this.

CHAPTER TWENTY-SEVEN

THEA LISTENED to the crunch of hooves on gravel without lifting her head. She sat with her arms folded atop her knees, her forehead resting against them. The first rays of sunlight had been welcome. Company was not.

The hooves stopped and for a time, the soft breath of the horses was the only thing she heard. Eventually, her visitor spoke.

"You left your coat." Rilion. She'd hoped and feared that it might be him. "And your bag, and..."

And everything she'd thought she loved. The thought was hollow now. She didn't have any tears left.

The prince cleared his throat. "I'm going back to Danesse. It may be difficult to manage two horses on my own. I hoped you might help me manage Molasses."

She slowly raised her head. Her eyes burned and her cheeks were raw from tears in the cold, but he didn't flinch when he faced him. "And in Danesse?"

"I suppose we'll continue with our arrangement. A shop for a Threadmancer to conduct business, within the spectrum of what Ranorsh laws governing artisan magic allow." He extended the mare's reins and her eyes drifted to the horses. Her bay mare and his dappled gray gelding. The red one was gone.

Rilion offered a tentative smile. "He's gone ahead. There is... much to be done."

And coming for her hadn't been part of it. She shut her eyes and scolded herself. Finding comfort in the arms of a king was a foolish fantasy. Even if she wanted him to come for her—she wasn't positive she did—it wasn't as if it could mean anything. The kisses they'd shared had set her heart afire, but Gil, the assassin, had never existed. He was Gaius, the merciless king, and the lives of kings held no space for disgraced nobles.

Thea pushed herself up and took the reins. "I'll need help obtaining things. Fabrics, thread. Fibers for spinning."

He nodded. "Of course. Everything will be seen to, and I'll ensure you're able to stay at the guest house we departed from until your building is ready. But we'll worry about that when we reach home."

Home. The word plucked something in her chest. It reverberated inside her, bittersweet, as she wondered if anywhere would ever feel like home again.

She climbed into the saddle and they rode.

Rilion was polite, but stiffer with her than he had been, and they spoke little as they passed through the mountains, even when they made camp at night.

By the time they reached the Ranorsh side of the range, winter had set in fully. Thick blankets of snow covered the landscape, slowing their travel, but providing an abundance of fresh water whenever they had time to stop and melt it to drink.

With nothing but mundane work ahead of them, there was little reason to spur themselves in travel, and they meandered for far longer than the trip into Angroth had taken. They took shifts in the lead, so one horse at a time worked to break a path. Now and then, Thea found herself watching the road for signs of passage, but there were none. A lone horseman would struggle in the snow, which fell often and heavy, and cold winds scoured the night.

"Do you think the people from that burned settlement will come back?" she asked as they left the foothills behind and the mountain river that fed the lake beside Danesse came into view.

"Who knows," Rilion said. "We likely won't know until spring. I imagine someone will take over that fortress and declare themselves leader. They had plenty of provisions, and no one will get back into those mountains to clear them out until the snow is gone."

"Will you attack them?" Part of her felt sorry for the commoners left behind. They'd abandoned their homes in pursuit of a better life. It was no different than what she'd done, and they didn't have a Third Prince to help them.

"Not without a direct request we do so. They're on Angroth's side, so they're Angroth's problem. I'll pen a letter to Angroth's queen. If she asks for our help in clearing the place, we'll be obligated to offer it, but who can say what she'll do? She's young, and Angroth is so isolated that no one knows much about her methods."

"Then I hope her choices cause you no trouble," Thea said.

Rilion nodded as if to accept her good wishes, but offered nothing more on the subject.

Eventually, the lake itself came into view. The snow was shallow enough in the river valley that the horses progressed with little trouble. The roads became a jumble of slushy footprints and she gave up hope she might see some indication Gaius had reached the city before them. It didn't matter, she told herself, though none of her believed it. Gaius would return to Kentoria, and once again, he would be king. She turned her thoughts to the things she'd need for her new dressmaker's shop and refused to dwell on anything else.

When they reached the guest house they'd stayed at before, the windows were dark. Ina met them at the door and seemed pleased by Thea's return.

"I kept all your things in your room," the maid said as she escorted the two of them into the house. "You'll be pleased at how cozy it is in the wintertime. I'll bring up a rocking chair. It'll be a perfect place to work on your mending, right there by the fire."

"Thank you. I'm sure it will be." Thea stopped in the entryway and watched Ina hurry past to find the chair she spoke of.

Rilion lingered by the door. "I don't relish going to see my father in the wake of everything that's happened, but I can't put it off." His smile was strained, more a grimace than a look of cheer. "Give me a week to settle things. I'll have your building by then."

She couldn't smile, either. There was a sense of finality to the way he said things, and she supposed there had to be. Despite all they'd dealt with, she hadn't been certain she could count him as a friend. Standing in the entryway of the royal family's guest house, she knew they couldn't be. Third Princes were not friends with Threadmancers, or any other sort of working folk. "Thank you for everything, Rilion. I so deeply appreciate everything you've done, just saying thank you doesn't feel sufficient."

"Believe me, it is. I have everything I need already. I'll have keys, the address, and instructions for ordering supplies ready for you in a week." He opened the door, but hesitated to depart. For a moment, Thea thought he'd say something more. Then he clamped his jaw, gave a stiff nod, and left.

The moment the door closed, the house felt empty.

She stood in the middle of the entryway, twisting her fingertips until she was certain he wouldn't return.

"I've found that chair, milady," Ina called from the stairs. "Shall I bring your bags up for you?"

"I've got them. And please, call me Thea." She turned to climb to the room she'd stayed in before. The room farther down the hall beckoned her, but there was no point in going to look. It was empty, and unlike her, Gaius had left nothing behind.

"If you say so," the maid replied.

The room was just as she'd left it, save the addition of the rocking chair. She dropped her things onto the bed and contemplated the basket she'd stowed there before. She'd finally have time to fix that dress, at least. Perhaps Ina could take her scissors to be sharpened. They still rode in the sheath on her thigh, the closest thing to a weapon she'd had for the last leg of their travels.

Rather than drawing the scissors, she unfastened the sheath from her thigh. As it came away, she inspected the dirt beneath her fingernails. "Ina, do you think you could heat a bath for me?"

"Of course, milady. Thea." The name was an afterthought, tacked on too late. Nothing out of the ordinary for her life anymore.

"Thank you," Thea murmured, all the same. The house was gloomy and she was alone, but at least she could count on the warmth of the water to lift her spirits.

There was no hope for fixing the dress. The cut was too ragged, the bottom of the bodice too frayed. The seam would be visible and the skirt too short. Instead of trying to put the two back together, Thea settled in the rocking chair beside the hearth and finished the task of turning it into two pieces.

After the sewing she'd done during the trip, making something without magic in it felt strange. Stranger, in a way, was holding the garment after Gaius had cut it. It was her duty to put it back together, like the pieces left of her shattered life. Work gave her a sense of serenity she hadn't known during the trip back to Danesse. She never pricked herself once as she turned the trimmed edges of the shell and lining to the inside, pinning and repinning sections until it was perfectly even.

The needle and thread glided easily through the fabric.

Without the tingle of magic in her fingertips, she could work for longer periods and do finer work. Her magic might have been what appealed to most clients, but the quality of her craft in which she took pride. She closed the whole bottom with tiny hidden stitches, then added a tidy line of top stitching along the edge to hold everything in place.

Ina appeared when the bodice was nearly finished, carrying a tray of food and a pitcher of warm cider. A tiny basket hung on her arm. "It's hard to fix food in proper amounts for just the few of us, but Cook will see to it, don't you worry. Supper will just be a bit late."

The food on the tray was more of what she'd had at noon; buttered bread and a selection of cheeses and preserved fruit. Thea didn't mind at all. It was far better than dry travel rations. "Thank you, this will be fine. What's that on your arm, though? It looks like a sewing basket. Are you going to join me?"

"Oh, no, milady Thea." Instead of the maid using one or the other, the two had somehow blended together. Thea decided she didn't mind that, either. Perhaps it was hard for her to imagine the Third Prince would host a common Threadmancer. "I'm all right with a needle, but I fetched this from the market for you."

Thea knotted off the last of her thread and lowered the bodice to her lap as Ina brought the basket near. Inside lay an assortment of thick crewel threads in at least a dozen colors.

She touched a hand to her chest. "Oh, Ina, these are beautiful."

"I know that shiny cotton stuff is more popular in Kentoria, but wool is Ranorsh, through and through. I thought you might like to give it a try." The maid deposited the basket in Thea's hands, then drew back. "I'm off to help Cook now, but you let me know if you need anything, and I'll do my best to see it done."

Thea scarcely got out a thank you before the woman disappeared. She touched the threads in the basket, marveled at their softness, then retrieved a needle large enough to accommodate them.

She worked embroidery until her fingertips grew sore, before and after supper and across the next several days. Maple leaves and the colorful flowers that once grew in her mother's garden bloomed across the bodice until they disguised the bottom edge.

After that came the skirt. She gathered it to a new waistband, then it, too, received leaves and flowers blooming all along the hem.

By the end of the week, when a messenger came, the dress was good as new, but two parts instead of one. She wondered at that briefly as she descended the stairs to hear what the messenger had to say.

"His Highness, Prince Rilion sends his regards," the messenger said stiffly. He extended a thick paper envelope with both hands. "He also sends information regarding your permanent residency and accommodations. I am to escort you to your new domicile and provide you with the stipend the Third Prince has approved for the establishment of your services. Are you prepared to go?"

"Of course." Thea took the envelope, her fingers exploring its folded end and the striped cord that held it shut. "Just let me get my coat."

"I'll fetch it, milady Thea," Ina called from somewhere in the house. Where the woman went for most of the day, Thea didn't know, but she resurfaced a moment later with the bright-collared Ranorsh coat in her arms. She helped Thea don it, then disappeared again as quickly as she'd emerged.

The messenger opened the door and motioned for her to precede him. "After you, Lady Thea."

Had they all decided she was some sort of noble? She considered correcting him, then thought better of it. Perhaps it had less to do with her and more to do with Ranorsh culture, something of which she knew little.

He led her through the cobblestone streets at a steady pace, granting her enough time to familiarize herself with the route back to the guest house.

Eventually, they came to a stop before a tall two-story house built of stones within a log frame. Its peaked roof seemed to scrape the pale sky when she tilted her head back to look at it. Drifting snowflakes swirled around it, shadows of silver against the light.

"His Highness did not know the appropriate verbiage to advertise your field and felt you should commission a placard for the front on your own," the messenger said as he unlocked the door and ushered her inside.

Thea crept in and clasped the envelope to her stomach. The storefront's tall glass windows let in plenty of light, but the interior was dusty and cold. The room hosted nothing but a tall wooden counter. "That will be no problem." She didn't know what the sign should say, either. Should she advertise her work as a Threadmancer? Or would it be better to keep her head down and focus on ordinary clothing until she understood the regional climate regarding artisan magic?

"Here is your key, and here is the stipend His Highness has promised." He extended both hands with palms flat, the key on one and a fat sheepskin purse on the other. "Do you wish me to carry a message back to His Highness?"

Thea plucked them from his hands one at a time. "Tell him I said thank you, and I will let him know when I've decided what I must do next."

"Of course." He bowed from the shoulders and excused himself from the storefront, shutting the door soundly behind him.

She turned back to the vacant room, key and money in one hand and the envelope in the other.

She should have been happy. This was what she hoped for, the new start she'd needed. Why did it feel so empty?

Slowly, she crossed to the counter and put down everything she held. The contents of the purse were obvious, but she still didn't know what waited in the envelope. She untied the striped cord and shook out the papers it held.

Documents with information on taxes sat on top. She snorted in disgust at the reminder of the problem that had started everything. Below that was a list of merchants selling cloth and other supplies. She paged through those for a moment before something else caught her eye, a small, folded document with colorful borders poking out from the bottom of the stack. She set aside the list and tugged that document free.

The marriage license.

A sharp ache shot through her chest and she squeezed her eyes closed. It made sense for it to be there. She knew why it had to be. But she'd fought hard to keep her thoughts away from her false husband. He'd delivered everything she asked; she had no right to be upset now, as she stood in the middle of the new life he'd presented as a gift. Yet her heart still twisted at the thought of him.

Before long, he'd send something else, a document declaring that marriage license null. A statement of his death, or some other political chicanery? Strange, morbid curiosity stole over her as her fingertips parted the edges of the paper. She'd never seen it after she'd signed, never knew the name he'd used for his false identity.

She unfolded the page and a scrap of paper dropped to the floor. She started to glance down, but something on the open document caught her eye.

Gaius.

He'd signed it *Gaius*.

By the Light, the man had used his real name!

Thea covered her mouth and didn't know if she was going to laugh or cry. She blinked hard and made herself draw a breath, then bent to take the paper from the floor. The back was blank, but a few small lines of writing decorated the front when she turned it over.

. . .

If ever you have need, speak to Rilion and it will be met.
My heart remains yours, but you deserve the best.
Do not settle for less.

The last line blurred before she finished reading and she sank to the floor. Cry. She was definitely going to cry. Her chest tightened until her ribs ached, but instead of tears, all that escaped her was a soft exhale. She laid a hand flat against her stomach, just beneath her ribs. The raised outlines of embroidered leaves and flowers greeted her fingertips. They grounded her in the moment and drew her eyes downward.

A ring of leaves and flowers encircled her, her skirt spread on the floor. Everything she thought she wanted surrounded her, yet she was hollow, incomplete.

Her hand drifted down her bodice, to the now-separate skirt. Divided by circumstances and put back together again.

Two pieces, one whole.

She had to go back.

CHAPTER TWENTY-EIGHT

THE SNOW WAS unkind to travelers. Even with the escort Rilion had assigned, Thea's contingent found progress slow, and winter deepened before they made it across the range to Heartroot.

Most of her escort peeled off there. Some would continue back to Danesse; others would wait for the lone rider who continued into Kentoria beside her.

When they reached the river outside Samara, he departed, too. She hadn't felt their presence necessary, but the prince had refused to let her go alone. It didn't matter that she'd learned to fight. She didn't have her dagger any longer, and though he'd confessed that her combat skill with a pair of scissors was impressive, Rilion was unwilling to take risks.

He had explained the plan for her return before he allowed her to set out. News of what had happened would not pass easily between the kingdoms until spring arrived. For a group of Ranorsh soldiers to press too far toward the capital could be viewed as a threat, no matter how amicable things were between himself and Kentoria's newly-crowned king.

Or, re-crowned, Thea thought. She'd heard nothing about the state of things in Samara, and while part of her wished to ride straight to the palace, she couldn't predict what might be there waiting. Gaius, she hoped, but she didn't know, and she doubted he would forgive her if she rode straight into danger.

Instead, she tied Molasses in the stone-walled garden behind her old home and brushed snow from her skirt. Her illusory trousers underneath had kept her warm, but her dress represented something now. She couldn't see herself wearing anything else.

The mare had become a gift, since Rilion didn't know how to get the horse back when she was done. Thea didn't know what she was supposed to do with her, either, but it was a problem for another time. The first thing she had to do was find out if the posters calling for her capture had been removed.

She unlocked the back door and let herself in. To her surprise, the kitchen was warm.

Had someone else taken her home? No, that made no sense. They would have changed the locks. Curious, she tip-toed to the doorway to peer into the front room.

The lanterns were lit and the room was bright. At the far end of the room, her cousin sat, concentrating hard on a seam.

Had Elia kept the shop open all this time? Bless her! Thea retreated a few steps and wiggled out of her boots. No matter how eager she was to see her cousin, she wouldn't approach her in disguise. She shimmied out of her trousers and winced when she bumped the corner of the table.

"Hello?" Elia called.

Perhaps she should have gone in the front.

"It's me," Thea said. She shook snow from her skirts and crept around the corner to find her cousin poised like a bird ready to take flight.

"Thea! Oh, Thea!" Elia bolted across the room to seize her in a crushing hug. The moment she'd squeezed all the air out of her, she stepped back and took Thea's face in her hands. "By the Light, when we saw the posters, we thought you were dead! Where have you been? What's happened?"

"The posters," Thea wheezed as she tried to get back her breath. "Are they still there?"

"They vanished about a month ago, when King Gaius came out of hiding. Light! Were you hiding, too? Thea, what happened?"

Thea's heart skipped a beat. So he was there. She extricated herself from her cousin's hands and brushed over her dress again. "So much has happened, I hardly know where to begin. Oh, but what about you? You've kept the shop going by yourself, all these weeks?"

Concern rose in Elia's eyes and her excitement faded. "Well, sort of. I'm not sure if... that is, I've done my best, but there's a problem, and..."

After all she'd dealt with at this point, Thea couldn't fathom what it might be. "What? Angry customers? A late wedding gown?"

"No. It—" The clock chimed before Elia could finish. "Light! Is it that time already? I have to—oh!" She clapped her hands together with a gasp and hurried across the room.

Thea turned to watch her. "Where are you going?"

"I have somewhere to be!" Elia pulled on her cloak and flipped the sign on the door to show they were closed. "But this is perfect. You have to come with me. You'll be able to settle this in no time."

"What are you on about?" Thea asked, but her cousin grabbed a satchel and then grabbed her arm before she could object.

"You'll see." There was a light in Elia's eyes again, a hint of excitement Thea couldn't understand.

Her cousin dragged her out the back door and into the street.

"But I haven't got any shoes on!" Thea protested.

"We don't have time, we'll be late. Hurry!" Elia dragged her along through the streets. They were clear, but wet, and Thea's socks were soaked through in no time. Her toes burned with the cold by the time she realized where they were headed.

The red granite palace at the heart of Samara lay just ahead.

"Wait." Thea tried to stop, but her cold feet gave her no purchase. "Wait, I'm not ready!"

"We don't have time," Elia insisted. "You didn't get a chance to see him last time, are you really going to throw away a second audience?"

"I can't! Not like this!" Not in a snow-damp dress with mud-stained socks and no shoes, and no idea what to say.

"My father tried to petition the council while they led the country, while the king was rumored to be dead," Elia explained. "Then the king returned, so he took his audience with him, instead. Even with my father's station, it was fruitless. Father wasn't in line to inherit the property, he said. The shop is set to be possessed by the crown. They're right about him, Thea. Everything we've heard. He's absolutely heartless."

And as heartbroken as Thea was, if she'd learned anything at all. Selfishly, she prayed it was so.

"But we're not giving up. I asked for this audience right after, and if he is mean, at least he's fast."

"You're late," the guard at the palace gate called as they approached.

"I'm not late! I'm on time, but barely." Elia pulled a paper from her bag and waved it at him as she passed. Thea stared at it, dumbfounded. Her cousin caught the look and gave her a lopsided grin. "I guess that's one thing that runs in the family. No sense of time at all."

Thea couldn't find the will to argue. By the Light, what was she supposed to say to him? She was supposed to have time to gather her wits, collect her thoughts, maybe ask to speak with him in private. Instead, her cousin dragged her up the stairs and into the palace. Behind her, the guards wheezed with laughter at her appearance.

"I can't," Thea gasped, one last effort to save her dignity. She was a mess, her hair tangled and limp, her feet leaving wet marks on the floor—

"You will." Elia shoved a handful of papers into her grasp and then planted her hands on Thea's back to thrust her through the doors and into the throne room.

The doors banged open and she stumbled onto a plush carpet she didn't remember from her first visit.

Thea froze.

Gaius slouched on the throne and conversed with a guard nearby, his face so cross she hardly believed it was him, and so handsome she couldn't help but stare.

Taxes.

They'd never seemed so trivial.

His eyes flicked her way, returned to the man beside him, then snapped back. He sat up straight.

The papers spilled from her hands and drifted across the floor.

"Thea!" Elia scolded in a whisper. She bent to snatch the papers from the rug, her face pinched with distress.

Thea couldn't make herself move. What should she say? What *could* she say? Every thought whirled away the moment she tried to grasp it, like maple seeds twirling in the wind.

Slowly, Gaius rose.

"Say something," Elia cried at her back, the words scarcely more than a breath.

Thea unstuck her tongue from the roof of her mouth. "You said if I had need, to let Rilion know."

Elia froze with her hand on a paper.

"Rilion couldn't help me." Her eyes prickled, but she drew a deep breath. She would not crumble now. "I need you."

He descended from the throne with long, sure strides and swept her into his arms.

"I dared not hope," he whispered beside her ear. She'd heard him say it before, but not like this, not with her face buried in his neck and his hands tangled in her hair, his breath but a catch in his chest. "After all I've done, after how badly I've wronged you, how could I ask—"

"You never had to ask," she said. "I'm yours."

Gaius took her face in both hands and kissed her so hard, she thought he might never let go again. She rose on tip-toe to meet him, sliding her fingers through the short hair at the nape of his neck until she could cradle the back of his head.

"Marry me," he gasped when they parted.

She leaned up so her answer brushed his lips. "I already did." Her hand went to the bag she'd had no time to remove. She found the paper she was looking for and pulled it free. "You signed your real name? Truly?"

A single laugh escaped his throat. "Honestly, who would have believed?" He glanced down at the paper as she held it out, then leaned back to let his eyes travel farther. "Where are your shoes?"

"In my shop. Which is still burdened by improper taxes, I'll have you know."

"By the Light, that still hasn't been fixed?" His eyes darkened like thunderheads, like the storm of him that had drawn her in and left her dizzy, consumed her and yet made her whole. "Let it be known, my wife is not to be taxed!"

Thea laughed as he crumpled the license between their hands to lace his fingers with hers.

Elia and a dozen courtiers stood around them, mouths agape in varying degrees of confusion.

"Thea," her cousin said slowly, eyes drifting between her and the king. "What is going on?"

Madness, part of her thought, though the best kind, the sort that drove one to the sort of reckless and magnificent behavior that had come to dominate her life.

Love.

She drew back a step, but Gaius kept an arm around her, as if he'd never let go. Maybe he wouldn't.

Thea cleared her throat and offered a smile as she presented the man beside her. "Elia, I'd like you to meet my husband."

Gaius flashed her a smile. "Charmed."

ABOUT THE AUTHOR

Beth Alvarez has enjoyed writing since childhood and is a ravenous reader.

A visual arts major, Alvarez has worked as a freelance web designer, graphic designer, illustrator, and video game programmer. When not writing, she enjoys drawing, playing video games, driving, and sewing for her unusual collection of Asian ball-jointed dolls. Her collection can be seen on her YouTube channel, Lomi's Playground.

Raised in southern Illinois, she now resides in the suburbs of Memphis, Tennessee with her husband, daughter, and a very mean cat.

If you enjoyed this story, consider signing up for Beth's author newsletter so you'll never miss a future release:

https://www.ithilear.com/newsletter.html

OTHER BOOKS BY BETH ALVAREZ

FANTASY BOOKS

Gale's Gift

Of Blood and Rain

To Steal the World

To Steal the Crown

To Steal the Queen

Serpent's Mark

Serpent's Tears

Serpent's Bane

Serpent's Wake

Serpent's Crown

Serpent's Blood

Spectrum Blade

Paragon of Fire

Paragon of Water

PARANORMAL BOOKS

Keeper's Finder

Her Midnight Cowboy

Her Midnight Wedding

Her Midnight Hunter

The First Hunt (Newsletter Exclusive)

Death of the Sun

Born of the Moon

Printed in Great Britain
by Amazon